Those
Delicious
Letters

Also by Sandeepa Mukherjee Datta

Bong Mom's Cookbook

Those Delicious Letters

Sandeepa Mukherjee Datta

aka The Bong Mom

HarperCollins *Publishers* India

First published in India in 2020 by
HarperCollins *Publishers*
A-75, Sector 57, Noida, Uttar Pradesh 201301, India
www.harpercollins.co.in

2 4 6 8 10 9 7 5 3 1

P-ISBN: 978-93-5357-459-8
E-ISBN: 978-93-5357-460-4

Typeset in 11.5/15 Perpetua Std at
Manipal Technologies Limited, Manipal

Printed and bound in India
Manipal Technologies Limited, Manipal

For the three feisty girls in my life,
Sharanya, Ananya, and my Ma

1

Yesterday was my birthday.

It was also the first day of Boishakh – Poila Boishakh – the beginning of the Bengali New Year. A Bengali takes his Noboborsho very seriously. All that drinking and waking up with resolutions and a hangover might be good for the first of January but on Poila Boishakh, Bengalis wake up crisp and fresh, ready with their well-thumbed *Gitobitan*, a tattered diary scrawled with Tagore's songs, and an iPhone that is squeaking under the pressure of 'Shubho Noboborsho' – Happy New Year wishes scattered over millions of WhatsApp groups. If a dusty harmonium is present in the attic, this is the day it sees light.

For Bengalis, mid-April is all about looking ahead and no one so much as glances back to bid adieu to the year that was.

But for me, this New Year unfurling brings a lot of anxiety. I am not particularly excited about the brand-new days lying ahead. They do not hold any mystery for me. Instead deep in my heart, there is this dull ache. No, no, I am not having a heart attack! My heart is actually pretty good according to my last wellness visit. My cholesterol is within range and BMI is fine for my age. I even exercise regularly. Okay, the last bit is a lie. But I do have a valid gym membership, so I can exercise regularly if I want to.

Anyway, this ache is different. The kind of ache that you feel only when you stand still, close your eyes and hold your breath tight. Right there in your soul. It is there that I feel the ache, a deep trough of sadness for not just the past year, but for all the thirty-nine years I have spent on earth doing nothing.

Nothing. Zilch. Nada.

I turned forty yesterday. I had never thought I would feel any different about this birthday. I mean I still feel thirty-two, or even twenty-two for that matter, just with a bad lower back pain. My frizzy black hair has only now started to show bits of grey. Teeny, tiny grey lost in the frizz. Anyway, I am not the kind to lose sleep over the colour of my hair, so that is not my primary concern.

The thing is, I don't feel forty. In fact, I don't feel any age at all! I don't even think of age 364 days of the year. What is there to think, you tell me? If not for yesterday, I would not even have sat here moping and telling you about my apparently futile thirty-nine years.

Let me tell you what happened yesterday. It is all Sameer's fault really, he threw me a birthday party. A surprise one at that. I am sure there are women who love that kind of thing, but not me. I hate surprise birthday parties. I have always felt sorry for the birthday person, the supposed star of these parties. Particularly, the deer caught in the headlights look on their face, when every other person in the room cheerfully shouts 'Surprise!' Oh, how that tortures my soul. I have always tried to imagine how stressful it must be to prepare for a cosy evening of Bollywood reruns in comfortable pyjamas, and then being thrust as though by a catapult, into a crowd of friends and almost friends, who have no greater desire in their heart than to wish you happy birthday. I always felt immensely grateful when year after year passed without a single surprise being sprung on me. Cakes? Yes! Gifts? Bring them on! Surprise? No thank you!

So, at the party yesterday when Sameer gave me what could be dubbed as the triumphant look of 'see what I pulled off', I naturally gave him a dark scowl. You see, I wasn't prepared for it. I had made other plans for my evening in fact. I was feeling particularly peppy with the first signs of crisp green that spring brings after the long, tortuous winter in the East Coast of the United States. We were to go out for dinner at this Turkish restaurant that had opened just last month in Washington, DC to great Yelp reviews – an hour's drive from our home in the Maryland suburbs. I had picked the place and made the reservations. But I had some time in hand before that, so I had applied oil in my hair and a homemade yogurt pack on my face which is supposed to clear it of all black spots, and then sat down to watch the *Real Housewives of Beverly Hills*. The last one is my guilty pleasure. I don't see much of reality TV but occasionally I reward myself with an episode of trashy drama.

I had just eased into the comfort of my couch, trying my best to keep my oily head stiff and upright like a Manipuri dancer, careful that the pristine white couch wasn't sullied by coconut oil, when the doorbell rang. I waited hoping someone would open the door, but of course no one did. No one ever does. I hold the honorary doorman position in this house alongside my umpteen other honorary roles. The bell rang again. It must be the UPS guy, I grumbled, and went downstairs, thoroughly irritated at this disruption. And so, when I opened the door to a shrill chorus of 'S-U-R-P-R-I-S-E', my yogurt-smeared face was contorted in a frown and oil was dripping off my forehead, in a greasy trickle along the uneven ridge of my nose. I could even feel my acne scars glow with all the attention that the oil gave them. My first thought while staring at those excited, make-up laden faces before me was: 'God please don't let them put photos on Facebook. Please!' I must have mumbled desperate prayers to all the thirty-three crore gods in my religion, with little hope.

I am pretty sure this whole surprise party was Piyu's idea, Sameer could have never come up with something like this. Piyu, my fifteen-year-old firstborn – the fulcrum of the Sen-Gupta family. She is the one maintaining the family balance among her puberty-struck, feisty, twelve-year-old sister, Riya, a workaholic, jet-setting Dad and an awesome mother, yeah, that would be moi!

But then again, it could very well have been Sameer's plan too. He has been so busy the last few months that we hardly get to see him. He has been either travelling for work, in office at work, or burrowed in his study at work. Maybe this was his way of redeeming himself. I would rather he redeemed himself by flying us all to Tuscany for a weekend. Now that would have been nice. I could do with some tagliatelle al tartufo and a glass of Chianti amidst the rolling Tuscan hills. Mmmm … just thinking of a truffle sauce makes my mouth water. But no, he had to go and throw me a surprise party. I mean, seriously?

Though I must confess the food at the party yesterday was damn good. No, no, not Tuscan. Just plain old Bengali. But so lip-smacking good and delicious. Sameer did an outstanding job with it. I mean, with the ordering of food. He is the only one I know who can cajole the neighbourhood Bengali caterer to cook a lentil stuffed kochuri and aloor dom just like the famous Putiram's, a tiny store around the corner in Kolkata's College Street. Sameer has a penchant for cooking and though he doesn't get the time to do it any more, he sure can guide the caterer to cook exactly what he wants. 'Go low on garam masala but increase the fresh ginger' is the kind of instructions he can belt out. And we could taste the delicious result yesterday.

The aloor dom had that zen-like balance between sweet and spicy, with the delectable gravy lovingly clinging to tiny round potatoes like a baby clings to its mother. And the kochuri had just the right amount of stuffing, not so little that you will miss it nor too much to weigh it down. Just perfect.

For dessert, there was a layered chocolate cake with complicated frostings and decorations. Piyu and Riya had baked it – 'from scratch' they had said. I am not sure where they got this talent from. Certainly not from me. And then there was much drinking of wine and a few cocktails.

My snippiness was gradually wearing off and I was kind of warming up to the surprise. Life was good. I had managed forty years on this beautiful planet without any major crisis. I had two lovely daughters – well, lovely for the most part. I had a husband who loved me enough to throw me a surprise birthday party. Not exactly what I had wanted but he did have good intentions. What more could I wish for? We have been married for almost eighteen years and I couldn't expect him to sweep me off to Seville or Tuscany or somewhere for a passionate birthday romance. We had responsibilities and mortgage and irritable bowel syndromes. I looked around at the happy faces sitting around in my family room, huddled on my red and blue kilim rug, lounging on my tufted Pottery Barn beige sofa and felt happy, the kind of happy that you feel when you bite into a perfect kheer kodom and discover the juicy part inside. I deserved a pat on my back for making this ordinary life work. We all did.

But as the evening progressed, with the 1960s' Chardonnay being opened and poured liberally, things started to go slightly off-key. Too much wine does that to you. With long fingers tapping on the stem of her fourth glass of Chianti, my vivacious, brilliant and beautiful friend Anju started talking of bucket lists.

'How many things have you ticked off your bucket list, Shubha?' she quizzed me. I have never been very fond of Anju. She is one of those friends I just put up with and secretly love to hate. Anju knows everything, has an opinion on everything, is best in everything she does, the world loves her, blah, blah ... she is that annoying. She had once told me that she had perfected all the poses from *The Joy of Sex* and was so good at them that she could make a YouTube video tutorial.

'I don't even have a bucket list.' I rolled my eyes.

'Oh! Then this is going to be fun,' she squealed, and pulled up a '40 Things to Do Before 40' bucket list on her iPhone. It was apparently doing the rounds on Facebook. I still don't know how she is the first to come to know of all things trending on social media.

Anju started reading out the list, her lilting voice framing each word of it in perfect accent. With her silky hair cascading down her face, her halter-neck blouse plunging to mysterious depths, her vibrant blue chiffon sari flitting across her shoulder, she was a vision.

'Go on a humanitarian aid trip.'

'Check, Uganda, the most fulfilling trip for me.' Anju sniffed. A few of the others checked it off too exchanging notes on their three-week social work stint across slums and pavement dwellers in India and Nepal.

'Learn to play an instrument.'

'Check, saxophone,' said Anju smugly. Minal said, 'Viola!' Minal's husband said, 'Check, flute.' Anju's own husband had recently picked up drumsticks (not the KFC variety), and he with a few others was forming a band to play at the local Durga Pujo.

I remained silent pondering over my instrument-lessness when Sameer said 'harmonica'. I almost guffawed but checked myself in time. Sameer had last picked up a harmonica in fifth grade when it was known as mouth organ. I looked at him, my mouth agape, but he avoided my gaze, staring hard at Anju's creamy shoulder instead.

I wished Neela was there. Not that Neela is my best friend cum saviour or anything. Well, she is kind of my best friend but that is not the primary reason I craved her presence. It was because Neela is like a black hole of conversation. If she opens her mouth, all other speech gets sucked into oblivion. She could talk about her sofa, her dog, her son and, if all else failed, her husband, and silence any other person in the room. All this list-wist would have just swept away if Neela started off about her son playing the sax. But no, she had to choose right this time to take a vacation.

'Run a marathon.'

'Check. Full marathon for each of the last four years.' Anju smiled. Running marathons seemed to be a popular idea because almost everyone said they had run a full marathon or at least a half one and agreed it was a liberating experience.

'Shubha, you should sign up for one. What do you do all day?' Anju asked me, her eyes innocent but lips forming a twisted smile.

I didn't know what I did. There seemed to be plump golden afternoons of nothingness in my days which I could have converted into sweaty gruelling marathons. But I didn't. So, I smiled weakly.

After a few more of that bulleted list, none of which I seemed to have ran, played or achieved in the four useless decades I spent on the planet, Anju dragged the list to an end.

'Get a dream job.'

'Senior VP at Dream Company. Check,' Anju said with a patronizing, smug smile.

'You have really done well for yourself, Anju. The dream job I applied for rejected me but now I am at a better place, so it worked out well,' said Minal who was the owner of a successful headhunting company. Soon the others went into a heated discussion about whether their job was indeed a 'dream' one or not.

I sat quietly, my glass of red wine turning warmer in my grip. What was my dream job? Why did none of those points in the list feature in my life? Had I been too easy-going? Had I wasted all my life's precious hours packing lunch boxes, snipping coriander, sitting outside Piyu's ballet classes, and waiting in the parking lot on cold winter evenings for Riya's swimming lessons to be over? I could have finished running multiple marathons in the sum of those hours.

I felt a sudden panic. What had I done with my life? It had looked so peaceful and ordinary until this list came along. And yes, maybe it wasn't perfect but then I always thought no one's is anyway. I had no idea of all the things I had missed out in all these years while everyone had gone ahead and had a smashing innings on the world pitch. I was like Sumedha Sarkar, the girl in my sixth grade who always came trailing in last during tracks, oblivious of the rest of us who had passed her a whole thirty minutes before. We would all look at Sumedha with suppressed giggles when she finally showed up. Where was Sumedha now? I should look her up and apologize. Maybe she too has shot past me in the real-life race.

Fifteen years ago, I had quit my job as an architect at a well-known architecture firm in New York City because I wanted to be with my kids. Being a mother at that time seemed all-encompassing. Far more important than designing buildings. Sameer travelled a lot and I was going crazy balancing work and day care. After a particularly sleepless night, I had woken up one morning and sent off an email which had turned out to be my resignation letter. 'I quit' was what I had written and started on my dream job.

But now my life sounded more 'Mother India' than 'Marilyn Monroe'. And I didn't like it. Not at all. I was destined for more than this. Much more than the tiny publishing boutique where I was recently moonlighting and earning practically nothing. I cringed at the thought of Anju rolling her eyes on hearing about our floundering company. So, I kept quiet.

'Hear, hear ... here is the last one on the list,' Anju said, her face shiny and content with the knowledge that she had finished all the tasks on the list and could now die in peace. 'Learn to cook at least five things that your mother cooked.'

'Gokul pithe, paayesh, mishti pulao...' the voices washed over me.

Voices from far away, whispered in my years, with a tinkle of bangles. '*Ki re, Shubha, aaj luchi khabi na pulao?*' the voice asked with a sweet lilt, 'Do you want luchi today or pulao?' It has been almost twenty-five years since I heard that voice. Twenty-five years since my mother passed away. All that remains now is, as the Portuguese say, 'saudade' – presence of an absence. And I have never learned to make a luchi or pulao. In the beginning, it was too painful to cook those same dishes that she conjured with such love. It seemed wrong to even touch her lovingly curated jars of cumin and coriander, to simmer a fish curry in her absence, and so I just avoided it. Now the pain had dulled and yet I was afraid to try them.

Over the years I have painstakingly learned to cook foreign flavours, food that does not carry the aroma of my mother's kitchen. I make risotto with mushrooms, pasta in a creamy Cajun sauce and even roast a whole turkey on Thanksgiving but when it comes to anything more Indian than rice or dal, I stumble. I wait for later to open Pandora's box.

Boishakh
(April – May)

When I enter the office today, late, at 11.30 in the morning, I can immediately see the excitement on Claire and Samantha's face. Our office is tiny, its shaggy beige carpeting almost threadbare, walls a yellow that reminds you more of puke than daffodils. One look at those walls and you know the bank account is dwindling. Samantha and me try to cosy up the space every now and then and have successfully managed to cram the 450 square feet with pictures, pots and mirrors that no one wanted at garage sales. However, there is not a lot of space or steel and concrete to mask emotions, if any. Hence, it's no wonder that emotions often run high in here.

Claire, the part-time intern, with her straight silver-grey hair and freckled face, holds up a bluish rectangle thing in her hand and gestures wildly at me. She is in her mid-twenties and still filled with a childlike exuberance. Given that there is hardly a distance of ten feet between the door, where I am standing, and Claire's desk, I really don't think such frantic measures are necessary to get my attention. So, I merely smile and then proceed to very calmly peel off my floral spring jacket to hang in the closet.

'Shub…ha,' hisses Samantha, clearly agitated by my nonchalance. Samantha Swaminathan is in her early fifties and going through a hissy menopausal phase. She is a taekwondo instructor when she is not cold-calling clients for us. Believe me, a hissy taekwondo instructor can be quite intimidating!

But my new mantra is to be calm, to go with the flow and not be agitated by any external force. That is the new me at forty. Lotus pose, here I come.

I, therefore, keep smiling and take long strides towards my desk by the window. Don't get caught off guard by the window. It is not a corner office situation. It is just that no one wanted to sit there because in summer the sun blazes in from eleven to three, and in winter when the temperature drops to freezing, the window can get draughty. But I like it. To see the lone tree outside change colours from blinding parrot green to crackling magenta as the earth traipses around the sun. To hear the ice melt on the line of red roofs across the quiet side street. To furtively glance at the mother who steps out at noon, like clockwork, to pick up her little boy getting off the yellow school bus.

Claire and Samantha are by my desk, even before I reach it, for my strides are in fact not that long. Claire puts the rectangular, pale blue piece of paper in front of me and taps at the postmark with her long green nail. I hate long nails. They freak me out. But whatever the nail is tapping at freaks me further.

I see a browned head of Gandhi. Just below that in neat inked uppercase letters, my name, SHUBHALAXMI SEN-GUPTA. 'Sen-Gupta' and not 'Sengupta' as in I was 'sane' before marriage, I like to tell people.

Yes, that's me all right. Shubha, short for Shubhalaxmi. Age: forty; height: 5'1'; build: slender – more like 'not fat' but always with those 5 lb to lose; eyes: brown with flecks of black; hair: frizzy.

I turn the blue aerogramme letter over to check the sender's address.

253/5 Panchanantala Lane
Baranagar
Kolkata – 700036
None of it rings a bell.

'It is for you, Shubha. Aren't you excited? Our first international mail in this office. Not an email, a postal letter!' shrieks Claire with a childlike innocence that is typical of her.

'At least not another bill or junk advertisement.' Sam rolls her eyes.

Well, I am definitely excited. I have not seen an aerogramme or inland letter in God knows how many years now. This piece of blue paper was how we remained connected with family all the years that my father was transferred on his job and moved around the country. My mother wrote long letters in blue inlands to her parents in Kolkata from the cold valleys of Leh, the hot plains of Jamshedpur, the beaches of Chennai. Sometimes she had so much to say that her rounded letters in Bengali script, filled all the space and spilled over to the scrimp where she perhaps unwillingly signed off, only after giving pronams to the elders and love to the younger ones.

It was those letters that told my grandparents about my exams, my first prize in art, my new school and my annual report card. And it was one of these that one day bore the news that Dida, my grandmother, was no more.

I gently pick up the letter and run my fingers around its edges. I then hold it close to my nose and sniff lightly. It smells of coffee and stale flowers.

I wet the glued edges, carefully prying them open as I had seen my mother do all the time. She almost never cut off the edges with a paper knife as there was always something written on the scrimp.

As I open the letter's folds and try smoothing the edges, a few dry petals and stamens of orange marigold tumble out.

Instinctively, I reach out to catch them and in a gesture of respect lift them to my forehead.

Tiny Bengali script in a lavender ink fills the blue paper. That ink colour is my favourite. What was the ink that we used in school? Sulekha, I think.

———

Dear Moni,

How are you? We miss you all so much.

Yesterday I went to the Dakshineshwar temple for Poila Boishakh. Uff, what a mistake! The place had such long queues that it was worse than our neighbourhood cinema hall. It was almost two hours before I could even get a glimpse of Ma Kali. Can you imagine? Even heaven can be reached faster than that.

Anyway, I am sending you blessed flowers from the Goddess' feet. Keep them safe, I might not go there any time soon and the flowers are not exactly hygienic so wash your hands after touching them.

Moni, do you celebrate Poila Boishakh in the US? Or do you say in English – Bengali New Year?

When you were in school, you and your friends would dance and sing and put up a show every Poila Boishakh. Right under that huge mango tree, on a makeshift stage. Far away in America, do you ever think of those days, Moni?

Remember that one time, the Kalboishakhi, the fearless storms in the month of Boishakh, stormed in just as you all were getting ready. The dark storm clouds descended on the north-west horizon and lightning crackled like cymbals. Soon the gusts of winds gathered strength and blew away all your mother's saris that you had draped as stage curtains. The mango tree swayed to rhythms of the storm while its mangoes were plucked by the wind and thrashed around. Then came the rain, fat large pellets of it, drumming on the courtyard, flooding the makeshift stage.

All your friends started crying but you were not too bothered. Instead you tugged at my sari and asked, 'Didan, can you please make your hing'r kochuri and aloor tarkari for dinner. Yours is the best in the world.' Food was your solution to all problems.

Ah, I remember those days so clearly. You know, lately I realize my mind is becoming like wool — soft, jumbled up. Some days, I forget if I have brushed my teeth or had breakfast. But the past? That I always remember so clearly that it floats in front of my eyes more crystal clear than pictures on that new television your eldest uncle gave me.

Now, that is why I am writing to you. You know my mother's cooking was some kind of a legend. All that thakurbarir ranna and everything you hear these days, well, their recipes were no match to hers. Or at least that is what she claimed. But she was a legendary cook anyway.

I learned whatever I could from her and then there is also that thing called genes so I was a pretty good cook in my time. And, of course, your Dadu loved food so I would make sure that we had a feast on all occasions. Fair white puffed luchi with aloor dom, misti pulao fragrant with just a hint of javetri and jaiphol, kosha mangsho that had cooked for hours and was soft and succulent.

Those were the days. Now I have no one to cook for. Your Dadu isn't around. Even if he was, I don't think I would be able to cook. Some days I can't seem to remember if it is cumin or coriander that I added in my kosha mangsho, but then suddenly it all comes back to me and I try to write it down. I am getting old, Moni, and I fear that something is dying in my brain. I forget. The past is lucid in my memory but on some days the present gets all foggy like a December morning.

But I digress. The thing is after your youngest aunt was born, my mother gave me a notebook with all her recipes written down in her own beautiful handwriting. Her 'Rannar Khaata' – her handwritten recipe book. Pages and pages of precious gems. I know none of my children will treasure it as much as I do and I don't want to pass it on to just one of them and let them fight over it. I wanted you to have it but the problem is, now I have forgotten where I have kept it. It must be some place very safe but I don't remember anything. I am afraid if I don't find the book those rare recipes will be lost.

So, in the meanwhile, I will send you my special recipes – what I remember from my memory. That way my legacy will live with you. There might be some slips, some mistakes, but I know you will be able to figure it out.

Take care of them like your own. Remember, food does not only feed the body, Moni, it feeds your soul. My blessings will always be with you.

Bhalo theko,
Didan

The letter ends with what looks like a detailed recipe of hing'r kochuri and aloor dom in the postscript.

'Who gave you this letter, Claire?' I ask, chewing on my lower lip, the letter still open in my hand. Dida, my maternal grandmother, had passed away long back. Even Thamma, my father's mother, was no more. I have no relatives who could have sent me this letter. 'Moni' wasn't even a name anyone called me by. I am certain this letter is for someone else and has been wrongly delivered by the post office. It seems like an uncanny mistake, but I assure myself that these things happen.

'Dunno,' says Claire, 'looks like it came in the mailbox, United States Postal Service.'

'Kajol might know but she is away in Aruba,' chimes in Samantha. Kajol, my friend, the 80 per cent owner of Right-to-Write – this tiny, independent, wannabe publishing house, is a fiery, independent spirit (I am the wimpy secondary owner of the rest 20 per cent). Single and unencumbered, she has her hand and heart in several different ventures and good-looking men. My mother, if she had known Kajol, would have called her a jack of all trades, master of none. Only Kajol doesn't even want to be the master. It is all the different things she dabbles in, from global hunger to eclectic art, which breathes life in her. Actually I am a bit in awe of her. She is like Joan of Arc, shushing everyone with her personality, throwing around her hands animatedly and talking with her big kohl-rimmed eyes. Actually I am not sure if Joan of Arc did that, but you get the idea, right?

As I fold the letter, my stomach rumbles and I feel this teeny shard of pain at not having Dida around. She was an artiste in the kitchen – chopping, grinding, stirring, her life revolving around feeding her children and grandchildren. Her flaky khasta kochuris stuffed with spiced lentils, which we always carried by the jarfuls after the winter holidays, were the best I have ever had. It has been so long since I have tasted anything like that. I often wish that I had learned to make them like her.

The thing is, cooking is not my forte. Never has been. Chopping onions had me in a tearful puddle; the sizzle of red chillies in hot mustard oil made me sneeze like crazy; and tossing cauliflowers in hot oil had left many a burn on my arms. When Ma was around, she hardly ever let me in the kitchen, shooing me away every time I wandered in.

'Go study now and get into a good college. I will teach you to cook when you need it,' she would say, dismissing me with a flutter of her hands. Well, she didn't wait to see if I needed it. She was gone even before I went to college! I always felt angry that she did not keep her promise, cheated that now I would never know what secret spices she put in her fish curries. And then later, I never felt the urge to pick it up on my own.

But I had always liked good food, a carefully crafted meal, the family sitting down at the dining table at the end of the day. In the first few years of my marriage, I even hung on to that warm glossy image, carefully laying a table, arranging flowers and placing the right silverware every evening. In that fancy set-up I served egg curry and rice, day in, day out. Sameer said little and I thought he was enjoying my routine meal until one day he blurted out the truth. 'Shubha, you don't have to go through this every day you know. Why don't you relax while I cook dinner from tomorrow?'

I had agreed with secret relief. So, Sameer started cooking our meals, exotic dishes named methi murg, badami fish, makhmali paneer tikka, from his collection of cookbooks. He was good at it.

Slowly, however, our roles shifted. After the girls were born, Sameer got busier at work. I quit my job as an architect and became the driver-cum-cook-cum cleaner – the all-in-one mother. Only, I resorted to quick thirty-minute meals which we all ate at different times, sitting in front of the TV, leaning on the counter or in the study. If I was bored I would dabble through a Sanjeev Kapoor or Madhur Jaffrey cookbook but never did I attempt to cook the Bengali dishes my mother used to. I was afraid I could never do justice to those recipes.

Today, the time has come to amend all of that and start afresh, I tell myself. There is something in that letter which convinces me that I should. 'Go, Shubha, take a leap of faith, try it out even if only once,' I whisper to myself.

It has been two weeks since my birthday, only fifteen days since Poila Boishakh, and we are still fairly new into the Bengali year. We need to celebrate. Piyu and Riya need to know their traditions. If that can happen by deep frying kochuri in my kitchen, so be it. I am sure my mother will appreciate it from wherever she is. And how bad can I possibly be at rolling dough? After all I did learn to make ravioli in that Italian class the girls gifted me last Mother's Day.

With my mind held high and determination in my chest, I message Sameer to come back at least an hour early. He has been coming home after ten lately, way past the girls' dinner time. Then I stop at the Indian grocery store on my way home. Carefully ticking off items from the recipe I had jotted down, I manoeuvre the shopping cart through the narrow aisles of Patel Grocery. A box of saffron yellow hing from Rajasthan, pungent mustard oil, tiny cloves, pale green cardamoms, fiery red chillies, a packet of maida. Tick. Tick. Tick.

Even chubby old Mahesh Patel, the elder of the Patel brothers is surprised by the stuff in my cart. '*Koi can nahi lena?*' (You don't want any canned food this time?) he asks me, unable to keep his curious Indian mind in check.

Back home, I take a quick shower and brace myself for the evening.

1. Measure two cups of maida and half a cup of atta in a large bowl. Add a little ghee or vegetable oil and rub it to the flour with your fingers.

    I measure out the flour in my big salad bowl and then rub in oil as per the instructions. Easy-peasy!

    But the flour is soon in crumbles and I start having the first inkling of doubt. How is this going to ever come together? Was the old lady totally in her senses when she wrote the recipe?

2. Slowly add water and mix with your fingers to form the dough. Without giving it a thought, I pour a jug of water. Biggest mistake! The whole thing now looks like a flour soup, greyish in colour with small dumplings of flour swimming around. By no law of physics or chemistry could this ever be transformed to dough.

    Man, making these kochuris is not easy. And definitely not for someone like me. I dump the whole soupy mess into the bin, scrub the salad bowl clean and start with Step Number 1 again. 'I can do this,' I repeat after myself. If I say something enough number of times, someone had said, I can convince myself to believe in it and then actually do it. Sounds like load of rubbish but no harm in trying, I decide.

    On my second attempt, I notice the keyword 'slowly' and add the water gradually, each time mixing the flour with my fingers. It slowly comes together and this time I know the moment when the water is just right.

3. Knead the dough well. Pummel and knead with the heel of your palm until the ball of dough looks smooth like a baby's bottom. I punch and pummel and knead thinking of Anju and Kajol and it seems to work. I am getting this right. My dough isn't exactly like a baby's bum, well, maybe a very wrinkly one. But it is close.

4. Cover the dough with a damp cloth and let it sit for twenty to twenty-five minutes.

Dinner was getting late. Today is usually our taco day when I serve ground chicken chilli and black beans with crispy taco shells bought from the store. The girls make their own tacos, topping them with lettuce, salsa and sour cream. It is easy for me, and the girls love it. My salsa is quite good actually. Around nine, Piyu comes wandering into the kitchen and is not too welcoming of my dinner idea. 'But we always have tacos on Tuesdays,' she sulks. Uggh, what have I done to my girls? Made them such boring slaves of routine.

'Today, we will have kochuri. It is deep fried and yum. Just wait for it.' I try to make it sound exciting though for all I know we might end up eating just plain bread and jam for dinner instead.

'But Mom, that is tonnes of artery-clogging oil. You know how harmful it can be. Can you visualize the layers of fat that will be deposited in your blood vessels from that single deep-fried bread?' She grimaces, her face innocent and young but her tone desperately trying to be adult.

I am taken aback. That is not how I had ever looked at kochuri. It clogs my heart no doubt, but with the weight of its love. 'Ha, nothing like that will happen,' I assure her as I roll out the dough flat. I do not have time to make the stuffing spiced with hing, that will have to wait until next time.

Riya is more supportive. Not that she would eat more than a bite but this 'kochuri-making' has excused her from homework, and so she stands around cheering me. 'Mamma, it is not that hard. It is like play-doh. You can do it.'

'Well, I can't help,' quips Piyu and stomps up to her room.

The strains of Tagore's song '*Esho he boishakh, esho, esho…*' from my iPhone washes over my modern kitchen, falling flat and lifeless, while Riya and I roll out the dough in all shapes and suspend it in the hot oil. Some of it puff up just like I remembered it should. The soft kochuris, their belly plumped with a paste of dal flavoured with hing, would levitate on the small kadhai until my mother gently lifted them up with her 'jhanjri', ladle. Some fall on their face, flat and crispy. We keep plodding along, undefeated.

By the time the kochuris (or rather luchis, as I skipped the stuffing), are all done, I am exhausted and have no energy to make aloor dom.

Around 9.45 at night Sameer texts: 'Running Late. Sorry.'

I am not sure if he really is sorry. Texts don't show emotions. And Sameer never uses emojis. This is an annoying habit of his. Given that we communicate mostly over texts, how was I to know exactly what he felt?

'Sameer, you need to use those little emojis. The sad face, or the angry face, or the happy one. They are there to show your feeling, your mood,' I have told him repeatedly. 'Shubha, you could just murder someone and send three red hearts and a hug. They don't mean a damn thing.' He has always shrugged it off in his usual Sameer way.

It is getting late and I can't let my luchis go cold. My arms ache and I wish Sameer was home to see this magical stack that we have conjured. 'Let's just have them with ketchup,' I declare cheerfully to the girls.

I update my Facebook status.

Shubho Noboborsho. Errm ... belated. #bengalinewyear

50 likes. 50 hearts. 30 sad emojis.

Hing'r Kochuri

Hing'r kochuri is a very popular Bengali stuffed bread that is deep fried. The stuffing is made of urad dal (called 'kalai'r dal' in Bengali) paste spiced with a good sprinkling of hing or asafoetida, grated ginger and a touch of fennel powder. Hot off the oil kochuris served with chholar dal and aloor dom is a popular Bengali breakfast. To make the experience that much more perfect, don't forget to end the meal with jalebis and steaming cups of hot tea. This recipe serves four.

Making the Stuffing

Urad dal/kalai'r dal/biulir dal – 1 cup
Green chillies – 3
Ginger – 1" knob
Asafoetida – ¼tsp
Grated ginger – 1 tbsp
Ground fennel powder – ¼tsp
Mustard oil – ¼cup
Salt – to taste
Sugar – to taste

Soak the urad dal overnight in water.

The following morning, put the dal in a blender along with the green chillies and chopped ginger. Add very little water to make a coarse paste. Not very coarse, but not smooth like a vada batter either.

Heat mustard oil in a kadhai. Preferably one with a non-stick surface. To the hot oil, add the asafoetida, grated ginger and fennel powder.

Pour the dal/lentil paste that you made. Add salt to taste and a pinch of sugar. Mix well.

Now comes the part where you must keep stirring like a maniac, so that the dal paste does not stick. You might also have to add some more oil in the process.

Eventually the paste will slowly start coming off from the sides and will get drier. It will also no longer taste or smell raw but will taste pretty good. If it does not, adjust the spices and keep stirring. Add a little more hing if you feel the aroma is missing.

But take heart, this whole process takes a mere twenty to thirty minutes of your lifetime and life gets better after this.

Once you have the stuffing, keep it aside and make the dough for the kochuri.

Making the Dough

All-purpose flour – 1 cup
Whole wheat – 1 cup
Vegetable oil – 1½ tbsp
A pinch of salt

In a wide-mouthed bowl, add the flour, salt and oil.

Rub the oil in the flour with your fingers. Then gradually add warm water and knead the dough until it is soft. Cover the dough with a damp towel and let it rest.

Making the Kochuri

Vegetable oil – 1 ½ cups for frying
Make about twenty balls, the size of a gooseberry, out of this dough. Dip the tip of a ball in oil and then flatten it between your palms.

Now roll it out into a 2" circle. Take a little of the dal stuffing and put it in its centre. Bunch up the sides of the dough disc to form a purse-like formation. With your fingers, close the top of the purse so that the stuffing does not come out. Flatten it between your palm and you are ready to roll.

Roll out the stuffed ball into small discs about 3" in diameter, the same size as a luchi or puri.

Heat enough oil for frying these in a kadhai. When the oil is hot, dip the rolled-out disc to see if the oil bubbles. If it does, slowly release the disc in oil and press with a slotted spoon, coaxing the kochuri to puff. Once the kochuri puffs up and becomes a shade of pale brown, take it out and repeat the process for the rest.

2

The day dawns stiflingly hot and muggy. Warm for mid-May in the East Coast. Technically, it isn't even dawn yet. The eastern sky has just turned a shade lighter, like a slate grey dhonekhali sari with pink border and scattered twinkling sitara work. The seamstress seems fickle-minded, switching the twinkling slate grey for a peach grey canvas now.

I lie awake, looking beyond the huge maple tree outside the window. The birds are already up, busy and chattering. The baby green leaves on the maple are yet to catch the morning light and the tree looks like a huge blob of dark green paint. Beyond that I can see stars in the sky, switching off one after another as the morning light spread its wings.

Usually I am not a morning person. I am the kind who puts the alarm to snooze for the umpteenth time and then goes back to sleep again. I love my morning sleep too much. My father who believed that the time between 4 and 6 a.m., brahma-muhurta, was the best for young brains to absorb knowledge would regularly make my life hell while in school. 'The early bird catches the worm,' he would thunder, holding the screeching chrome alarm clock to my ears.

I wish there was a voice like that near me now. Forty per cent thunder, 10 per cent disgust, 50 per cent love. I would have bolted through life like an arrow. Instead I have this New Age alarm clock which throws at me waves from the shores of the Atlantic. I groan and try to prop myself up. The Tempur-Pedic or some-such-pedic mattress doesn't make it easy. My lower back has a dull ache. I should seriously start sleeping on the floor like my yoga teacher has suggested. Hard floor, no pillows, entire body in the same line, relaxed muscles. 'Relax like a corpse and your body shall be rejuvenated.'

I slam down the alarm and glance at the other end of the bed. Sameer's side is smooth, without a single wrinkle. The pillows are propped up and puffed. It doesn't look slept in at all. Unlike me, Sameer is an early riser. He is also a late nighter. I mean he is the kind of person who goes to sleep after midnight and is up by five in the morning. He can get by with little sleep and yet remain energetic throughout the day. Oh, how I envy him.

He is not the kind of person my yoga teacher would like, I presume. He doesn't have problems. I mean he does have problems, but he doesn't acknowledge them. Sameer likes to solve his problems on his own. Like that time when he was writhing in stomach ache and kept trying his own remedies; until I dragged him to a doctor, and it turned out to be appendicitis.

My yoga teacher on the other hand thinks he has been born on earth to solve other people's problems.

Mental Stress? Pranayama

Constipation? Vajrasana

Sexual malfunction? Gomukhasana

World peace? Sukhasana

If all else fails? Shavasana, my favourite.

But the fact that Sameer didn't sleep the whole night bothers me. At first, I feel guilty that I slept peacefully through the night without realizing Sameer's absence. Does it make me a bad wife? What makes a good wife? Errm ... I don't want to know.

Then I panic. Did he even get home last night? Lately he has been working so late that I am often snoring by the time he returns. What if he had called my phone and I had missed the call? What if he was in the middle of a heart attack and called me for help? Or what if he was in an accident last night and the cops could not reach me as I was snoring? I feel a shiver of fright shoot through my spine. Oh no, no. Please God, I will take any kind of pill to stay awake from tonight, but please let Sameer be okay.

I bolt out of bed, with an alacrity that would have made Baba proud, and rush to the catwalk hanging across the two-storey family room. It is a beautiful room with huge glass windows that bring the outside greenery into the house. But right now, I am not seeing any of that.

'Sameer!' I almost scream, my stomach in a tight knot. I am leaning so precariously far that half my body hangs over the banister. It is a dangerous thing to do, this leaning. A little shift in my centre of gravity and I could just topple over. Plop! I would land straight on the terracotta tiles of my kitchen floor; the tiles I had chosen after days of search and research simply because terracotta reminds me of warm, luxurious summer days. Probably my skull would break open and my new, gleaming stainless steel dishwasher would be spattered with blood.

For a fleeting moment I think 'What if that happens? What if I am not there tomorrow? Would my family just go on with their morning routine after calling 911? Who would clean the bloodstains on the dishwasher?'

'Sameer, are you downstairs?' I yell again, still thinking of the gory details of my hypothetical fall. 'Mom, shhh ... don't scream. Baba is on a call,' shouts my fifteen-year-old daughter Piyu, munching on a protein bar. I feel a wave of relief but also a whole tsunami of irritation. All that panic for nothing! I turn my focus on Piyu instead.

Today is her early practice for tracks. Her bus comes in five minutes and she is not even dressed. In the last one year, Piyu has grown taller than me. At 5'3", she towers two whole inches over me. Her face is scrubbed clean as always, no make-up. Thick strands of not-much-cared-for hair hangs loosely down her back. No time for brushing, Ma, she tells me every time I pick up a comb and bottle of coconut oil. I can feel her becoming a whole different person, like an arrow at the tip of being released from the bow. She is just waiting, waiting, for the last pull to peel away.

'Piyu, why are you not dressed yet? Your bus comes in five ... no, four ... minutes.'

'I am,' says Piyu as she scrolls down on her phone.

She is wearing a T-shirt that looks straight from the laundry hamper. I am sure if I sniff at it, it would only confirm my belief. Her shorts have frayed ends and look like something that the cat dragged in last night.

'Piyu, you didn't do your laundry, did you? Seriously, when will you learn to do your own stuff?'

Piyu rolls her eyes, gathers her hair up in a ponytail and grabs her backpack. 'Mom, think of the earth. Each load of laundry depletes the earth's water resource by 20 per cent. I am saving the earth. And when you do my laundry, remember to not use the dryer. Dry them on the clothes line outside. It saves power. Think green.'

With that parting shot, she strides out on to the driveway to wait for the bus. Piyu thinks of the earth more than anything else. She shuns plastic and styrofoam and is always lecturing me to stop buying hand soap from Bath & Body Works. I just pour out the Japanese Cherry Blossom Gentle Foaming Hand Soap in mason jars and tell her it is organic and home-made by my neighbour's cousin. There is so only so much you can listen to your teenager.

I can see Sameer in the study, pacing the length of the room, his hands animated, his fingers dancing around, explaining some secret of the universe to an invisible audience. Until a few years back, his fingers danced for me as we would have lengthy discussions on everything from food to fractals. But then his career took off like a rocket. He went from being an expert software architect at a traditional technology company to being the CTO of a shiny new start-up. He says they are an idea farm, selling ideas and then getting venture capitalists to invest in those ideas. Honestly, the whole idea sounds vague to me.

As he rose in the corporate elevator, his time with us slowly dwindled and now we are at a point when I don't even realize whether he has been to bed or not. His face looks thinner and the nose angular. There is a slight paunch where the T-shirt would lie flat earlier. The shadows under his eyes seem to be darker, making his eyes look afloat in a hollow well.

'Shubha, what are you thinking? You always seem lost these days.' Sameer's deep voice snaps me out of my reverie. I was so engrossed thinking of him that I hadn't noticed him coming out of the study. He leans over to switch off the gas, where my pot of tea has been bubbling away for the past fifteen minutes.

'Maybe you should try yoga,' he says looking distracted, 'meditation, tai chi?'

'I have been doing yoga for the last two months,' I reply stonily, suddenly aware of my very non-yoga-esque persona.

'Really?' He narrows his eyes and peers at me, not quite believing my yoga claim. I get a whiff of the fresh scent of his cologne. Always the same, citrus and musk, the one I buy for his birthday. I feel an ache in my heart. I want to reach up and nuzzle him, ask him where he was all night. But his smugness irritates me, so I keep quiet. I wait for him to say something.

Instead he moves away and gets his oatmeal ready. If nothing, Sameer is supremely self-sufficient. Very unlike the usual mollycoddled Bengali sons. If he wants, he can cook a seven-course meal and change fitted sheets like a pro. It is another thing that he doesn't 'want' to do it and so I am left with all the drudgery of housework. But if I just happen to vanish from the face of the earth tomorrow, he will sail through life without worrying about where the next meal will come from or what washer setting is best for delicate cotton.

'You are sooo lucky, Shubha, I always tell Saty. Had I met Sameer while I was single, I would have married him straight away. Saty toh cannot even vacuum right. He doesn't get the corners at all. Babe, you cannot imagine how easy your life is,' Anju repeats in her nasal voice every time we meet. I am not sure what she wants – a Hoover or a husband. It always strikes me as strange that someone like Anju would marry Saty. Her husband Saty aka Satyajit has the looks of a hunk, but if I may say so, is a bit off in the head. He seems to have no voice of his own and is always nodding to whatever Anju has to say, like a puppet with a bobbing head.

Sameer gulps his oatmeal down, all the while tapping on his phone. He is done in two minutes and is wearing his jacket, grabbing the car keys and leaving. Leaving just like that, with a terse 'Bye, Shubha'.

Seriously, 'Bye, Shubha' is all he has to say? No explanation of his all-night binge? Even if it is only work? My eyes sting with tears. I want to actually throw the pot of tea at his back.

'Mom, did Dad leave without saying bye to me?' wails Riya. I suddenly realize she is still in her bedroom upstairs instead of being dressed and ready for school. This puberty thing has made the poor girl super-sensitive! She finds every freaking reason to moan and wail. What is with kids these days? They hit puberty by twelve and then hang on to all the teenage drama until nineteen!

'Honey, he did say bye. Now you come down or you will miss the bus,' I quickly try to assuage her and pack her lunch. Riya is on some self-proclaimed diet recently and all I can give her is sautéed broccoli sprinkled with Feta and chopped almonds. The broccoli must be steamed just al dente and look bright green, so I do it fresh every morning.

Riya wails some more and then bangs the bathroom door shut, staying there for the next twenty minutes doing God knows what. I feel the stress creep up my shoulders with every tick of the clock. 'Riyaaa!' I let out my patent blood-curdling growl, 'Down in the next five.' Riya comes down sulking, wearing one of those cold shoulder tops, where half of the shoulder and arm is bare. She is petite and looks small for her age. Her thin, knobbly shoulders jut out of the opening, like a hanger, and I really wish she would eat rice and butter for lunch instead of steamed broccoli. But there is no time for arguments. I hand her a fig bar for breakfast, the lunch box, and then shove her out right at the moment the bus rolls in.

Phew! Every-frigging-day this is how my morning goes. Rushed, stressful, mostly catastrophic.

After everyone leaves, I make myself one more cup of tea. This time, I let the water come to full boil and steep my Earl Grey for full three minutes. I take down my favourite mug, the one with a turquoise rim and orange ikkat print, pour out the tea and add a teaspoon of sugar. The house is quiet with only the hum of the refrigerator giving my thoughts company. I plump the turquoise and gold pillows studded with shimmering sequins and straighten the rug in the family room. I step out onto the back deck and can hear faint sounds of small children from far. The mint bushes in my backyard are growing like crazy with the warm weather and the air is sweet with its smell. They carry a whiff of methi parathas and pudina chutney from a friend's lunch box from many years ago in another continent.

This area where we live, the 'burbs of Maryland', is what typical American suburbia looks like. Everyone lives in almost identical three-thousand-square-foot houses with a neat lawn and have two cars in the driveway. At ten on a weekday morning, the place is almost deserted except for the resolute jogging mommies with their toned arms and iPods and nannies pushing baby strollers. The way they go running in every weather you would think they are training for the Olympics.

I check the newsfeed on my phone and a trending article tells me 'Five Ways to Keep Your Relationship from Fizzling Out':

1. Spice up your life, your love will be refreshed.
2. Share a common interest. Play the same Facebook game.
3. Don't forget using emojis in your texts. God didn't make those for nothing.
4. Take a selfie. It helps you to get closer.
5. Have a drink together every night.

I have that empty feeling inside me again. Usually my sugary cup of tea is my picker-upper, but not today. Today something is missing. I feel like I am in deep waters, desperately trying to grasp something – something that will prop me back to firm ground, but everything seems to be slipping away. Mossy green relationships. Years. Experiences. Achievements.

What did I do with my forty years on earth? Why is it that my life suddenly has no meaning? Why do I feel like Sameer and I are moving apart?

I feel bare, stripped, sinking. Scared, I try to run through my mind looking for a common interest for myself – for us – something that will propel me towards the next day – and find nothing except a list of chores to be ticked off. I must check with the landscaper about those spider mites I noticed the other day. Dentist's appointment for Riya is next week. I have to shop for an anniversary gift for Neela. Need to sign up Piyu and Riya for their summer classes before the slots fill up. None of them have the potential to be tagged as #couplegoals.

Maybe I should try taking a selfie with Sameer after of course having a drink together!

I update my Facebook status.

Why, oh why? #seekingpurpose

23 likes.

Jaishtha
(May – June)

I had barely parked my car in the rear parking area of our office building when I saw Claire's excited face in the upstairs window. Claire is like an exuberant dog. Always excited, always yapping. As soon as she saw me, she took the two flight of stairs and burst through the metal door and into the rear parking lot. Her hand was held high, like the Statue of Liberty holding aloft a torch, and clutched in her fingers was a rectangular piece of blue. She didn't have to say anything, I knew it. The letter. A second one from the stranger at 253/5 Panchanantala Lane – a little more than a month since the last one, I mentally calculated.

I felt a surge of excitement rush through me. A sudden high. My heart began beating a tad bit faster and I leapt out of the car.

It reminded me of the times, about eighteen years ago, when Sameer used to write letters to me from his work trips abroad, soon after our engagement. Phone calls were expensive and we didn't have laptops or smartphones. No WhatsApp or Skype either. How did relations survive then, I wonder. His letters were short, written on the back of picture postcards, in scrawny handwriting. '*I ate smoked salmon today. I don't know if you would like it. It smelled very strongly of the wild sea,*' he once wrote on the back of a postcard with a photo of the Little Mermaid on the other side. He signed off with 'I love you', words we rarely uttered loud then. I thought the way he made a heart out of the 'o' in l-o-v-e was extremely romantic and very unlike him. Just that single letter would make my heart go swish-swish.

'Kajol is here, she saw the mail,' Claire whispered conspiratorially. I hadn't told Kajol about the last letter. I had concluded it was clearly a postal delivery faux pas and nothing that Kajol would be aware of. Also, the letter seemed very personal and yet not really mine. I was going to send it back soon anyway. What was the point of telling her?

Now this second letter throws a bit of a wrench in the situation. I had never expected that there would be a second! It seems a bit queer, this wrong delivery once again.

'She might want to find a story in this. You know how desperate she is.' Claire added in a hushed voice.

Kajol was indeed desperate. She had started this small publishing company in the hopes of publishing a Booker Prize-winner some day. Forget a Booker, we had not been able to get a single author to publish anything with us. The local church and neighbourhood stores were our only clients. Their annual brochure, monthly newsletters and colourful flyers were all we had managed to publish till now. In dire situations, Kajol had even decided to write the great Indian-American novel herself, but with her flitting mind and hundreds of other interests, she was unable to find a story to tell.

Last year around November, it was at a Bengali community Durga Puja that Kajol had sought me out. Dressed in a black chikan kurta, leggings and dangling silver earrings which were shaped like a damru, she had popped up while I was standing in queue for the puja anjali, my palms folded around damp marigold and rose petals.

'Aren't you Shubha? Arch '97? Hostel Leelavati, room #42B?' Trying to scramble my memories I had fumbled guiltily.

'Kajol.' My memories immediately sorted themselves out at that name. Who could forget the girl who had bet with the cafeteria cook and devoured all his fish chops in a record fifteen minutes? Later at the hostel it had been a harrowing night for all of us as Kajol retched and vomited and writhed in pain, promising she would never touch a fish chop again! Kajol was more a fellow hosteller than friend when we were in college but that incident had brought all of us in the hostel closer.

'Kajol Banerjee? Comparative Lit '96? You still don't eat maach'r chop, do you?' I beamed.

Now Kajol, as typical of her, had started this tiny publishing company a few months before we met. She had been through a bitter divorce, left her job at a Page 3 kind of magazine, and had just ventured out to live her life anew. Right-to-Write was her baby and she had invested almost all her savings in it with no clear business plan.

I was unemployed and volunteering at the local library at that time. When Kajol asked me to join her with no salary but a 20 per cent stake in the company I had agreed without so much as even asking how much the profit was.

Turned out there was no profit!

Looked like all she wanted was an ally, someone she could trust and didn't really have to pay, to come on board with her. Typical Kajol! But I didn't mind. I took up her offer. If I don't like it, I can leave and anyway it's only a few hours a day, I assured myself. And so, for the last four months I have been spending my golden hours when the girls are in school, at Right-to-Write. Other than me and Kajol, there is Claire, our exuberant intern, and Sam, who comes in three days a week to edit copies and follow up on clients in her gruff voice. After paying Sam and Claire's paltry salary, rent, utility and miscellaneous expenses there is almost nothing left for us, the so-called partners, and yet I have stuck around.

This has turned out to be a creative haven away from home, a hideout for me. And though I have no buildings to design here, I channel my knowledge to design layouts and write copy for the few flyers and yearbooks that keep our business barely afloat.

Now, the back-from-vacation-with-new-boyfriend, tanned and glowing Kajol waved at me excitedly. 'Shubha, what is this? You keep getting letters from India, I heard. What is it? Is it a manuscript from an Indian author? We can publish her if she wants.' Kajol's big kohl-lined eyes pierced through my very epicentre. I averted her gaze and made up my mind to keep this my secret. At least for now.

'They are from a relative, a distant grandmother, my grandfather's first cousin.' I found myself uttering a blatant lie clutching the letter in my hand.

'I thought you didn't have any relatives on your side any more, other than your aunt.' Kajol wasn't going to let go of this easily. She could be irritatingly persistent.

'We know very little about the people around us, isn't it?' I was saccharine sweet, as I fired up my laptop busily, signalling an end to this conversation.

I know Kajol has been a bit tense lately. This month we lost a client. One of the two churches in the neighbourhood whose newsletters we published, closed doors. No one believes in God any more, they said. 'There are not enough donations coming in. Folks would rather invest in real estate than God,' the elderly pastor told us.

I kept the letter aside and got to work. It was the middle of the month and the newsletters had to be composed before sending out to the printer. It wasn't exactly a creatively challenging job but to break the monotony I changed the font now and then, and looked for fancy synonyms of simple words. Last week, I had used the word 'suspire', when all I meant was breath!

I often think about going back to a real job, I mean the kind of job that pays good money and paid vacations. I am not that old for the workforce. I have a college degree, I can get myself an interview and maybe even a job – a 'dream job' in Anju's words. I imagine myself throwing my head backwards and sharing my story of ticking off a 'dream job' from that stupid bucket list.

But then I am not sure whether I will fit in. I have been away from the corporate rat race, the fast life, for too long. I have come to like the slow pace here, the easy camaraderie between us four women. And the fact that I have 20 per cent share in this tiny business, is reason to live. I desperately want our company to survive. And one day, maybe just one day, that 20 per cent share will be worth some money.

It was afternoon by the time I could finally get to the letter. Claire had left for the day. Samantha was at her Tuesday afternoon taekwondo class, probably teaching a bunch of sixty-year-old ladies to break boards like Bruce Lee (wait, that's karate, but I am sure taekwondo has something similar). Kajol was nowhere in sight. I was all by myself in our tiny office. The sun spilled long shadows along my desk. The birds in the tree outside were quiet, probably napping on a hot afternoon. It was a sweltering hot day and except for the occasional screech of a car, the world around me was strangely silent.

I had called Pishi, my dad's sister and the only living relative from my paternal side, last week asking her if she knew someone who might have sent this letter. Or at least know where Panchanantala Lane was. But Pishi had no idea. She said if my great-grandmother would have been alive she would have written something just like this. Maybe it was her spirit that was writing this, she suggested. And with that she had veered to her favourite topic and asked me if I thought Sourav Ganguly, the famous cricketer and now a reality TV host, really knew all the answers to the questions he asked in Dadagiri. 'He must be smart,' she said, 'if after playing all that cricket he also memorized our history and geography.'

'I have to send the letter back,' I told myself, trying to concentrate on the newsletter.

God knows, what the old lady has written this time. Well, just a little peek isn't going to harm anyone. I can always glue it and send it back.

Soon my curiosity got the better of me and in the next minute I had wet the glued edges of the aerogramme and opened the letter very, very carefully.

———

Dear Moni,

How have you all been? It has been very hot here these last few days. The earth is spewing fire and the air is scorching and dry. My room upstairs is so hot that during the day I prefer staying in the room beside the kitchen. At least it is cooler.

My mother used to say that Jaishtha is the month of heat and hope. When the sun scorches the earth, shooting spears of fire, the only way to survive is to nurture hope for the monsoon.

The only good thing about this heat are the mangoes and jackfruits, which grow sweet and plump from Jaishtha's warmth. You wouldn't believe it but both the trees in the garden are laden with mangoes this year. The one beside the well in the north-east corner has mangoes dangling from practically every branch. I have no idea what to do with so many of them. I have already made three kinds of achaar, one of them sweet with jaggery. Wish you were here. You would have been so happy to pluck ripe golden mangoes from the trees and have them.

By the way, Moni, it is Jamaishoshthi next week. I might not have remembered it this year, but I don't read the Ponjika every day for nothing. I know you probably don't get the time to follow all our rituals there, but this is special.

A lot of people think it is only a day to feed sons-in-law, but that is not true. The sixth day of Jaishtha is also a day to celebrate the goddess of fertility and thus children. We call it Aranyo Shoshthi. Do you remember, you and your cousins would be visiting me for summer and I would let you all make the figurines of Shoshthi Thakurun with rice flour and then paint them with turmeric and bright water paint? You particularly liked the part where I fanned you all with a palm leaf fan and gave you new clothes to wear.

You know Jamaishoshthi was a big celebration in the neighbourhood of north Kolkata where I grew up. I never liked so much hullabaloo over feeding sons-in-law; but paying no heed to my protests, the very year that I got engaged Ma went ahead and invited my fiancé for Jamaishoshthi.

I had just turned twenty and was in my second year of college. My fiancé, Rajat, was a handsome lawyer, the only heir of a very rich family.

He had just cleared his bar exam and joined a very prestigious British company. Though we moved in different social circles, Rajat had seen me at our college's annual day function. Apparently, he was so smitten by my singing that his parents sent a proposal the very next day. Everyone said I was so lucky that he had chosen me — an ordinary girl with a complexion like the twilight sky, when he could have married any beauty in town. Honestly, I didn't feel all that lucky. I liked studying and was eager to finish college. Also, I loathed the fact that Rajat worked for the British, even while India struggled for independence

My parents were simple middle-class Bengalis and practically in awe of Rajat's rich and influential family. They thought it was only by some good karma that they had received an alliance like this. So, though technically Rajat was not a 'jamai' yet, my mother invited him home for Jamaishoshthi that year. Ma was a great cook and took pride in her culinary skills. She was fervid with excitement and toiling in the kitchen for two whole days creating the best dishes for the upcoming feast.

After much discussion over what would be a fitting menu, a seven-course lunch had been decided, that started off with fried green spinach, followed with a golden chholar dal with tender pieces of coconut, potol'r dolma where the pointed gourds were stuffed with minced meat, and then two kinds of fish. I think I made a prawn malaikari with coconut from our own tree and Ma made her famous aam katla with green mangoes and katla fish. The aam katla was my mother's summer special. Spicy and sour, it was a beautiful silky fish curry that we enjoyed only during the hot summer months.

On the day of the grand feast, Ma was edgy and I could feel her anxiety even as she polished bell metal plates and added the last teaspoon of ghee to the simmering dal. She revered her would-be son-in-law for his social standing but also dreaded the meeting at our humble home.

That day, when Rajat came to lunch wearing an expensively cut suit instead of dhuti-panjabi like most Bengalis, you should have seen the shock in her face! That was just the beginning. During lunch, Rajat asked for a knife and fork as he thought using fingers to eat food was 'nasty'. My mother stammered and sweated at the request. No one at our home ate with cutlery and we had to get a pair from the neighbours.

All through lunch, Rajat seemed bored and stiff. He hardly enjoyed the food my mother had cooked so lovingly. 'Too oily', 'very spicy curry', he kept saying. 'You know, this Indian food does not go with our weather. At home, we mostly eat ham sandwiches, mulligatawny soup and roast pork for lunch. You should try that,' he suggested haughtily.

My mother's face flushed pink with embarrassment. Her days of hard work were reduced to nothing in seconds. I felt anger bubbling inside me and wanted to give Rajat a piece of my mind immediately. But she gestured me to keep quiet. I knew then that just like the tender green pointed gourd bursting with flavours inside and sealed at the tips, my fate too was sealed — my parents were ready to turn a blind eye to everything else for this marriage to happen.

Today I am sending you the recipe for potol'r dolma and aam katla. The dolma is an offshoot of the Mediterranean dolma where grape leaves are stuffed with rice and meat. For this recipe, you can stuff the potol with keema or paneer. It is my mother's recipe and the best that you can find. Remember to get the finest tender potol for this dish, a lot depends on it. Remember, it will take time, be patient!

I think you will love it.

Bhalo theko,
Didan

I don't know how long I sat there with the letter. My mouth curled up in a smile.

I have no clue who writes these letters, but they have a key to open a part of my heart I no longer visit. Through those neat scripts I could trace thirty years back to a house, in a narrow lane with frangipani blooms in the front courtyard, where it was summer just like in the letter. That house too had a huge mango tree from which hung mangoes that would turn vermilion as they ripened. I would spend my summer holidays in that house, climbing trees, plucking mangoes off branches, swinging from the pale branches of the guava tree and then as dusk fell and conch shells resonated in the neighbourhood, I would tuck my wings and return to my Dida as she cooked dinner and narrated stories.

I wanted to tell Samantha and Claire about Dida, my grandmother. About the letter that came a day too late to our bungalow in the tea gardens of Darjeeling. After Dida was gone, my mother lost her flair for writing letters. There were the curt, occasional ones sent to my baba's parents, the annual Bijoya ones to the myriad of relatives whose addresses were neatly noted in her address book. But almost always they were written on a postcard and sent off bare, stripped of any enigma or love. She had nothing to fill three sides of inland with.

I can fathom the deep love with which these letters are written and the special bond the elderly lady must share with her granddaughter, Moni. A part of me wants to find Moni and hand over her rightful legacy, but the sly other part wants to believe, even if just for a few days, that these letters are written to me – the unconditional love pouring out on paper was also for me.

———

When I stopped at our Indian grocery store on my way back home, I knew what I was there for. Goaded by the taste of a forgotten mango chutney, I had to pick the mangoes. The firm raw green ones for the chutney and the ripe sweet yellow ones to hold in my palm and suck the juice. And the potol, pointed gourd, only the tender fresh ones, the color of jade, deep green painted across with faint pale stripes.

For dinner, I made potol'r dolma stuffed with grated paneer, as the letter said. I had watched two YouTube videos carefully to understand the steps. It was no easy task, scooping out the seeds and flesh from inside the potol, stuffing each carefully with grated and spiced paneer, then frying it. The scent was familiar and though my shoulders ached from all that peeling and frying, I felt a happiness, similar to that of drawing a complex blueprint. I then made a silky gold mango ombol with the raw green mangoes, spiced with panch phoron, and a soupy gravy just the kind I loved as a child.

My kitchen smelled like my mother's did from another country, many years ago. Piyu came sniffing, her nose in the air, drawn in by the simmering chutney. The scent must have worked some magic on her. 'Mom, looks like you have a new hobby now. You keep trying different things every month,' she said, bending down and inhaling the flavour of the whole spices, 'mmm ... this smells so good. What is it?'

'You will see.' I smiled contentedly, sprinkling the last pinch of aromatic bhaja masala. I felt light, like a helium balloon, ready to float with buoyant joy. Even Sameer was home early for a change and I imagined how stunned he would be at dinner.

Indeed he was. 'You cooked all of this, Shubha?' Sameer's voice carried a note of astonishment. To be fair, my family had never seen me cook like this. I was surprised myself. 'You really made potol'r dolma? My mom used to make the best dolmas,' he added wistfully.

Well, now I was getting irritated with his questions. I get the surprise part, but he seemed to be doubting that I had cooked all this food by myself. Okay, so maybe I had never made it before, but people learn, don't they? Didn't I learn French in just two days when we went to Paris for our honeymoon? Okay, only one cute waiter at the café had understood what I had been speaking, but still.

And was it even necessary for him to bring up his mother's dolma? My mother-in-law is undoubtedly an amazing cook, but she is also one of those overtly self-assured ones who thinks her progeny will starve without her cooking. 'Sameer will never eat eggplant', 'He only likes how I make chingri malaikari' are the kind of things she likes to remind me. I never ask her for recipes.

Pick your battles, Shubha. Pick your battles.

I didn't want a rare, perfect dinner to turn caustic and so I shoved aside my irritation. Instead, I laughed lightly and said, 'It is Jamaishoshthi around this time. I don't think you are lucky enough to have in-laws who will feed you a lavish meal for it. This is to make up for all these years.'

I was very excited with all the effort I had put in and couldn't wait for Sameer to rave about my potol'r dolma. It was a killer! Well, it had nearly killed me with all the hard work.

We had just sat down for dinner when, 'DING!', a notification popped up on Sameer's phone.

I bristled in annoyance. Really? Using the phone again at the dinner table even after my repeated 'no gadgets during dinner' argument?

Sameer grabbed his phone quickly, his face twitching in a slight smile but his mind was no longer on the food. You could see it. There was something in that just arrived text which distracted him from my dolma. I tried not to open my mouth and remind him about electronics and family dinner time, etc. Instead I took a bite of the potol and decided to resolve this peacefully, with love. The dolma was really good, if I say so myself. Tonight, I will tell him about the letters and he can tell me what is worrying him, I assured myself brightly. Maybe I will even take that selfie as HuffPost had suggested.

'What is Jamaishoshthi?' quipped Riya.

Just when I started telling Riya and Piyu about this Bengali tradition, Sameer excused himself from the dining table. 'I will be in my study but don't disturb me unless the house is on fire,' he declared to no one in particular! Just like that, no explanation. He pushed back his chair, making a screeching sound on the terracotta floor.

'Sam-ee-r!' I called after him in frustration.

'Have to change the rubber tips on the chair,' he muttered absent-mindedly and then marched off towards the study. The screech lingered in my mouth like a bad aftertaste.

Would it have killed Sameer to say the potol'r dolma was as good as his mother's? I felt a flicker of resentment quivering deep in my heart. If he wasn't interested, I wasn't going to tell him anything. Fuck that selfie! I was startled by myself, I am not the kind to sprinkle the F-word liberally like garnish, even in my thoughts.

'But why feed the son-in-law and why do women need to have kids? Such anti-feminist stuff.' Riya rolled her eyes, still stuck on Jamaishoshthi rituals.

'It was a different time, Riya. Women were valued only because they kept the family tree alive.' Piyu's voice was grave and sombre. I was surprised by her maturity.

After dinner, I showed Riya how to hold a ripe mango between her palms, tear off the top with a sharp jerk of the teeth and then suck out the mango juice. After a few unsuccessful attempts, the juice squirted out in an arch and hit her straight in the face. She was thoroughly annoyed with the sticky mess and refused to attempt it again.

I, however, still remembered my skills and as the sweet mango nectar trickled down my throat, my spirits soared and I knew there was something sweet waiting for me in life. Only, I had to take charge of my own happiness.

I posted a picture of the potol'r dolma on Facebook.

Don't depend on others for your happiness. Find your own. ♥
#therapyinfood #newrecipe #jamaishoshthi #potoldolma

There were 29 likes and 32 comments. Anju asked, 'Babe, did you make this? Seriously?'

Potol'r Dolma

Potol'r dolma or dolma is a very popular Bengali dish made with the summer vegetable potol or pointed gourd. The word 'dolma' is derived from the Turkish 'dolmak', which means 'to fill'. Dolma is a common dish in Persian and Iraqi cuisine where several vegetables and fruits are stuffed with a mix of rice, minced meat and saffron.

It is believed that dolma came to Bengali households holding the hands of Armenian families who were originally from Persia and had followed the trade route to finally settle in Chinsurah, near Kolkata. While the original dolma was stuffed with minced meat and rice as mentioned earlier, the fusion potol'r dolma in Bengali households was stuffed with minced meat, fish and even a vegetarian stuffing of paneer and coconut. This recipe serves four.

Ingredients

Potol/Parwal/Pointed Gourd – 12

For stuffing the potol

Paneer (crumbled) – 1 cup
Fresh grated coconut – ½ cup
Salt – ½ tsp
Raisins – 1 tbsp
Sugar – 1 tbsp
Green chilli – 1
Bhaja masala – 1 tsp lightly packed (dry roast 1 tsp whole cumin, 1 tsp whole coriander powder and 1 dry red chilli and then grind to a powder)
Vegetable oil

For making the gravy

Tomato – 2 medium

Ginger – 2" knobs

Green chilli – 2

Put all the above in blender and make a puree.

Turmeric powder – ¼ tsp

Kashmiri red chilli powder – ½ tsp

Cumin powder – ½ tsp

Coriander powder – ½ tsp

Mix the above powders in 1tbsp of yogurt and keep it aside.

Cashew – 2 tbsp. Soak in water for 10 mins and then make a thick paste.

Sugar – 2 tsp

Mustard oil – 2 tbsp

Ghee – 1tsp

Salt to taste

For tempering

Green cardamom– 2

Cloves – 2

Bay leaf – 2

Whole dry red chilli – 2

Hing – a pinch

Prepping the potol

Wash and dry the potol. Chop off the tip from both ends of the potol. Scrape the skin very lightly using a peeler or knife, so that the thick skin is removed and pale green stripes remain.

With a scraper or metal spoon handle, carefully scoop out the seeds of the pointed gourd from inside. Keep these aside for later use.

Making the stuffing mixture

Make a paste of grated coconut, green chilli and potol seeds in the food processor. Grind to a coarse paste adding splashes of water, as needed.

Heat 1 or 2 tbsp oil in a frying pan. Add the coconut paste. Sauté for a couple of minutes. Add the crumbled paneer, raisins, bhaja masala, salt and sugar.

Mix and sauté until the stuffing is cooked and does not stick to the sides.

With your fingers, mix the stuffing gently to make the texture uniform.

Stuffing the potol

Heat mustard oil in a deep frying pan or kadhai.

Shallow fry the potol until it starts to turn light brown in colour. Sprinkle salt while frying. Remove and keep aside. Fill them with the stuffing, gently pressing in with your fingers, making sure that the potol innards are tightly packed.

Making the gravy

Heat mustard oil in a kadhai or any other heavy-bottomed deep frying pan.

Temper the oil with all the spices listed under 'For tempering'.

Add the tomato + ginger + chilli puree. Sauté till there is no raw smell.

Add the cashew paste and the spice paste. Sprinkle a little water into it and cook for two to three minutes.

Add about 1½ cups of water. Add salt and sugar to taste and let the gravy come to a slow simmer. Gently add the stuffed potol to the gravy, arranging them in a single layer in it. Cover and cook on low-medium flame for about ten minutes.

Once the vegetable is done, add a sprinkle of garam masala and ½ tsp of ghee and gently mix. Serve with hot steamed white rice.

3

Sometimes I think Sameer is having an affair. Well, I am not just imagining things, I have surely seen signs. For one, in the last six months he has been coming home insanely late. Often after the girls have gone to bed and the dishwasher is humming at its last cycle.

Don't you roll your eyes and tell me a lot of folks work late. This is not quite the same.

It's not only that he comes home late. He doesn't even volunteer to tell me where he has been exactly. I used to nag at first but then stopped asking when three months ago he told me, in a very dismissive tone, 'Where else but at work, Shubha? You have been out of real work too long to know how it is in the corporate world.'

It stung like hell when he said that. So, what does he think our tiny little company does — gossip and kitty parties? I am very sensitive about my small biz and prickly at best when anyone sounds patronizing about it. Okay, I get it, it's a struggling business and there hasn't been any profit and so I have not been paid or anything yet. But still this was going too far so I lost it completely and shouted in rage. He did apologize but words are like arrows, how do you take them back and heal the wound they caused? I was so hopping mad that I promised myself to never ask about his whereabouts again.

Third, he is almost always on the phone, his facial muscles yo-yo-ing between a burrowed frown and a hint of a smile as he taps on it. So, it is most likely that he is texting work-related stuff, but I cannot be absolutely sure.

Anyway, HuffPost says that these are signs of midlife crisis. His. Not mine. When you have a midlife crisis it can often lead to an affair, the HuffPost blogger elaborates.

Well, deep inside I know, he will never do such a thing. I mean the 'affair thing'. He is too honest to cheat. And I do love him too much to doubt his integrity. It is just that things are different between us these days. I can't quite put a finger on it but the connection seems to be slipping away. And so, lately this thought hovers over the back of my head, like a nimbus cloud. A cloud pregnant with possibilities.

The HuffPost blogger with her blunt-cut hair and cool voice whispers in my head, 'What if there is in fact someone in Sameer's life? What would you do if that is the truth?'

Strangely, I don't feel revenge or despair at the thought. Only a mellow sadness, a thin layer of fluffy sadness for I don't have anything to explain the rift that I feel is growing between us, and to blame it on an affair with another woman seems to be better than to admit that we are growing apart because of ourselves. To admit that would pump my heart with cold Arctic wind laden with icicles.

He ditched me again last night. And that too at the very last moment.

'I am caught up at work, Shubha. Won't be able to make it to the party at Neela's.' He called at around six in the evening on a Friday. Friday! At six! Practically on a weekend!

'You knew about the invitation since a month. It is Neela's anniversary and you know how she takes these things to heart,' I grumbled, the anger bubbling at the nape of my neck.

'Why don't you go along? I am sure Neela will understand. I really have to go, Shubha, the clients are waiting.' His voice was getting antsy and desperate to get off the phone.

Visions of the client floated in my brain. Whoever it was, sure had Sameer wrapped around their little finger. Maybe a brunette? Sharp, intelligent, demanding. At times too demanding in her black slacks and Miu Miu heels. I rubbed the back of my neck, which was stiff with all the imagination.

Until a year or so back I knew all of Sameer's colleagues and clients by name. I even knew the name of his office janitor, Mrs Morgan. At our dinner table we would laugh over how, one of his German clients, Wolfgang, had this insane love for American Ding Dongs. But then things started changing, Sameer kind of started clamming up about his work. Suddenly his clients were calling all the time … literally all the time … he had to get on to conference calls even in the shower! The poor guy was so busy that I didn't want to pry. Perhaps, I should not have let things go. Perhaps, if I had asked more questions and been persistent, things would have been different.

I rotated my head in a slow clockwise motion to relax my muscles, and tried to bring back the evening in focus. Think of your wardrobe, Shubha, instead of brunettes in Miu Miu heels,

I chided myself. Maybe the client was all right, it was just me. It was just in my nature to overanalyse everything.

Two hours later I was at Neela's party. Finally, I drove down all by myself. Piyu made some excuse about a project on the weavers of Mexico that she had to work on and Riya wanted to stay back because she found such parties boring. It is strange, how these fruits of your womb, the ones that lived nine whole months inside you, become teenagers and then want to be as far away from you as possible!

I wasn't too enthused myself about this whole party but managed to dress myself up in a turquoise Kanjivaram that had a thin silver zari along the border. It is one of the few saris from my mother's wedding trousseau that I had brought with me many years ago. In moments of indecision, I drape one of them and try to think what my mother would have done. Now, I try to imagine her walking into Neela's house, all by herself, into a party thrumming with almost all the Bengalis in the area. These Bengali parties can be onerous at the best of times. You are judged at many levels, the sari you drape, the kurta you buy, the grades your children didn't get. It's like walking a tightrope. It is fun when you do it right. But God help, if you don't. I am a 'worrier', so the whole thing stresses me out.

I was also dreading meeting Neela. Although a good friend, at times her 'all-knowing' persona irritates me. I knew the moment she noticed that Sameer wasn't there with me, she would go, 'Shubha, you let go too easily. You should have dragged Sameer from work, no? One evening would not have killed him.'

And Anju, the perfect Anju would pull a sad face and say, 'Tsk, tsk, the poor guy, how much he has to work. Shubha, you must take care of him you know?'

I secretly wish that in the near future she has a daughter-in-law who pours pesticide in her tea. Nothing potent enough to kill her, but enough to leave her indisposed or something.

By the time I reached Neela's home, her driveway was already packed with cars. There were Beemers and Porsches spilling along the curb too. The only parking spot I could find was two houses downhill by a big bush of blooming azaleas. Gosh, now I must walk all the way uphill in my heels, I grumbled to myself.

I parked my car, careful not to get scraped by the azalea branches, gingerly lifted my right foot from the brake and planted the left one outside the car. I did not feel that usual thrust. The ground felt too close. Did I just shrink? People do with age, but I was only forty! It can't happen this fast.

And that is the moment I looked down and realized I wasn't wearing heels! Like, really, no heels, not even a fancy pair of sandals. I was wearing my white and blue flip-flops! Hawai-chappals that I wear when I potter around my garden. I must have just slipped those on while rushing out to the car. How did I not even notice? How could I be so careless? My brain was losing its edge. I should start taking gingko biloba, I quickly made a mental note.

To tell the truth, I was mortified to enter Neela's home. I would be the joke of the Bengali society. I would be the woman who would go down in the history of 'Bongo Sammelan' as the lady-who-wore-flip-flops-with-her-Kanjivaram! But what options did I have? It was already late and there was no way I could go back home, change my footwear and be back. Nope, this would have to do. I pulled my sari lower and flip-flopped all the way up the sidewalk to Neela's gorgeous home, fervently hoping that no one would notice my flip flops or my sudden drop in height.

Two cocktails later, however, I had forgotten about my footwear. Everyone was too busy about their own looks and so no one noticed either. Even Neela's 'gyan' glided smoothly over me without making the slightest dent. I was warming up to the party and the bedazzled men and women milling around.

Neela looked dazzling herself, in a sequined black-and-white creation. She is five feet four inches, has a flawless peach-and-cream complexion, gorgeous hair and looks every bit a Bollywood heroine. Well, except for the inches around her waist, but those extra inches make her look sexy in a sari. Bottom line is she looked stunning, I must admit.

Flashing the solitaire on her finger every now and then, she was serving bite-sized kebabs, pancetta-wrapped shrimps and tiny samosas. 'Keto-friendly,' she whispered to some reed-thin lady. Avinash, her husband of fifteen years, was mixing cocktails and throwing looks of admiration in her direction. He is a nice guy. Slightly bald, polite and soft-spoken, he is one of those guys who make better husbands than boyfriends. He smiled at all the jokes Neela made at his expense. I found them to be the perfect couple. Neela, stunning, gregarious, outgoing like an Andy Warhol pop art. Avinash, calm, dependable, a bit boring even, like the frame which holds the art.

'Congratulations on your fifteenth anniversary, Avinash,' I said. He smiled shyly like he always does and handed me a cocktail. I felt a pang of jealousy. My marriage could have been like this. Sweet and smooth like the wine.

I took my wine and walked towards the breakfast table where the women were huddled, dishing their respective husband. 'Shubha, you seem to have lost weight. And did you get shorter? Anyway, you are so lucky that you don't have to cook like me. Sameer even makes his own breakfast, and look at my husband, he cannot even boil an egg, always so dependent on me,' complained Maitreyi di, an elegant lady, tall, fair and very regal-looking. Her husband is a professor at the local college and reminds me of Lalomohan Ganguly, the portly writer from Satyajit Ray's Feluda detective series. I tried to imagine him boiling an egg and it did not seem incongruous. Maybe a couple of disasters initially but if Maitreyi di just lets him do it without criticizing, he could manage fine.

'But I don't see Sameer much these days. Shubha, is everything okay?' asked Minal with a frown.

'Yeah. He is just too busy at work,' I blurted out. My fake attempt at defending him. From the corner of my eye, I could see the faint smirk on Anju's face.

'I can totally understand. I wasn't sure if I would be able to make it either. I told Saty, why don't you go along while I wrap up my presentation. But after all it is Neela's party na so I had to come,' said Anju smugly, her perfect figure wrapped in a short shift dress. Only she can carry off a tiny dress amidst sari-clad Bengali women.

'My son got a perfect score on his SAT, and he doesn't even study. All the time he is playing video games...' I could hear another voice rising from a separate group. There it goes, I told myself.

I slowly backed out on to the deck where a few people sat scattered, beer bottles in hand. The sky was clear and a million stars spread across its pitch blackness. I stood at the far end, where a magnolia tree with its wide leaves and huge white flowers towered over the deck. It is surprising how these trees survive the freezing temperatures here. I was so close to the tree that the leaves brushed my hand, but I liked it. I felt protected in its presence, it was so hardy, resilient and strong.

'Don't go too close, there might be caterpillars,' murmured a deep male voice in the dark. I got a bit irritated. Seriously? Can't a woman get a moment of peace and quiet here?

'I can take care of myself,' I snapped.

'Aha, so that's why you are wearing chappals. In India, we don't need exterminators to kill bugs, our hawai chappals work best.'

I wanted to get angry, but his voice was so frank and candid that I guffawed at his comment. So, he was the only one who noticed? Maybe I had made the phat-phat sound when I walked across the deck.

'Hello, I am Joy. Not the "Joy" of your life, but you know the Bengali "Joy" who conquers. If I were a non-Bengali, I would call myself Jai,' the voice introduced himself. It was a friendly voice, calm with a touch of humour. Not a loud or overbearing one. I decided I liked the voice.

Even in the dark, I could figure out that the owner of the voice was tall and slender. The hand he had extended towards me had long fingers and when I took his hand to give a polite shake of greeting, I noticed his grip was firm and light.

'I just moved here last month from India.'

I had heard about him, in bits and pieces, from the Bengali grapevine. Joy, or Jai, worked at the same company as Neela's husband and had moved to the US from India. He was single and people had assumed that he had had a divorce after which he had decided to move. Though it seemed highly strange that a freshly divorced Bengali man would shun all the maternal pampering and attention that he could have lapped up back home and move to a country where life was going to be anything but easy. Now if it was a divorced Bengali woman, it would be a different story altogether.

But I didn't tell him all this. Instead, I nodded and introduced myself. I was getting worried about all the banal small talk I would be forced to do. I was in no mood for that.

Well, I shouldn't have worried. Jai turned out to be one of those people who could easily start a conversation and ask the right questions to keep it going. I didn't have to think of the next thing to say, things ebbed and flowed and took its own course, as we talked of our small-town childhood, college, books and food. I could feel my muscles relax and my laugh become louder, the wine was snaking up my veins, relaxing my nerves, lifting my spirit.

It has been so long that I have had a proper adda like this. A proper adult conversation that did not involve kids, husbands or mothers-in-law.

As we picked through dinner, Jai turned out to be a very earnest foodie, discerning about the cut of meat and flavour of the gravy in the mutton korma, finicky about the pulao which lacked sweetness. 'These restaurant-made mutton curries are no match to the Sunday mutton curry we grew up with.' He added wistfully, 'My childhood Sundays were always perfumed with the smell of goat meat curry wafting through the rooms and my mother's turmeric-stained sari as she cooked the mangsho.'

Marinate mutton, a little mustard oil, some cloves of garlic in the pressure cooker, fresh ginger and gorom masala towards the end – I could hear the words rising from within me like bubbles in a soda can. I couldn't believe that it was me speaking aloud. I have hardly ever cooked a mutton curry, but the steps like a flow chart are embedded in my brain from Ma's kitchen, aeons ago. I never thought I would want to talk about caramelized onions or grated ginger so much one day, seems those blue letters had unlocked some secret chamber in my heart and here I was giving out recipes like a pro.

'Is this curry organic? Was the goat local?' I could hear Anju's shrill voice quizzing the servers. I quickly grabbed dessert and retreated back into the darkness.

The heat around us was oppressive and even in the cool darkness under the tree you could feel the earth breathing fire. 'It is going to rain tonight,' Jai said while clutching a bowl of nolen gur'r ice cream.

'When it rained back home, you know what my mother would cook? Khichuri.' His voice was distant and dreamy. 'I don't know why she did it, even if her refrigerator was full of other things. "*Badla dine khichuri khete hoy*," she would say. Khichuri is a must on a cloudy day! It seemed like a sacred commandment followed through generations.'

As he spoke, his words evaporated and spun a picture around me. It was like a hologram and I could see Baba in our kitchen on such rainy evenings. Back from work, he would be busy getting our dinner ready. This was after Ma passed away, for he never cooked anything when she was around. On those evenings, the cook would have left early anticipating the rain, and Baba was happy to take over the kitchen. He would be singing and chopping potatoes, onions and green chillies to go into the masoor dal'r khichuri. I would sit at the dining table vigorously beating eggs to a frothy yellow that would make the perfect omelette. This simple meal, a medley of rice, lentils and vegetables, was something he loved more than a lavish meal at any five-star hotel. 'Put a spoonful of ghee and the khichuri becomes food of the gods,' he would declare, plopping a ladleful of ghee in the boiling pot.

By the time I left Neela's home, I was feeling light-headed and happy. The future seemed to carry a promise, a fragrance of ghee melting in a sunny khichuri.

It was almost eleven by the time I reached home. Sameer was still at work, apparently. Riya had already gone to bed, but Piyu was waiting up for me. She was sitting on the single couch by the window, an ikkat red and navy blue throw wrapped around her. Her nose was deep into her MacBook. She was writing up one of her reports probably. The soft glow of the lamp on the side table bathed her in a warm yellow radiance. Sitting like that, the glasses resting almost on the tip of her nose, she looked so much like my mother.

'Did you have fun, Mom?' she asked. She looked at me for a full minute and said sternly, 'I think you had too much of wine. You shouldn't have driven.' Piyu, my fifteen-year-old, maths club president of her school, go green champion, was becoming the mother I did not have.

'Don't worry, baby, I am okay. I didn't take the highway or anything, just the back roads.'

Giving excuses, I felt ashamed and even a bit guilty. But also, I was feeling so much happier that I didn't mind. I am sure it had nothing to do with Jai, it was the alcohol really. Maybe I should drink a glass of wine every night. To relax my nerves and fill my head with dream bubbles. Is this the reason everyone at AA gives?

Facebook

Friend request from Jai G. The Joy who conquers sent me a friend request. Should I hit accept?

Asharh
(June – July)

Dear Moni,

Asharh started last week. It is the first month of the monsoon season and I hope we get some respite from the heat. We have had a few showers but they were nothing more than mere droplets for the parched earth. I am trying not to get my hopes high each time I see dark clouds gathering in the sky, but I do wish that those clouds would open and drench the earth for once.

I don't think I have ever told you but I first met your Dadu one such rainy evening of Asharh. It was almost the middle of the month and the rains were yet to come. Everyone complained about the oppressive Jaishtha heat. As summer progressed, the sticky 'pyach-pyache' humid afternoons, the long power cuts in the evening, the sun that burned you like a sinner in hell, stretched more and more. By the end of Jaishtha, one would wait for rain as if the rains were the messiah to save us from suffering.

That evening the sky was dark with clouds just like today. Those monsoon clouds, their pregnant belly weighed down with fat baby raindrops, had started appearing on the south-east corner of the horizon, the ishaan kon, in the wee hours of the evening. The wind was soft and sweet carrying whispers of rain.

I was around twenty years old at the time and you know how a young twenty-year-old feels all melancholic during monsoon. I stood in the covered balcony looking out on the road, humming Tagore's 'Abaar esheche Asharh...' to myself.

My wedding date had just been fixed. I wasn't sure whether I should be happy about it or worried. Rajat had a certain arrogance about him, which I did not like. Accustomed to flattery and praise, he assumed that he was the best in everything. When I told my parents this, they said it was all my imagination and I should not spend time thinking such thoughts.

While I stood there, my head full of contradictions, the rain started. Hesitant at first, shy on their nimble silver steps, the raindrops soon got bolder and raucous. Huge blobs of water hit the warm earth rapidly, drumming the Pilu raga on the veranda railing. I stood there, letting the rain soak me.

Soon the rain was coming down so heavily that even the kirshnachura tree opposite our house looked like a daub of red and green paint. People in the street were running to take shelter from the rain and many of them had gathered on our small porch. Amidst all this, there was a loud banging on our front door. 'Dekh to ke,' my mother said from the kitchen immediately, asking me to check who was at the door. I could hear the sizzling sound of frying and the strong smell of mustard oil wafting from the kitchen.

Irritated at being disturbed from my thoughts, I went downstairs to open the door anyhow. My hair and sari were wet but I didn't care. When I opened the door, a stoic gentleman was standing outside dripping just as wet. His eyes were sharp and shone with humour and his complexion was dark like mahogany.

He avoided looking directly at me and said, 'I work with sir, your father. He will leave office only after the rain stops and, so, will reach home late. Told me to inform you.'

'Okay,' I said and slammed the door shut in his face.

'Who is it?' asked my mother, still busy in the kitchen, frying beguni and pumpkin blossoms to celebrate the monsoon.

'A peon, I think, from Baba's office,' I answered.

Later that night when Baba came and sang paeans in praise of a certain new boy who had joined his office that week, a brilliant student *and yet so humble that he had offered to bring home the news that Baba would be late tonight, I quickly retreated to my room. The boy's dark and handsome face kept smiling at me in my dreams. I knew it was wrong of me to even think of him, now that I was engaged to someone else and yet that face kept coming back to me, the next day and the next.*

Later, your Dadu would often tease me about the day when we first met. It seems he had heard the frying sounds from the kitchen and was hoping for some cha and fritters when I had banged the door shut. He always loved fried food. Begun bhaja, fried eggplant, was his particular favourite. Served with khichuri and dollops of ghee on a rainy evening, it was his favourite meal.

'No one can make khichuri like you,' he would often say. 'What is there to make in a khichuri?' I would reply with a shrug, 'It is just a mix of rice and dal.' 'And you can make a simple thing like that so delicious because of the magic in your hands,' your Dadu would insist.

Those were the days ... oh ... how I miss them. Hold on to your time, Moni ... and whenever you get the chance, make memories. Those are the only things you will struggle to hold on to in your old age.

Bhalo theko,
Didan

My eyes were damp by the time I finished the latest letter. It was a depressing cloudy day and the sky looked ready to open up any minute. I made myself a cup of black tea, without sugar and milk, and settled down at the kitchen counter. This third letter had been lying in my Vera Bradley handbag for the last two days. I had all the right intentions to go to the post office and return it. Trust me, I did. In fact, if I hadn't been feeling so low, this one would already have been on its way back to the sender. But now, the overcast sky and the tender love between the strangers in the letter had made me all maudlin and nostalgic.

Eighteen years ago, in Kolkata, the day Sameer and his mother were to come see me as a marriage prospect, it had been a cloudy day just like today. I was appalled at the idea of 'seeing' and refused to play any part in the whole matchmaking game. I was freshly out of college with a degree in architecture and into a job that I really enjoyed. I looked down upon so-called arranged marriages; secretly nurturing a dream that one day my soulmate would come running towards me in slow motion, his muscles rippling under a tight T-shirt and his hair slicked down with hair gel.

Instead this seemed like an arrangement from some 1960s' film where the prospective groom from the US would be sitting in my living room, shoving shingaras and chomchom and asking me questions like 'How many pressure cooker whistles does it take to cook mutton?'

My dad wasn't too keen either but Sameer's parents were his sister's friends and she thought it would be impolite to refuse. With my mother not being there, I guess he was also nervous thinking of it as his responsibility to get me a good husband. 'Give him a chance, Shubha,' Baba had said, 'it is not that we are forcing you to marry anyone.'

Annoyed, I acted more haughty and rude than usual. The rain had started by the time Sameer arrived. He was by himself, dressed in a plaid shirt and jeans, his hair ruffled and his muscles invisible.

'Where is your mother?' Pishi, my aunt, had enquired.

Sameer had replied with a shy smile, 'It is I who is getting married. What does she have to do with this?'

To be honest, I actually liked him in that first meeting itself – shy, intelligent, eyes twinkling and yet calm like the lake across Pishi's house. He didn't have the muscles I had been dreaming about but he was tall at six feet one inch and lanky. And he never asked me about the pressure cooker or the mutton.

Instead he picked up a shingara, smeared it with the thick, dark tamarind chutney, took a few bites and chatted with Baba and Pishi as if he had known them all his life.

As he had methodically munched through the shingaras, fish fry and gur'r rosogolla, I sat there thinking – how much this guy eats! Does he have a girlfriend in the US? Has he slept with her? Is he looking at me? Would my mother approve of him? I don't know why I was bothered, given that I didn't even want to get married.

The rain had danced around in the lake across Pishi's flat, making concentric circles, each circle giving birth to another, until they grazed the bank. I stared on blankly, trying to make up my mind. Hoping for a voice in my ear to tell me what I should do. Spend my life with a stranger or wait for the man of my dreams to appear some day? It was clear that Sameer was not exactly the 'man of my dreams' but even back then I couldn't deny that there was something in his calm eyes that had soothed my ruffled heart.

'This gur'r roshogolla is just amazing. You know, Kaku, what I miss in America? This food. That paneer butter masala has totally numbed the American palate. That is what the West considers to be Indian food. How I wish they could taste something like this! And by the way, Shubha, would you like to come with me to

Coffee House on Friday afternoon?' He had asked gulping down
the last sweet.

I wasn't even sure if he was asking me out on a date. It seemed
so very unceremonious. Pishi was vigorously making gestures
with her head telling me to say yes.

I had agreed to go out with him. To walk the narrow lanes of
College Street, weaving our way through shops piled high with
books and then climb the dingy stairs of Coffee House; to sit
at a greasy table under high ceilings with clattering ceiling fans,
eating chicken pakora and sipping cold coffee served by waiters
in tall turbans and rubber sandals. I had been to Coffee House
umpteen times before with my friends but never had I imagined
this busy place with a permanent hum in the background to be
the site of my so-called first date. In fact even when I was there I
was not sure if it was a 'date' at all.

'Don't you think this place is so much cooler than any five-
star restaurant?' were the first words he had uttered excitedly as
we had sat down.

I was slowly warming up to this stranger from across the
seven seas. His energy and enthusiasm about everything was
electrifying. Every time he looked at me with his frank, honest
eyes, I could feel the muscles in my lower abdomen tighten. I had
not wanted that evening to end.

I don't know the exact moment when I started falling in love
with Sameer. Was it at Paramount when we realized that we both
loved their chocolate malai? Or was it at Nokur's Mishti, where
we both reached out for the kheer roll at the exact same moment.
Or was it much later? What I do remember clearly is that I had
mouthed a 'yes' under the influence of chelo kebab at Peter Cat.
I was sure by then that Sameer was the only man with whom I

was willing to share moist kebabs on buttered rice with a fried egg on top.

'You didn't know anything about Dad until your aunt asked him home? Did she set you up?' years later Riya had asked with an incredulous look on her face. Stepping into her tweens, she had publicly declared that she hated love, marriage and boyfriends. Her friends had started developing crushes on boys, but Riya thought it to be a huge waste of time. Arranged marriage was likely to be at the top of her list of things to shun.

She had prodded me further with a serious look on her face. 'Did you go weak in the knees when you met him?'

'Er … nope. Well, maybe a tiny bit. He was handsome, you know, with that mop of curly hair and twinkle in his eyes.'

'Did you feel like he was the only one you wanted to spend your life with?'

'Not really. I mean I didn't look that far into the future but I was happy to spend time with him then.'

'Then what was it, Mom? Why did you say yes?'

I still don't know. It just seemed the right thing at that moment. He was nice and fun and I had told myself that things can go wrong with anyone so why not take the risk? And it worked out fine. We did fall in love in the days after our marriage, if not before. Maybe there was some magical fairy dust sprinkled over us that did the trick.

It has been eighteen years since we first met and I don't know what happened in the course. Seems we lost some of the magic along the way.

I sighed and looked at the kitchen clock. It was almost seven in the evening. The rain had petered down but the grey sky made dusk darker than usual. Sameer was working even on a Saturday but had promised to be back for dinner. Toying between a quick pasta and khichuri for dinner, I finally decided to go with the latter. Sameer loves khichuri and always made a pot of it if the sky had even a hint of dark clouds in the horizon. I have no such fondness and the few times that I have tried making it, it has ended in a congealed mass.

'Shubha, how can you mess up even khichuri? It takes extraordinary skill to go wrong with it. It is that simple a preparation!' he would say disappointedly. Sameer doesn't get any time to cook these days and we haven't had khichuri for over a year now.

I was afraid that I would make a mess of khichuri again. But then, I convinced myself; after all I had Didan's recipe with me. Even as the thought crossed my mind, I chided myself. Who was I calling Didan? Who was Dadu? Who were these strangers whose letters I read and whose life I glimpsed into?

Lost in my thoughts I washed the little red pearls of masoor dal in water, chopped the cauliflower in perfect florets and quartered the potatoes precisely. I followed the recipe, all the while admiring its rounded penmanship, and tempered the hot oil with specks of dusky brown cumin seeds and tej patta with three perfect veins. I roasted the rice and lentils just like the letter said and waited patiently for the aroma which would tell me the right time that it would be done.

When the khichuri was done and I had poured the last dollop of ghee in it, the kitchen smelled divine. I took a photo of the golden bubbling dish to post on Facebook later. Summer holidays had just started and the girls were away for sleepovers at their friends' homes. In their absence, the house was eerily silent. All I could hear was the softly falling rain and the steady sound of the cicadas in the garden.

I settled down on the sofa and waited for Sameer to come home.

I was determined to bring back the magic tonight. I would shower, shave my legs, wear my sexiest nightdress and then serve steaming khichuri. Maybe I should fry something to go with the khichuri. Fried food ignites passion. Or was it flatulence? I was not sure but I felt lulled by what the night held in its folds. I imagined the dumbstruck look on Sameer's face when he saw me wearing that skimpy, lacy negligee from many years ago. But I should first check if it even fits me any more, since I haven't worn it in so long. But my negligee is not the point, it is the passion with which he will tear it apart that is more important. I could feel my cheeks getting hot at that thought. I also smelt something ... something smoky ... not smoking hot ... but burning.

I touched my cheeks, half expecting them to erupt in leaping flames. But they were the same as always – squishy and a bit sticky.

The smoky smell got stronger and I could hear an angry hiss now. I thought I saw a shadowy figure coming closer and my heart thrummed wildly against my chest. I tried to make out the face. Was it Sameer? Was it Jai? Why was Jai even here? I leapt up from the sofa in panic, only to find the pressure cooker was steaming like a mad volcano ready to erupt any moment and there was not a single soul around. Did I just doze off sitting there thinking of Sameer and my negligee?

I gingerly approached the stove and realized that I had lowered the flame in hope of keeping it warm and forgotten all about it. Shucks! I managed to salvage the pressure cooker, but the khichuri had a burnt deep brown bottom and a smoky flavour throughout. It was barbecued khichuri, which, needless to say, tasted awful.

There was no way I could serve this for dinner. I sighed and picked up the phone to order takeout and saw Sameer had called some twenty minutes back and left a message.

'Shubha, flying out to San Fran. Urgent client dinner meeting. Will be back tomorrow afternoon.'

I felt tired and drained of all energy all of a sudden. How could he do this to me now? When I was all set to woo him with his favourite food. Okay, so the favourite food part didn't work out as intended, but still. I wanted to sit on the floor, spread out my legs and cry my heart out. If effing Sameer was having a mid-life crisis, damn it, I could have one too. Maybe a bigger one. But I was already in crisis. My life seemed worse than the burnt khichuri and I didn't know how to make it better.

Facebook

My life is like khichuri on a rainy day. Where is Panchanantala? *#therapyinfood #newrecipe #searchforpanchanantala*

15 likes. 25 hearts. 30 wows.

Masoor Dal'r Khichuri

Khichuri or khichdi is a simple one-pot dish made of rice and lentils, very popular across India. Its name has its origins in the Sanskrit word 'khicca', which translates to 'a dish made with rice and pulses'. It has a rich history that can be traced back to mujaddara, a Middle Eastern preparation from the tenth century.

The Bengali khichuri is of two kinds – the bhog'r khichuri made with roasted moong dal for the gods and the masoor dal'r khichuri made with red lentils mostly during monsoon. It is best served with fried vegetables like eggplant and potatoes, papad, fried fish or an omelette. This recipe serves four.

Grains

Rice – 1½ cup
Red masoor dal – 1 cup
Yellow moong dal – ½ cup

Vegetables

Onion – 1 small chopped into slices
Potato – 2 small peeled and quartered
Cauliflower – 8-10 large florets
Sweet peas – 1 cup
Tomato – 1 medium-sized chopped fine
Garlic – 2 fat cloves minced
Ginger – 2" minced
Green chilli – 3-4

Spices

Bay leaf – 2 small or 1 large
Cardamom – 2

Clove – 2

Cinnamon – 1 thin stick

Cumin seeds – 1 tsp

Dried red chilli – 2 cracked

Roasted cumin powder – 1 tsp

Red chilli powder – ½ tsp or to taste

Salt – to taste

Sugar – to taste

Oil – for cooking

Ghee – 1-2 tsp

Wash the rice and dal in several changes of water.

Heat some oil in a thick-bottomed deep pan. Lightly fry the cauliflower florets with a sprinkle of turmeric powder. Once they turn a shade of golden, take them out and keep aside.

Pour some more oil into the same pan. Temper it with the whole spices.

When the spices start sputtering in the oil, add the minced garlic closely followed by the sliced onion. Sauté till the onion is soft and pink with a little browning at the edges.

Add the chopped tomato and fry till there is no raw smell. Put grated ginger or ginger paste in the mix and fry for a minute.

Follow this with the potatoes and peas. Fry with a sprinkle of turmeric for a minute or two.

Add the rice and dal and fry for the 3 to 4 minutes mixing everything together.

Pour about seven cups of water. Add red chilli powder and salt to taste, followed by roasted cumin powder. Mix everything well together and let it cook. Remove the cover intermittently and give a good stir.

When it is halfway done add the cauliflower florets and mix. If needed, add more water. I like my khichuri on the runny side so, usually, I add more water; it depends on your preference.

Once the rice, lentils and vegetables are all cooked, taste and adjust for seasonings. Add 2 tsp of ghee on the top and mix well. Enjoy your khichuri with papad, fried eggplant or an omelette.

4

It is a hot day in late July. Humid too. It is almost 6.30 in the evening and the sun is still blazing strong. I peer into the mirror above the sink in the laundry room. It is one of those cheap ones with a wrought iron frame. When you look into it, you can notice the slight shift in the reflection, the tip of your head tilts by a nano-fraction from your face, giving it a magical quality. It is so simple to glide from one face to another, one role to another. I don't know why there is a mirror in the laundry room of all places. It was the previous owner. Back then, we had raised our eyebrows at his taste and had thought of getting rid of it the moment we moved in.

My mind flashes back to the summer from fifteen years ago. Piyu was this wee little baby, Sameer was still working with that tech giant, which had not sucked up his life, and I was on maternity leave from the architecture firm I worked at. We lived in a much smaller condo and Sameer was adamant to move to a house with a large backyard, 'big enough to host a football team' he would say. Lugging Piyu in her car seat or on a sling attached to our chest, we would go house-hunting every weekend. Her soft baby chin rested against my neck as we checked out wainscotting and discussed the merits of one wood floor over the other. Sameer expertly changed her diapers in strange bathrooms with Victorian wallpapers and sweet potpourri. We were still flush with pride that only new parents feel and added to that was the thrill of finding just the right house. The moment we saw this house, we knew this was it. The red brick façade, the moss green window shutters, shining brass lamps on the porch and the sunlight streaming through every room – it was perfect. I had looked at Sameer, who was mesmerized by the glowing maples in the front yard which dazzled as they caught the last rays of the sun, and in that moment my heart had bloomed with love for my little family.

There was so much excitement the day we closed the deal and got our keys. So much to hope and live for. Every day brought new challenges and we were in it together. Sameer and me. Working as a team. Painting the nursey. Taking turns to feed Piyu. Planting that cherry tree in the corner. Selecting the right painting to hang in the foyer. Three years later, Riya was born in this very house. We were so happy creating our little universe.

It has been fifteen long years now, and the mirror still stands. A part of our life has become stagnant just like that mirror. We never got around to changing it.

I look at it again while sorting Sameer's white shirts from the coloured ones. The person looking back is quite unlike how I imagine myself. Are those wrinkles under my eyes or am I squinting? What is that look on my face – tired or bored? Where is that confident and excited Shubha who had wanted to lead the winning project for her company fifteen years ago?

I pull up my hair, tilt my chin and glance sideways, like the selfie face. This looks better.

'Mom, what are you doing?' Riya walks in with her eyes narrowed and tone suspicious.

'Er, I am trying to see, do I look younger this way or that?'

Riya rolls her eyes and says, 'Mom, chill. Either way you look somewhere around forty-five.'

'Forty-five? But I just turned forty!' I almost wail. In my mind I am still thirty-six.

'Plus or minus five years is not a big deal!' She quickly moves on, showing zero interest in analysing my age any further, and jumping from one foot to the other asks, 'Mom, so are we going anywhere for the summer?'

'Ask your dad.' I shove all the shirts together into the washing machine with vengeance. I don't care if the colours bleed and Sameer has to wear a tie-dye shirt to his next meeting. He is travelling and is somewhere in Europe right now, probably Basel. I wish I were in a café in Basel, sipping Swiss coffee (I don't know if that is even a thing) made with cream from those famous Swiss cows, instead of doing laundry in a sweltering laundry room.

'Can we go to Machu Pichu? Alena is going to Machu Pichu and they will go for the two-day hike. Or maybe Alaska? Remember you said your one dream was to go visit the Denali National Park. Can we go? Pretty please,' she pleads, scrolling through her phone. 'Here, see Swati is in Alaska right now.' She thrusts her phone in my hand. An Instagram post of a young girl in front of gorgeous snow-capped mountains in Alaska stares back at me. For Riya, at twelve, life is easy. You want to go somewhere, you just go.

'I told you to ask your dad.'

'I asked Dad. I texted him last night. He said it was fine.'

'He did?' My heart skips with joy. It has been two years since our last vacation together. Memories of those ten days of sun and aquamarine waters in Hawaii lift my spirits. I can feel the taste of fresh ahi tuna in a bowl of spicy poke. A vacation will solve all our problems. Sameer, me, Piyu and Riya – all together like before. Why didn't I think of this earlier? Maybe we can do Corfu this time – way more relaxing than Machu Pichu. Yes, it will be bit hectic with the last-minute booking and all, but it is doable. Just one island, where we can all relax by the sea, sip on some Ouzo and eat flavourful souvlakia on the stick. Sameer works too hard, once he can loosen up and spend some time with us, everything will be okay. I was being too harsh with his shirts, maybe I should sort them again. I can already feel the excitement.

'Yeah. He has lots of work trips this summer, so he can't come along but he said his travel agent will arrange everything for us...' Riya continues, looking at me expectantly.

I dump the rest of the laundry along with half a bottle of Tide liquid and start the washing machine. A scrap of paper folded twice slides out from the clothes pile and sticks to the side of the orange detergent container. The washing machine starts on its low rumble and its whirring sound dulls my brain.

Sameer is too busy for us.

Well, I should have shown him that I can be too busy for him too. I should have never left my job.

I could have run that marathon and saved people in Uganda instead of doing laundry.

Angry word clouds whirred around at fast wash speed in my head.

'Mom, so is it a yes?'

'I am signing you up for the town camp. It starts next week. They will take you to the water park maybe.'

'You are being mean. Why am I stuck with such parents? Not fair,' she grumbles loudly and storms out of the laundry room. At just twelve, her emotions run real high. I want to stomp my feet and go to Machu Pichu too. Or Corfu.

'One more word from you and you don't even go to camp, Riya,' I shout after her, putting an end to the conversation. I can hear her voice fall down by two notches as she mutters under her breath. I feel bad for her but I want to go on a family vacation, not chaperone two teenagers in wilderness.

I look in the mirror again. Maybe I should colour my hair! That is when I notice the folded fragment of paper by the bright orange Tide container. I pluck it out and hold it close. I am not sure if I should open it. I have a premonition that it will not be the bearer of good news. I open the fold and smooth out whatever remains of the paper. Looks like the original paper had been carelessly torn and this piece has somehow stubbornly survived. The major part of the letter is missing and this bottom piece has only three sentences. In a slight slant, feminine handwriting it reads: '*Hope I am fulfilling what you wanted. Does she know about this? Love, F.*'

For a minute, I can't make sense of it. It is like my brain has been wrung out dry like the clothes in the machine. Slowly my neurons start sending messages and my first instinct is that this is some kind of a joke and Sameer will have the funniest story to explain it. My next thought is who the eff is F? Faria, Faith, Frida, Fatima ... I can't think of many names starting with F. And why the heck is this Frida or F-whoever wondering if I knew about 'this'. What was this? And what was she fulfilling?

Wait ... was Sameer getting blowjobs at work? Was that what fulfilling meant? It was not a nice thing to think about your husband but you know these things happen. Even the President did it. One day you are a perfectly charming gentleman, and next day – boom! – you are all over the media sucked into #metoo scandals. A chill runs down my spine at the thought. My heart flutters like a tiny bay leaf curling up in smoking mustard oil. What would my daughters say? I cannot let them down. I have to stand by Sameer and defend him, whatever happens. Not for me, but for Piyu and Riya.

I feel sick at the thought. Maybe I am just overreacting!

I bring the letter to my nose, close my eyes and sniff hard, trying to unearth clues like those sniffer dogs, but it smells clean and sweet, of detergent. I am not sure what my next steps should be. No one prepares for situations like these. No one tells you, 'If you come upon a love note in your husband's laundry, here are the steps to take.' I can call Sameer and demand an explanation, but what would I say? I don't want to be the nagging wife who is always suspicious. I used to hate that kind and now I was becoming one! Nope, confronting Sameer right now was not a good idea, not when we were in different continents and time zones.

It will be only fair, I think, to wait for him to come back and give him a chance to explain himself. So yes, I am thinking of the worst-case scenario and of a brunette in Miu Miu heels, but it could be that this is a totally official above the board letter. A perfectly justified, official communication. Perhaps, it was some old lady from HR, not competent with emails, who wrote it. Or maybe it was just a guy, a straight one with feminine calligraphy. But who signs off work letters with 'Love, F'? Maybe a millennial then? A juvenile intern?

I wish my mother had not passed away so early. It has been so long that I don't really miss her every day as a person, but I think someone like her could help me in times of indecision like this. I like to think how my life would be if she was around. Maybe I could have called her and had a heart-to-heart chat and she could give me some sage advice on handling such a situation. Maybe she would have laughed it off as silly midlife crisis. Or maybe she would have shared some similar experience of doubting my very gentlemanly father and we would both have giggled over it. Then again, I am not too sure.

The phone rings and jolts me out of my reverie. Sheesh! I have stood there in the laundry room for the last thirty minutes doing nothing! The machine is already in its gentle last cycle. I pick up the phone and see Neela calling me.

'Hellooo, Shubha, sorry, I should have called earlier. Thank you soooo much for the gift. You shouldn't have really, na.' Neela coos over the phone.

'Oh, the party was so wonderful and the food was too good. I enjoyed myself so much.' I speak in that usual fake tone that most phone conversations start after a party.

Good ol' Neela wastes no time in diving straight into my mind; frank and uninhibited as always. I love her for her no-nonsense nature but never can I be like her. 'So what is with you and Sameer?'

'Umm ... nothing. Actually, nothing. All good.' I check my breathing and calm my voice. I can't tell her about the note I have just found. *The note does not mean a thing; it is merely a form of communication, an inconspicuous form of communication.*

'Stop lying. I have known you for almost twelve years now. You seem so lost these days. And I hardly see Sameer. When did I last see him, maybe six months back?'

'Not lost re, just the usual. Sameer has been very busy. I hardly see him too and it all gets too much for me, I guess.' *Yes, that is it. I miss Sameer. I miss seeing him, talking to him and that is why I am making a huge deal out of three sentences in a letter.*

'Aye, but it is his work. What can the poor guy do?' Neela tries to console me.

'It is not the work alone. Things have changed. He was so involved in everything before and now he seems to have so little time for us. Piyu and Riya are older now so they are okay with it, but what about me?'

'That is how relationships progress, the peaks after marriage slowly settle down to a steady flat line with minor ripples. This is how it unfolds.' Neela sounds like the guru of the 'art of marriage'.

'I guess we have become two different people with little in common. Now that the girls are older, we hardly have anything to even talk about. For all else, we have WhatsApp.' I am wistful.

'So? What is wrong with talking on WhatsApp?'

'But you don't understand, we are like, what is that set theory thing ... ah, a Venn diagram — our intersection set being only that which involves our daughters. It seems we are precariously hanging on two ends of a thread created by the kids.'

'You are expecting too much from marriage, Shubha. And don't give me all that set theory ... I scored only 59 per cent in math in high school! A marriage is not always for the great love or something. You are lucky if you get the great love but often it is the companionship, the co-dependency, the children. There is so much in the equation.'

'But I don't like settling down for anything like that. This feels like settling for a two-minute Maggi, when biryani is what's on my mind. I want more.' I give a rueful grin, while emptying the dryer.

'See, this is the problem with our generation. We grew up with "*Dil Maange More*" without knowing where to stop. We want more money, more houses, more of boobs and even more from marriage. Sheesh!' I can imagine Neela shaking her head while dispensing her gyan to me.

I can't help laughing, there is no one like Neela to clear the fluff. She was right, that is what was happening. I was expecting too much from our relationship. Maybe my relationship with Sameer at this moment is not exactly how I want it to be but that in no way means he is having an affair at work. Ridiculous. Poof! There goes my worry.

'But Neela, Avinash and you have such a perfect thing.'

Neela snorts and says, 'Yeah, except the in-laws. Who, if you have forgotten, live practically next door from us. But I did hit the jackpot with Avinash. I was all set for the worst and then got the best.'

I should be jealous of Neela at this point, but I am not. I am genuinely happy for her. When she told me her story, twelve years ago at the party where we had met, I was so intrigued that I knew I had to forge a friendship with her. Since then, every time I hear her tell it to anyone new, I feel a warm glow for her and Avinash.

———

Fifteen years ago, Neela was striking, smart, twenty-two and very, very poor. So poor that as she often recounts they would not know if and where the next meal would come from. Neela herself worked odd jobs and went to night college. Naturally, there was no money for marriage but proposals came in plenty for Neela with her gorgeous and bountiful hair, glossy pink skin and features that looked sculpted at Kumortuli.

One day, there came a marriage proposal from a Bengali family settled in far-off America, through a matchmaker, which even Neela thought would be foolish to refuse. There was too much at stake, monetarily. So, her mother bought her a ticket, with the money the groom's family had sent, and sent her off to the US to meet this NRI stranger and get married to him. It would seem that no mother could do something like this to her own daughter. Imagine the perils of it all. But desperation makes you take drastic steps, it seems.

So Neela had arrived single, but not ready to mingle, at JFK airport on a cold winter morning in January. With no money and only a single VIP suitcase, she waited at the airport for the supposed groom to arrive.

She had never seen him, in real or virtual. She wasn't his Facebook friend. Wait, there was no Facebook back then. With every Indian man that passed her by, and given it was JFK there was no dearth of them, her heart would take a leap. But no one stopped for her. Finally, after she had waited for more than half a day, she gathered courage and placed a collect call to the phone number her mother had scribbled on a piece of paper. The voice on the other side said wrong number.

Hungry, tired, scared, Neela had broken down right there in the airport arrival lounge. Fortunately, an elderly Indian lady with wilting flowers in her hair was also waiting right there for her family to arrive. When she heard Neela's story, she grabbed her hand and took her home. They were Tamil Iyengars from Madurai, now settled in upstate New York. The lady took her home, fed her hot sambhar rice, made steaming filtered coffee for her, and then called the supposed groom's number again. When yet again no one answered, they were extremely kind to the young, beautiful Bengali girl, and asked her to stay with them until the groom heard the voicemail and called back. No call ever came and Neela continued staying at the Iyengar house without so much as a peep from anyone. She had a tourist visa for the next six months and the Iyengars were kind people who treated her like family and took her sightseeing. However, all hell broke loose when a few months down, the lady's nephew, the youngest Iyengar son in the family, declared he wanted to marry her.

There was a lot of Appa, Amma, gothram, sanskaram hullabaloo. The Iyengars were staunch Brahmins who had done very well for themselves. Neela was like a mongrel stray cat encroaching their sacred household.

Thankfully, Avinash Iyengar had enough Iyengar blood in him to stand his own ground until his parents came around and grudgingly agreed to a Bengali daughter-in-law. I love Neela's story, it suits her perfectly.

——

'Okay, bye and be good. Don't go off all hoitering-loitering with someone else, like Anju. The hormones go all crazy once you hit forty.' Neela dispenses more nuggets of her wisdom.

'Wait, what? Anju? What did she do?' A whiff of some gossip piques my interest. I need that to divert myself.

'Arre, didn't you hear? Will tell you later. Gotta go.' Typical Neela to cut off the conversation just when it is taking an interesting turn. I am just about to hang up when Neela drops her voice and whispers, 'How is your sex life, Shubha?'

I fumble, not sure what to say. To be honest, it's far from stellar. Actually, it's been more than a month since we did anything! Sameer is either travelling or jet-lagged. And when he is not, I am not in the right mood. I didn't think too much about it, I assumed most couples married this long have it the same way.

'Okay-ish kind, maybe two or three times a month,' I lie through my teeth. I am not comfortable discussing my conjugal life, even with a close friend like Neela.

'Hmm ... that sounds far too low.' Neela's tone is now grave, which makes me gasp. Two or three times a month is 'far too low'? What am I? F... I stop myself, effing twenty-nine? I have renewed respect for Neela and Avinash now. No wonder they are so happy!

'You know what you need? A keratin treatment. Your hair is too frizzy. You need smooth, straight, silky hair cascading down, skimming your shoulders and stopping just around the shoulder blades. Think about it. Once you get that done, I will take you for a Hollywood wax. Sameer will be blown away.'

I fold Sameer's shirts, trying to make small, neat folds as I saw on the Marie Kondo show the other day, ruminating over what Neela said. It sounds practical but doesn't fill the chasm in my heart. I cannot seem to chase away that pesky scrap of letter from my head. An unknown fear lurks in my stomach, like a mild indigestion.

Who is F? I rummage in the different corners of my brain. Anyone that Sameer has mentioned before? But it's been a while since I have had even a proper chat with him. There is always some meeting he is flying to, some clients who have to be taken to dinner, some boss whose calls have to be always answered immediately. I can feel the growing distance between us and I can't figure how keratin or Hollywood is going to solve this problem.

Facebook

The peaks after marriage slowly settle down to a steady flat line with minor ripples. Don't expect too much. #marriagegyan #dailywisdom

85 likes. 45 hearts.

Shrabon
(July – August)

It hasn't stopped raining since last night. A nagging drizzle, very unlike August. It reflects my current mood – grey, dull, nagging. I have finally decided to resolve the issue of the wrongly addressed letters and I feel queasy at the thought. Over the last three months, the letters have given me a new goal in life. They have again connected me with a world that I thought no longer existed for me. I have come to wait excitedly for these letters from a stranger in a country that was once my home, to see what unfolds in her kitchen and life. In a way, that feels like home to me.

I had a feeling that the next letter would come any time this week. It has been about thirty-two days since the last one and if I have cracked the pattern right, there was one for every month in the Bengali calendar.

This time I would not open it. I would steel my heart. It wasn't mine. I was trespassing and in the court of law it could well be a crime. I will take the letter straight to the post office and mail it back.

All of last week I kept googling for 'Panchanantala Lane, Baranagar, Kolkata', without much success. Google Earth could narrow down to Baranagar, Kolkata, and some streets around it but when asked about Panchanantala Lane, it kept directing me to places like Behala and Serampore, which were nowhere near Baranagar on the map. So, either the address was a misprint or this was a narrow by-lane in some interior corner of Baranagar which Google Earth's satellite had missed. My worry was that even if I returned them, the letters might get lost in the network of postal systems and never reach the sender in India. But why worry about something that wasn't even mine, I tried to assure myself. It sounded hollow.

As predicted, the pale blue aerogramme arrives in the morning post. I push it aside, trying to concentrate on my work, but my eyes keep getting pulled by the blue missive. Finally, I put it inside a bigger brown envelope along with the last three letters and seal it firmly. I will take it to the post office at lunchtime and send it on its way to the real Moni. Yep, I am a good person who does the right thing. I feel like an angel with a fresh new halo!

Proud of my resolution, I focus on my laptop screen. The local middle school was doing a welcome book for September when school starts, and we had bagged the project. It was fun editing the comments of the senior eighth graders and laying out the design. 'Welcome to middle school. All that you need to survive is Google, Wikipedia and Cut & Paste', 'The only thing you need to remember in middle school is your locker code', etc. Last year, Riya had started sixth grade and been very nervous about middle school. These comments would have made her laugh.

I intend to finish all the edits by the end of this week, which means tomorrow. So, there is no way I can spend any time reading the letter anyway. Nope, I am not going to waste any more time nosing around other people's lives.

Two hours later, I find myself staring at the tree outside my window, my computer in hibernate mode. The tree is dripping water like a leaking faucet. Tip! Tip! Tip! My window is being slashed by fine needles of rain and I can barely see anything beyond the tree. On my desk lies the fourth letter, its pale blue paper opened at the fold, the lovingly penned Bengali fonts gazing up at me, mocking my resolution made only two hours back.

———

Dear Moni,

It is already Shrabon, the second month of the monsoon. My mother used to say that Shrabon is the month of steady rains and heartbreaks. The dark grey skies, the nagging drizzle, the tip-tip-tip sound of the raindrops as the days become damp and soggy with the rain. It is a month where rains bring Bengal alive with greenery, but also a time when the rivers run high and can get cruel and vindictive.

That year Shrabon was especially savage, with the rains being simply relentless. As I told you in my earlier letter, I was engaged to Rajat at the time, who I was starting to loathe. My wedding date was set for the cooler days of Karthik, but the preparations were already in full swing. I didn't know what to do.

My mother was busy buying saris for the 'totto' to be given to the many relatives of the groom. Purple-bordered, daisy yellow dhonekhali saris for the distant cousins, deep maroon and turquoise kanjiivarams with heavy silver work on their pallus for the groom's aunts, traditional red-bordered silk gorod for the grandmothers and the most exquisite dhakai jamdani weaves by the artisans of Bangladesh for the mother-in-law.

The wedding invitations had already been printed and every evening after office my father would write the addresses of the invitees in neat block letters on them, dotting each with his thumb imprint of sacred yellow turmeric. There was a frenzy in the air and my mother was being extra nice to me, always cooking the things I loved the most. I felt like the typical sacrificial lamb being fed only to be sacrificed.

As the days progressed, I found myself resenting Rajat's behaviour more and more. He always wanted things his way and expected me to change all my beliefs for him. A pucca bootlick, always grovelling to his British bosses and ridiculing me for supporting Gandhi. We were two very different people and I didn't feel I could live my life with him. Instead, I kept thinking of that boy who had stopped by our house on that rainy evening. He had come by a few more times and each time I liked him a little more. You have only one life, why waste it on the wrong person?

But it was difficult to confess that to my family. If I called off my engagement, my family would be the centre of ridicule of all our relatives and friends.

The only solace in that month of torture and heartbreak was the ilish. It is my favourite fish, and that year the markets were flooded with shining varieties of ilish from the River Padma. We had it in all forms for lunch and dinner. Every part of that delicious fish was cooked in our home with love and mustard oil.

The silvery pieces of the fish would be fried lightly in golden yellow mustard oil and put in a light mustard paste curry tempered with nigella seeds, called jhaal. On the days my mother made a creamy yellow mustard-coconut paste on the shil nora, the fresh pieces of the fish would be smeared with that paste, wrapped in fresh banana leaves from our garden and steamed in a pot of rice to make the bhapa ilish. The fat sack of fish roe, maacher dim, was fried in mustard oil and served with green chilli, the fish oil lashing the white rice with its bright yellow colour.

As the rains pounded the earth our whole house reverberated with the aroma of ilish. And then on those extreme days when you thought the earth would wash away in a great deluge there would be the grand finale — my grandmother's maacher tauk, where the fish head was *fried crisp and made into a sour curry with dark brown tamarind and jaggery. It was a beautiful dish, with a play of sweet and sour that spoke of deep secrets.*

But even all my love for the delicious ilish could not soothe the pain in my heart. Often relationships start out as a tender sapling, you need to nurture them ... but when you know that you and your partner are like two parallel lines that will never intersect, it is better to end it.

Moni, today I am sending you the recipe of my grandmother's ilish maacher tauk and bhapa ilish. The second one is very easy, and I hear these days you can even make it in the oven. The first one is slightly difficult — but don't shy away from it, do try ... you might just fall in love with it.

Bhalo theko,
Didan

A flock of memories along with the strong smell of mustard hits my olfactory senses. It has been ages since I have had ilish, or hilsa, the reigning queen of Bengali fish. My grandmother used to make a darn good ilish'r tauk too. It was a backstage kind of dish. I mean that while the choicest pieces of ilish were fried and served as a bhaja, the beautiful steak pieces steamed as a bhapa in clinging mustard sauce with fluffed white rice, the fish roe were fried and served with the oil and fresh green chilli, the fish's head (maatha) and tail (lyaaja) led a sad life waiting in Dida's kitchen until she was done with the bhaja, jhaal and jhol.

By then the sun would be high up, the crows sitting on the neem tree outside the kitchen would get tired of all the cawing, the neighbourhood cat would have had a princely meal of fish scales and be patiently waiting for the remains from the men's lunch plates who could never chew on the fish bones.

It was then that Dida would open a green lidded plastic jar that stocked a block of tamarind, brown, ripe and sticky, wrapped in a piece of old newspaper. Dida would put the wok back on the stove and pour some more mustard oil in it. Minoti'r Ma, her house help, would rub the tamarind in a bowl full of water to take the seeds out and prepare the thick sour liquid. The water would slowly turn a deep burnt sienna and the kadhai would hiss with scarlet red chillies and mustard seeds. The fish head and tail would nudge each other and smile; it was their moment. As they simmered in the tamarind gravy of the tauk sweetened with jaggery, I would wait patiently for the last course of my meal. My mouth waters even now just thinking of that sour fish gravy.

Maybe I will buy hilsa from the Bangladeshi store today and try making at least the steamed preparation – bhapa ilish. It seems simple enough. The thought perks me up and I can almost taste the pungent, sharp flavour of shorshe baata – the golden yellow mustard paste – on my tongue.

I fold the letter in a neat rectangle and put it back in the brown envelope again. I want to give Rajat a tight slap across his face. What an asshole! I wish she had ended up with that other boy she had met. It makes me sad that I won't know how this story ends and I fervently hope that Rajat treated her well after their marriage.

As much as I was falling in love with 'Didan' and her food, the right thing to do was to return the letters. Without letting my conscience and my heart battle it out, I sling my Vera Bradley bag over my shoulder, grab my umbrella and with the brown envelope under my left arm I leave for the post office.

Claire and Samantha are not in today and Kajol is in her office. Being the 80 per cent shareholder of the company, she has a tiny cubicle of her own.

As I tiptoe past her office, I can see her tall frame hunched over the desk with four mugs of coffee surrounding her. Unfortunately, the click of the latch is loud and clear as I try to open the door. Sheesh! All those times I've thought of putting some oil in this latch. No wonder they say all those bad things about procrastination.

'Shubhaaa…' Kajol wails. Her kohl-rimmed eyes look smudgy like a racoon's and her salon-styled hair is standing out in spikes. Clearly, she is in distress.

'Shubhaaa!' she wails again, in a higher pitch this time. 'I cannot do this. I simply CANNOT. Writing a book is so difficult, man. I am confused by my own characters. By the way, is that a manuscript you are carrying?' Her tone changes from distress to suspicion.

Kajol regards any printed A4 size paper as a manuscript. If it happens to be in a brown envelope her suspicion just confirms itself.

'Kajol you have got to stop this. Every piece of paper with something written on it is NOT a manuscript.' I raise my voice a little in frustration. But the miserable, hollow look in her eyes melts my heart and I decide to share my secret with her. I fling aside my bag, make myself a cup of jacaranda tea and carefully open the sealed envelope again.

With each letter that Kajol reads, her face mellows down and her eyes twinkle.

'These are gems, Shubha. These are gems.'

She keeps on repeating.

'The recipes! Handwritten and all!'

When she looks up ultimately, her eyes have gone from despair to hope. Sipping that awful jacaranda tea, that doesn't seem like a good sign to me. 'Shubha,' she whispers as if there are spies around us, 'I have an idea. A BRILLIANT one. We could become famous, make money. And not have to think of how to pay the electricity bill every month.'

I stare at her. The stress seems to have really got to her because she has lost it!

Kajol continues, her face flushed and animated, 'You don't understand. See, we can publish these letters as a book. A book of old letters about life from another era along with lost recipes. They are precious. Do you think anyone knows how to cook ilish'r tauk these days? People will go gaga over it. The only thing you have to do is string the letters together into a book.'

She fidgets around with the knick-knacks on her messy desk and then averts her eyes to murmur, 'And ahem ... of course if you could cook the recipes that would nail it.' I give her an incredulous look. What the heck!

'Well, there are two small problems that you have overlooked,' I say, gathering the letters, trying to sound sweetly sarcastic. 'First, these letters do not belong to me. So, there's the obvious copyright issue. Second, I can't write. I don't write. All I have written in the last fifteen years are notes for the school and edited the newsletters and flyers for our organization. Not enough expertise to write a book. I am not going to make a complete fool of myself by attempting to write one. There's a third problem too in fact – I never learned to cook authentic Bengali food. I cannot make an ilish'r tauk for you.'

Kajol is taken aback by my words. I think she got the sarcastic tone. 'Now, let me go to the post office to mail these letters so that their rightful recipient can cherish them.' With that I leave Kajol stupefied and breeze out of the door. I think I have made a forceful impact.

'But your short stories for our college magazine became so popular. Remember those?' Kajol's words ring out soft from behind the closed door. I pretend I have not heard anything. Today, I am sending these letters back definitely.

Facebook

Swim against the current. Be the hilsa. #ilishtales #dotherightthing

19 likes. Neela sent a 'thumbs up' emoji.

Bhapa Ilish or Steamed Hilsa

Hilsa steeped in a pungent mustard sauce steamed to perfection with a liberal dousing of mustard oil is almost a sensuous experience. An easy dish packed with utmost flavours, it can be cooked in a pressure cooker, oven or even microwave. This recipe serves four.

Mustard Paste

Mustard seeds – 2 tbsp
Poppy seeds – 2 tsp
Grated coconut – ¼th of a cup
Green chillies – 3 or 4
Yogurt – 1 tbsp
Mustard oil – 2 tsp
Turmeric powder – ¼ tsp
Salt – to taste

Fish

Hilsa fish – 5 or 6 pieces washed and scales removed
Salt and turmeric powder – to rub on the fish pieces
Mustard oil – 5 or 6 tbsp
Green chillies – 5

Step 1: The paste and the sauce

Soak shorshe (mustard seeds), posto (poppy seeds) and green chillies in less than half a cup of water for an hour. Drain the water and grind the three with coconut and a little salt to make a thick mustard paste or shorshe bata.

In a bowl, add the above mustard paste, yogurt, mustard oil, turmeric powder and salt to taste, and mix well. This is the mustard sauce that will be used for the fish.

Quick tip: *If you have a bottle of kashundi, add 1-2 tsp of kashundi to the mustard paste that you have made. This gives an awesome taste.*

Step 2: The fish

Wash and clean fish cut in steak-size pieces. Rub the pieces with salt and a sprinkle of turmeric powder.

Step 3: Bringing it together in two methods

Method 1 – In the oven

Smear an oven-safe bowl with a little mustard oil. Place the fish pieces in the bowl in one single layer. Pour the prepared mustard sauce over it so that it covers all the pieces well. Add 3 or 4 slit green chillies on the top and drizzle some more mustard oil on them.

Cover the bowl with an aluminium foil and at 375°F or 190C bake for 25 to 30 minutes. After the first 10 to 15 minutes, remove the foil cover and continue baking without it for the next 15 minutes.

Once done, serve hot with rice. This delicacy does not taste as good if stored and served later.

Method 2 – In the pressure cooker

Smear a pressure cooker-safe bowl with a little mustard oil. Place the fish pieces in the bowl in one single layer. Pour the prepared mustard sauce over it so that it covers all the fish pieces well. Add four slit green chillies on the top and drizzle one tsp or more of mustard oil on them.

Cook for two to three whistles. Once done, serve hot with rice.

5

Every first Tuesday of the month we have a potluck lunch at work. It mostly turns into a pizza party as everyone forgets to cook. Only Claire brings in a dessert every time. Yes, every freaking time. It is usually chocolate lava cakes, individual portions, baked in cute red ramekins. They are always perfect, with a gooey molten centre of dark chocolate and never too sweet. Her great-grandmother's recipe, passed on to her mother, and now to her. It always feels like a privilege to eat a spoonful of Claire's great-grandmother's lava cake, as if I am eating some precious antique, steeped in age and stories as it is passed from one generation to the next.

Given that our tiny company cannot afford to give its employees any benefits, this once a month potluck-turned-pizza party is a fringe perk that we indulge in.

Today was no different. We had just finished the last slice of the pizza. I had doused my slice generously with garlic powder and red chilli flakes and was trying to offset the heat of all that chilli with Claire's lava cakes. I had just dipped a spoon and taken the first bite, savouring the rich chocolate melting in my mouth and titillating my secret senses, when Sam came running up the stairs.

'Shubha, you have a visitor.' Sam was panting. 'He said he will wait for you downstairs.'

'He?' Claire looked at me with her mouth slightly open, the chocolate rich and brown on the edge of her pink lips.

Kajol, forgetting that we hadn't talked since the write-that-damned-book fiasco, turned sharply towards me and said, 'A he other than Sameer?'

Seriously! They were behaving as if I were a sixteen-year-old and they were my Victorian era guardians. But I was confused about the visitor myself. In my few months of working here, no one had ever come to meet me. No family. No friend. Not even Sameer. I mean, why would they? If I have to meet someone, there are many more convenient locations available and at my age, most folks prefer meeting in cafés or homes rather than at a tiny office. Unless of course what brings the stranger is strictly work.

I tried to crane my neck and look outside the window but the awning above the door concealed the visitor from view.

I wiped my mouth with a tissue and sauntered downstairs, hoping to take care of whatever business the stranger had in a few minutes. The building doesn't have a lobby and any visitor who comes has to stand outside the door and be buzzed in. When I pushed the door open gently, the mellow warm September sunshine jumped in and pooled at my feet.

'Hello, Shubha. I am sorry, I really didn't want to bother you but I was in the area and was wondering if you could help me,' the man standing right outside the door said in a very apologetic voice.

The sunlight was right in my eyes and I wasn't able to place the person. I was squinting like an old lady, when he scratched his head and mumbled, 'Jai! From Neela's party, remember? You told me where you worked so...'

Oh my God! It was Jai all right. The guy I had chatted with for hours about khichuri. How embarrassing that I could not recognize him. But in my defence, he was now standing in the sun looking all crisp and clean in blue jeans and a striped purple shirt, very different from the mysterious, shadowy stranger the other night. I mean he looked ... umm... fresh and handsome!

Compared to his 'Hello Sunshine', hunky fresh look, I was acutely conscious of the garlic in my breath, from the generous dose I had sprinkled on my pizza.

'Errm, no, it's fine actually. Tell me, how can I help. What can I do?' I said, acting nonchalant, still holding the door half ajar so that no one but me could cross the threshold.

'Well, it might sound very stupid, but I want your help to pick out some fish. I remember you telling me there was a Bangladeshi fish store somewhere nearby. I tried messaging you on Facebook too but you probably missed my friend request. Hope it is not too much trouble if I ask you to take me there?'

It did sound stupid actually. I could have just given him the directions to the store and told him to get it himself. Instead I said, 'Wait a minute. Let me get my bag and I will be back.'

Upstairs, I grabbed my bag, declared to no one in particular 'Will be back in an hour', popped a fresh mint gum in my mouth and after dabbing my face with a tissue for the second time, marched downstairs. I didn't look but could feel the six pairs of eyes piercing down my back. For a fraction of a second, I thought, should I apply lipstick? I was mortified by my schoolgirlish idea and hesitated for two minutes. And then I headed straight to the ladies' room and quickly sprayed J'adore on my wrist. I also applied my rarely used MAC Diva lipstick, a Mother's Day gift from last year.

When I finally stepped out, Jai was waiting in the parking lot with an apologetic grin on his face. He had faint dimples, I noticed. I remote started my Lexus, rolled down the windows to get rid of the ripe banana-stale muffin smell, and asked him to get in. The temperature was in the mild 60s but I was feeling hot, and could feel the patch of perspiration grow around my underarms. I had never driven men, whom I hardly know, to fish stores before. And then in my nervousness, I shifted the gear to drive instead of reverse to pull out. The car lurched forward and was about to hit a wall when I quickly pressed on the brakes in time.

'Is this how you normally drive?' Jai's voice was flat and face serious.

'Just wait and watch,' I tried to act cool, regaining my confidence. He laughed out loud, and his easy laughter cut through the tension in the air. There is always a first time, I told myself – of driving strangers to fish stores.

Ahmed Bhai's fish store was uncannily empty, which wasn't very surprising. One o'clock in the afternoon on a weekday is not the ideal time for fish-shopping. Ahmed Bhai, whom I had only discovered recently because of the ilish I bought last month, was watching some Bangladeshi soap on TV and wasn't particularly happy to entertain unwanted customers either. Jai quickly decided on a pack of rui, the river carp that thrives in the sweet freshwater ponds of Bengal, cut up in steak pieces, and we were out of the door in fifteen minutes.

'So, do you want to grab a cup of coffee before heading back?' he asked.

'I don't drink coffee,' I said and then added as an afterthought, 'but if you want some tea, there is a little chai shop just around the corner.'

In five minutes' time we had walked past the Zaveri jewellery store, a packed-to-the-brim dosa junction and arrived at 'The Littlest Tea Shop', which was pleasantly empty. Well, the shop had only two red formica-topped tables, six chairs and not a single person in sight except a bald, moustachioed man behind the counter who wasn't exactly delighted to see us. Looked like he was getting ready for a nice siesta and didn't like being disturbed. He reluctantly took down our order of two cups of chai and samosas and without a word disappeared into a dark cavernous space behind the counter.

We sat down at the relatively cleaner of the two tables. Outside the slightly grimy window, which covered the entire front of the store, a slow stream of people were trickling by. At this hour, everyone appeared to be walking with a purpose instead of wasting their time buying fish or drinking tea for that matter. I should have gone back to work too, I thought, instead of squandering my time like this.

Chatting with Jai had somehow come easy at Neela's house the other night, but in the harsh daylight I helplessly looked around for things to talk about. I wanted to sound fun and interesting but nothing came to mind. What's wrong with me?

'So, what do you plan to cook with the fish?' I asked finally, hoping I didn't sound too nosy. I am not great at frying these steak pieces of fish, which is a precursor to making any Bengali fish curry. So, I usually stay away from them. In the early days of our marriage, it was Sameer who would buy the tyangra, pabda and rui and cook a kosh koshe tyngra charchari dripping in mustard oil, the kalo jeere pabda jhol with tiny nigella seeds and dainty green chillies, or a fiery red rui'r kalia just like in a wedding menu. Now that Sameer has no time and the girls can't handle fish with bones, I always get a pink salmon filet or the pale-looking cod from clinical counters of our American grocery store, and just broil them in the oven with some olive oil, lime juice, garlic and pepper.

Jai had taken out his phone and was tapping on it intently. 'W.O.R.K.' he mouthed silently.

How old was he?

Maybe the same age as me or a couple of years younger. His face had an honest boyish charm. And I have to admit, his dimpled smile was very attractive.

Like Farhan Akhtar?

Sheesh! If only that guy had not married that hairstylist and then divorced and got entangled in all that mess My grandmother would have called her a 'napteni'!

Maybe I would still have a chance.

Wait, I meant Farhan Akhtar. Not Jai. I was speaking out loud by now. Jai looked up from his phone, a confused, quizzical look on his face.

I felt really embarrassed, and so took out my phone too and started checking for notifications and messages. Anju had posted a new profile picture with 193 likes. Sameer had sent a message: 'Flying out to London tomorrow and then Helsinki. I am tired, Shubha. I need a break.' Break? I wanted to text back 'Have a Kit Kat'. But I resisted. I wasn't sure what kind of break he wanted.

Sameer's text voice did not sound exactly kit-katty. On the contrary, the tone was sombre, as sombre it can sound in a disembodied text message with no emojis. Or at least I imagined it that way. He had been away for more than a month now. I never got a chance to discuss the scrap of a letter I'd found in the laundry with him and now I hoped it wasn't too late.

I could feel a soft lump forming in the back of my throat. Was this how clouds formed? Tiny droplets of tears that had long dried coming together to form a soft ball? I didn't understand what the last line in his message meant. It was kind of abrupt. Unforeseen. Sure, I had been feeling a dissonance in our relationship, a suspicion that something ominous was brewing, but I didn't expect him to say he needed a break.

What did he really want to say?

What did he want a break from?

Me? Us? What? Why?

Maybe I was overthinking again. I have this habit of leaping to conclusions. 'Impulsive,' as Sameer often said. Maybe he wanted a different kind of break; perhaps a break from his hectic travels. Yet something didn't fit right. Sameer loved his job. He loved sealing those major deals on his business trips. So why would he want a break from that?

I had read a survey in HuffPost the other day. 'Taking a break in a relationship' was a trending pattern amongst long-married couples these days. Anju and Saty were taking a 'break'. Neela had finally told me what was going on with them. Anju had gone ahead and convinced Saty that they needed to re-evaluate their relationship and for that it was necessary to take a break. They would still be married but it would be like a sabbatical, she'd suggested. And then she'd gone ahead and had a torrid affair with her Italian boss (can't blame her, he is just too handsome) till the boss's wife found out. Saty was in a state far worse than the boss's wife – moping and sniffing and vacuuming their staircase over and over again.

Did Sameer get this crazy idea from Anju? Was he having a torrid affair with 'Love, F', the client in Miu Miu heels? I tossed around the word 'torrid' silently on my tongue a couple of times. It tasted acrid like bile.

'Sorry, had to reply to some stupid email from the CTO. So, what were you asking? About the fish?' Jai was saying, putting away his phone, his long tapering fingers drumming on the table, the tea still nowhere in sight.

I nodded silently in response, my mind no longer interested in the conversation. I desperately needed the tea – a cup of steaming chai – to dip my face into its soft ginger steam and hide my tears.

'I am not yet sure, but I think I will try to perfect my doi maach. That and the malaikari. The last two times I attempted, the gravy got all curdled up…' Jai's voice trailed into intricacies of the gravy and his mother's doi maach with fish that was so fresh that it could be used raw in a curry.

I was thinking of Sameer. Of the life we had. Almost eighteen years. Two daughters. Twenty vacations. So many movie nights. Sameer's spicy scarlet dim kosha. My creamy Alfredo. Umpteen dining-outs. Millions of fights. Billions of kisses. Hugs. Tears. Pain. Joy. It was okay. Maybe it was not magical. But solid, good, nice. So nice that I wanted to hold on to it. I did not want a break.

I loved Sameer. Not in a *Qayamat Se Qayamat Tak* kind of way, but in the sense that I didn't want to grow old with anyone but him. We could work this out. We WILL have to work this out.

'I have to learn to make the best doi maach. It is my son's favourite. We always end up eating out when he visits, but his mother doesn't like that. This time I want to cook all his favourite food.' Jai's voice, weighed down with his terrible guilt, was cut abruptly by the moustachioed owner's bored 'Chai'.

Two terracotta cups in brick red, almost like kulhars but not quite, were put in front of us. The cups were filled to the brim and a little of the brown tea splashed on to the table. The moustachioed man didn't bother to clean it up. Instead he placed a steel plate on the splotch. Two samosas, their proud nose high in the air, sat on it. A small bowl of dark tamarind chutney stood guard.

Jai held his cup in the palm of his hands and gripped it tight. I sank my face to the level of my cup, taking a deep breath. A sweet and warm scent of ginger, cinnamon and maybe black peppercorns rose up my nostrils and nudged the cells in my brain, putting them back in order – pushing the sad cells to the back row, spiking up the sharp, curious ones.

'You have a son? He doesn't live with you?' I asked and almost immediately bit my tongue for sounding so inquisitive.

Jai was looking out of the same grimy window I was looking out of a few moments earlier. Life played out there. He continued staring at the sun-dappled pavement outside as he spoke softly, 'Ananda. Nine years old. Ananda means joy, the happy kind of Joy, unlike my winning Jai. Only, I didn't win.'

I took a long sip of my tea. Despite the moustachioed guy's apparent lack of interest, the tea was good. It was sweet, milky and had been simmered for a long time with the spices. The liquid felt good at the back of my throat. With each gulp, I could feel the warmth radiate through my veins. And finally, when the sharpness of the peppercorns, the sweetness of the cinnamon and the boldness of the ginger had reached my heart, I found myself saying, 'I will teach you how to cook the fish. You will be making the best doi maach in two weeks' time. Ananda will love it.'

Seriously? Even Piyu and Riya don't like my doi maach. Wait, I actually had never even cooked doi maach!

'Oh no, you don't really have to. You must be busy with your family and I don't want to impose or anything, I will try to find a recipe online,' he said, more polite than happy. 'So, how is Sameer? You both should come over some time.'

'I have plenty of time. It is Sameer who is busy.' I smiled bravely.

Facebook

Take a break. Have a Kit Kat. #idontlikebreaks

52 likes. Sameer is one of them.

I accepted Jai's friend request and then spent an hour looking through his photo albums. Ananda was indeed a happy little boy and charming too just like his dad.

Bhadra
(August – September)

Bhadra is the fifth month of the Bengali calendar. After Asharh and Shrabon, the two months of heavy monsoon, Bhadra is when the rain slowly recedes giving way to a stuffy, humid month when you pine for the dark clouds to return once again. Radha, Lord Krishna's consort, was born on the eighth day of this month.

I didn't know any of this of course. I googled.

It was already the second week of this month and there was no letter yet. Perhaps the old lady realized her mistake. Maybe she is now laughing with her granddaughter over the blunder she had made. I had been hoping that she would at least send a thank-you note for returning the mail but then I was also expecting too much. I was late by four months in returning them, wasn't I? She could have taken me to court for that, probably?

I missed the blue missive, the rounded Bengali script in navy blue ink. Its absence created a void in my life or maybe there was a void already and this just made it look wider. I had grown so used to those letters. Waiting for the recipes they carried and trying them out had been giving me a new zeal in life.

I had started believing that there was someone across the oceans watching over me, who wanted to share her precious stories with me. The letters had stirred up my 'hiraeth' for a home I can no longer return to, and at the same time had also made me brave to face my memories.

And the food! How do I live without those recipes now? They had helped me pick up where I had left off, to bring back the memories I was so scared to dive into. I was slowly morphing from Rachel Ray to my own mother in the kitchen, which would have never been possible without those letters.

I sat at my desk with these thoughts running through my head like slow-moving local trains, savouring the sights and tastes that the last four months of letters had brought. I was in a stupor, daydreaming, when Kajol rushed in, her jhola flying behind her, and dropped a thick brown envelope on my desk.

She panted heavily like an unfit marathon runner as she declared, 'I am coming from the bank. We have a deficit. I think we have to downsize. Since Claire was the last to join, she will be the first one to go. We cannot pay her salary any more.'

Her words sounded dark and ominous, like someone had dropped a bomb in our small office. Claire was an intern. She was paid minimum wage. What would we save by letting her go? It did not make sense. I found Kajol's decision erratic, just like she herself was.

'You cannot just decide like that. I have a 20 per cent say in what this company does and I vote for letting Claire stay,' I said, emphasizing on the words 'vote' and 'stay'.

Kajol let out a short laugh that sounded more like a whimper than a laugh really, and then said, 'Vote? Who is asking for a vote? Are you going to vote to raise money to take care of the deficit or is it going to come from your piggy bank?'

I turned red at Kajol's words and tried to keep my calm. 'Why can't we do something else, like increase our earning potential? We can diversify our services. Get more clients?'

'More clients? From where? No one wants to hire small companies like us any more. They can get the same level of job done way cheaper using an off-the-shelf product. And for more polished and expert services, they would rather spend money and go to the bigger companies who have the glitz and glamour. No author wants us to publish their book. They all want to go to the big names. If only we could get a break with a good novel.' Kajol sounded exasperated. I was not exactly sure how a good novel would solve our problem at this point, but I couldn't think of any other solution, so I kept quiet.

She pulled up a chair, put her head down on my desk and said in a resigned voice, 'I am so tired, Shubha. All I wanted was this business to survive. To prove that we could do it. That independent small businesses run by women can work. That we women are empowered.'

If you ask me, the last part of her rhetoric sounded like something one would say while giving a mayoral speech. But I knew she had legitimate concerns. Kajol then started snoring, her head on my desk, the brown envelope she was carrying still secure under her arms. I guess she had a long night with her nth boyfriend yesterday. Kajol was capricious and I didn't always agree with her whims, but today I genuinely felt sorry for her. This company is her child and losing it would be terribly hard on her. If only I could do something to help.

Maybe I should go on GoFundMe. But would people be convinced enough to fund us? I wasn't sure though; saving a failing business doesn't exactly stir up emotions in people like saving a cute puppy does.

I gently pried the envelope away from Kajol to get a good look at the bank statement; although lifting her toned arms was quite a task. And then I got a jolt. This was the same envelope I had sent back last month with the letters and my note. This was not the bank statement.

'Address not found' was stamped across it in purple. Was this a sign? Was God trying to tell me something? I had edited too many church newsletters to believe in signs.

I nervously opened the envelope and along with the four blue letters that I had sent back, out tumbled a fresh, new fifth one. As always, this too was addressed to 'Shubhalaxmi Sen-Gupta'. A shiver went down my spine and an electric spark of happiness was signalled by billions of neurons in my brain.

Kajol was still sleeping. I tried to shake her arms, but she only moved away and snored louder. I had to take a decision. I knew if I let this moment pass, my resolutions would just skitter away. Kajol's idea was probably our only chance to save Right-to-Write. And I would have to do it.

'Kajol, I will write that book for you. I will try my best to do what I can. We have to save Right-to-Write,' I shouted with my mouth near her ear. Kajol snored more sonorously.

I then googled 'How to write a book?'

There were 5,380,000,000 results in 1.07 seconds.

6

I am at the PTA meeting today at Riya's middle school. Well, I was kind of forced to be here. Don't get me wrong but I am just not one of those dedicated PTA moms. I don't have that kind of drive in me. My responsibility towards the PTA starts with paying the membership fee at the beginning of each school year and ends with the tray of cookies I send for the teachers' luncheon.

Years ago, when Piyu was in first grade, or maybe it was second, I had very excitedly signed up to be the PTA class mom. I had no idea what it entailed; all I knew was that it was a mandatory part of being the mother of a school-age child. The first holiday party that I was supposed to organize for the tiny six- and seven-year-olds was a Halloween party. I was over-the-top excited about it, drawing up menus and scouring the Internet for party game ideas. And then it started.

First, I think it was a text from Josh's mom, or maybe Kevin's. A little boy with blonde hair and a cherubic smile in Piyu's homeroom. 'Josh is allergic to peanuts. Please make sure that the snacks are nut-free.' Okay, no problem. I scratched off all the almond cookies and peanut butter blondies from the snacks menu.

Next it was an email from Diya's mom. Diya with the pigtails and glasses, who is now in high school and dresses like a hooker. 'Diya cannot have anything with eggs in it. In fact she cannot be near anything that has eggs and that includes egg-laying hens!'

I had wondered at the time if any of it was even real? What snacks could I even serve then that kids would love but had no eggs or nuts in it? No cakes or cookies for sure. I had ultimately come down to fruits and chocolates, and maybe chips. That would have to do, I had firmly decided.

'I think as a class mom you should promote the kids in the class to eat local, vegan and wholesome food. Please don't give Miles any fruit that has travelled thousands of miles or has been picked by underpaid migrant farm-hands. Thank you.' That had been a text from a certain Mrs Dextapose.

Seriously? Who were these people? What was I supposed to feed seven-year-olds on Halloween? Pumpkin? I had been so stressed out arranging that single party for eighteen six- and seven-year-olds that for a whole month I had been afraid of my own phone's message tone. I quit soon after, having decided to never go back again and the very efficient Mrs Dextapose, with her neat shoulder-length hair, had gladly stepped in. I never heard her complain even once.

———

But middle school is apparently a different game. The PTA moms here don't have to organize parties or arrange snacks; the kids are self-sufficient and full of angst. So, the PTA decides to have frequent meetings to discuss how to raise more funds and promote STEM. Or is it STEAM? I don't know any more. Too many new acronyms every year.

They made this meeting mandatory for all PTA members. I am surprised to see the number of mothers present at 9.30 in the morning on a Tuesday. All sleek and shiny moms in skinny jeans and sporting their newest boots with the first sign of fall. It is mostly mothers, a smattering of fathers maybe, sipping coffee or some healthy green juice from glass mason jars and looking very determined about STEAM. There is something about PTA and women, a close bond.

The first thing I notice as I look around is the hair. Smooth, cascading sheets of hair. Well, not always sheets, because a lot of them are wearing it short, but all of them are indeed smooth. Silky too. In different shades of colour. I don't know why I have never noticed these gorgeous heads before, it is not that they have all magically sprouted just today. Some are pitch black with hints of red, at least that I have seen before. Also the blondes with dark tips, ombre as Piyu says. But there are more. Silver blondes with lavender, red brunettes with gold, ash blondes with pale blue streaks shrieking for attention. It is gorgeous, all this hair; so well cared for.

I imagine all these women having a perfect marriage and posting smiling family photos on Facebook in colour-coordinated clothes that even matched their hair. Maybe they have perfect husbands too; the ones with perfect teeth and six-pack abs, who come back home every day at six to sit with them and watch the same show on TV. Okay, maybe not exactly watch TV; instead they probably have great sex every evening, but still.

Is it their hair doing the trick? Does my hair bother Sameer? I have never heard him say anything about it, but maybe that is what he wants to get away from. Maybe 'Love, F' has perfect waterfall brown hair like they show in Pantene commercials. I look sideways and then surreptitiously finger my own crowning glory. Yep, frizzy, dry, no character. All of a sudden I feel very conscious of my hair's characterless-ness. I need to get that keratin thing Neela had suggested.

While the PTA vice president drones on about how a robotics lab can help the kids, I type K-E-R-A-T-I-N in my phone. By the time the meeting ends, I have complete knowledge about all kinds of hair treatments and colours. I have even booked myself an appointment with Neela's stylist for a hair makeover today afternoon. It was not an easy feat. I had to slink out of that awful meeting for twenty whole minutes to get that appointment. Hair salons are busier than a doctor's clinic in flu season. They could only fit me in because there was a last-minute cancellation, as they pointedly let me know.

So, later in the afternoon I slip out of office for my appointment. It is one of those salons which look like a spa. There are terracotta pots in the lobby with water cascading down and potted green palms in odd-shaped brass urns. Only the name of the salon is a bit eerie – 'Hair today, Gone tomorrow', it is followed by the caption – 'That's why we are here!' I don't know if all these puns about 'hair' and 'here' is a good thing. Will they take my hair seriously?

My heart beats fast and I am second-guessing my decision. I have had frizzy hair all my life. I cannot imagine cascading, smooth hair on my head. What will that feel like? Will it be uncomfortable?

I walk up to the lady at the front desk, a young girl actually, who flashes me the perfect fake smile and asks me to take a seat. 'Kaila will be with you shortly,' she says in a sickening sing-song tone. Kaila? What kind of name is that?

Fifteen minutes later, a guy in a canary yellow muscle tee and man bun strolls towards me. His jeans are so freaking tight that it may as well be glued to his thighs. With an Iron Man-like body, he looks more like a gym trainer than an expert hairdresser. I hope he will concentrate on my hair and not notice my lack of a strong core. I try to focus on the positive though. Maybe Kaila will fulfil my dreams!

'Okay, so what do we have here?' he asks with a lot of enthusiasm and lifts strands of my hair to examine them closely. There are lots of tsks and hmms as he furrows his brows and examines my hair like it was a strand of rare DNA. I feel apologetic for both my DNA and hair.

He then guides me to the shampoo station with a raucous laugh. 'Sweetie, I will do my best with what has been given to me.' I can't figure if those are words of wisdom or he is joking about my hair, and so I give a meek smile.

Kaila washes my hair with his strong hands. His lithe fingers on my scalp feel very relaxing. Had he not been engaged (I noticed a ring), I would have married him. I don't go to a salon that often but when I do, I just love to give up myself to the shampoo person. Total submission. That is the best part before a cut. I can fall asleep on the shampoo chair. But I try my best to stay awake and concentrate on the perfume of some unknown tropical flower that engulfs me. I could be in Hawaii for all you know. I am almost on the verge of dozing off in contentment when Kaila asks, 'So, what conditioner do you use on your hair?'

'Er ... I don't know. Depends. Whatever is on sale when I am at the store!'

Kaila roars with laughter, spraying water all over my face as the faucet slips from his grip. Once again I can't tell if this is deliberate and if he is rolling his eyes at my answer. He will probably tell Neela later what a klutz I am.

'Would you like a colour with the keratin? It would look good on you and I could get you a discount. Purple and gold, what say?'

Purple and gold sounds very risqué. But then this whole keratin business sounds very risqué. Should I go for it? I debate in my head. 'Okay. Why not?' I am surprised at the sound of my own voice rushing out hurriedly. What has come over me?

'That's like a good girl.'

'Wait, I am not a purple and gold girl, am I?' I add hastily, trying to get out of it.

'You are definitely one, my darling. You have glitter and shine written all over you. Let me take care of this,' he says as he brushes out my hair in quick strokes. How can I say no after that? If I am glitter and shine, then I definitely need to go purple and gold. I feel all perked up by his words.

I must have gone to sleep through the whole two hours that had felt like eternity – the time it took for the entire treatment to finish. How did I manage that though – falling asleep with a million aluminium foils sticking out of my hair?

But I surely must have as I am jolted awake only by the whoosh blast of the hair dryer. Kaila looks immensely proud of his handiwork but I am really tense. What if I don't have glitter and shine written on me after all? What if it's dull and rust instead? He unwraps all the foils, blow-dries out the last bit and spins me around in the chair. I finally look into the mirror and draw a sharp breath. Although it's me I am looking at, I cannot freaking recognize me. If I had met myself around the corner I wouldn't have known who it was.

I am not even sure if it is good. It is just very different. My face looks smaller, the top of my head flatter, the volume that my frizz added to my face is gone and it looks young and vulnerable. My hair is smooth indeed and reaches my shoulders. The purple and gold is not as risqué as I had imagined it to be. The purple colour does not show that much on my black hair, the gold does. It looks sparkly, like tinsel, shiny and glittery. Oh wait, that is not my hair but bits and pieces of the foil that is still stuck on. The gold is like straw yellow woven in my dark hair.

Now that I am observing it carefully, the whole effect is pretty good. Very stylized. I look this way and that. This is a different person who's looking back at me, someone more au courant. Next weekend is the community Durga Pujo that we go to and I can't help imagine the look in the women's eyes. 'Did you see Shubha's hair? It is so freaking glamorous!' they would say. Sameer would be swayed by this new glam hair and lock me in a passionate embrace. I chuckle at the thought. Feeling confident, I start walking towards the lobby and then I see Anju.

Anju in a pinstriped trouser suit and stilettos, which go clack-clack on the tile floor. She looks disoriented and I can see lines around her mouth. Her hair is not in the perfect style that I am used to seeing. I don't really want to talk to her and so I look the other way. But Anju has seen me and is looking at me. I suddenly feel very proud of my new smooth hair with strands of the straw yellow colour.

'Hello, babes!' Anju squeaks in that voice of hers. 'What have you done to your hair? You should have asked me na, I would have recommended my stylist. See, they put a newbie to work on your hair, and now it will take you days to get back to style, tch, tch!'

I don't know what to say. My hand automatically flies to my head and pats it protectively. A part of me wants to squeeze Anju's slender neck but that part is all imaginary. The real part of me does nothing like that and gives an apologetic smile. I am not too bothered by Anju's comments, of course. The girl has some gall but I don't care because I know she has too much on her plate balancing Italian and Bengali. My confidence is a bit shaken, but otherwise I like my new look. I am sure Sameer will be surprised when he sees me. He is coming back late tonight, after midnight. In fact right now, his flight must be taking off on the Heathrow runway.

I am both excited and nervous about his homecoming. I am not yet sure what he meant when he said 'I want a break'. Sameer has been on a whirlwind trip the last couple of months. From London to Helsinki, then Hong Kong, Brunei, Japan and then back to London, his time zones and latitudes have been super chaotic. There have been a few dozen one-line texts but they were just mundane exchanges.

'How was Piyu's SAT?'

'Riya auditioned for school chorus.'

'The garage door got stuck again. We should install a new one.'

'Call the handyman to see if he can fix it.'

I never quite dared to ask about the 'break'. He never mentioned it again either. But the thought still burns like a slow flame in my mind. I keep recalling that one text with a sense of foreboding.

What if he really wants a separation? Like a trial run? What will happen to my children? Will they see their father on Wednesdays or Fridays? Which holidays will be mine? Will Durga Pujo be considered a shared holiday? I sway between feeling angry and humiliated, to stupidly hopeful, like when I think my new hair will solve all problems. But it is not the hair. It is never the hair.

If you churn a momentous issue over and over in your heard, after a while it almost always numbs the problem, taking away the sharp edges. I think this is what happened with me. I have pondered over it a million times in my head and have decided to act very cool and composed if he indeed suggests to break up.

So, this is my POA. I will try to work this out. I will hear what he has to say. If Sameer is honest with me, if 'Love, F' is nothing but the old HR lady filing alphabetically, I will give him another chance. Else, there is no point in holding back a man who wants to break free. Sooner or later the asshole will find a way.

Sameer is not an asshole though. He never was. And he can't just become one, unless there has been some genetic mutation, in which case I will have to either murder him or just let go!

Facebook

Ya Devi Sarbabhuteshu, shanti rupenu sangsthitha. Goddess Durga is the omnipresent one. She is the embodiment of power, peace and intelligence in all beings. And so are we women. #durgapujo #mightygirl

64 hearts. 25 likes.

Ashwin
(September – October)

I take a small detour while driving back from the hair salon and stop at our local Patel grocery store on my way home. Patel Bhai has developed a new-found respect for me these days. The huge bill that I keep racking up buying ingredients as I try and retry dishes has no doubt garnered his admiration for my culinary prowess. Today he comes rushing towards me from the freezer aisle at the back and says excitedly, 'I got that rice you had asked for. The one with the same name as the spice we use for tadka in moong dal.'

'Kalijeera!' I am excited that he has found the substitute for the short-grained fragrant gobindobhog rice I need for today's preparation.

'Yes, the same. Arre, you Bengalis have a strange way of naming stuff!' he says and then rushes off to procure a 2lb bag of kalijeera rice for me.

I want to try out a new dish for dinner tonight. I mean new for me to cook. Sameer will be home after almost a month, and whatever happens later, I want to at least celebrate his homecoming. So that years later when I look back and think of this day, the pain will be masked by the musky brown garam masala scent and subtle sweetness of the rice pulao.

I didn't have to think much; the letter yesterday carried a recipe straight from Ma's kitchen. All these years I had not dared to open my Pandora's box and let jewels like this spill out. I wasn't sure I could ever do justice to Ma's mishti basanti pulao, a pulao studded with cashews and plump golden raisins. Each grain of the rice glistening and separate. Pale saffron yellow in colour, 'basanti rong', like the sari which Ma would dye with stalks of the shiuli flower.

Ma would make the best mishti pulao in our entire neighbourhood, just the perfect balance of sweet and spice. The garom masala — pale green cardamom, woody clove, crackling bay leaves like the fallen leaves in autumn — would always be just the right amount, never overwhelming with their excess nor underplayed by scantiness. I can still recall the rice grains washed and set out to dry on the folds of a week-old newspaper in preparation for the pulao. The white grains of rice were smeared with turmeric so that they looked a pale yellow like the robes of an ascetic. But I knew that was just a decoy, it was only a short interval before they would all come together in a passionate embrace, in their one pursuit of making a beautiful dish, each cooked grain glistening in the same shade of yellow and each morsel of those grains fluttering between sweet and savoury.

I loved that mishti pulao so much that I could eat it just by itself every day. But it was not an everyday dish. Ma made basanti pulao only on occasions that demanded such delicacies, which meant birthdays and anniversaries. Since Baba's birthday was always on the fourth day of Durga Pujo, in the month of Ashwin, she always made pulao and a niramish kosha mangsho for lunch on Nabami. To accompany it there would be a ruby red tomato chutney, sweet and soured with a tiny bit of tamarind. What would I not give to return, if even for a day, to that lunch, throwing back my head and laughing at Baba's jokes, sucking the marrow out of a succulent piece of goat meat cooked to perfection by Ma.

It will take me a lot of courage to cook and serve the same dish today. But when the recipe same as my mother's came tucked inside the letter yesterday, I knew the time had come.

—

Dear Moni,

Do you know what month this is? Ashwin! My favourite month. After the humidity, the early autumn weather of this month is such a welcome change. The sky is scrubbed a perfect clear blue and even the clouds are fluffy white like those in a painting. By the lake, reed like kaash phool with their beige and white head are growing in abundance. Ma Durga is about to arrive in a week!

The loudspeaker in our neighbourhood Pujo pandal has been blaring 'Mahishasur Mardini' since last week. In my time, it was only heard live on radio early morning on Mahalaya — Birendra Krishna Bhadra's baritone voice piercing through the ether early at 4 a.m.

Ashwin is also special to me for another reason. So, you know the year I was engaged to Rajat, what year was that ... I think 1938. Anyway, that Durga Pujo, Rajat's mother invited me to accompany them on Nabami to see the Durga protimas around the city. They had a big Land Rover and would be going all the way to south Kolkata, where a new club Mudiali was doing its first community or Barowari Pujo. My parents were very excited about it and my mother had been giving me lectures for days as to how to behave in presence of my in-laws.

I felt no such thrill of course. I was desperate to get out of that relationship. I did not like the way Rajat behaved with me sometimes. He could be all nice and fancy until you disagreed with him on something and then he would flip, as if a switch was thrown somewhere in his brain.

His jawline would turn hard and his eyes would take on a ruthless look. I was afraid that he could even harm me when he was like that. One evening he took me to the restaurant Blue Fox for dinner, and there when I refused to dance the foxtrot, he created a huge ruckus and just stormed out of the restaurant leaving me all by myself. I wanted to tell my mother about that but I knew she wouldn't pay heed to me.

In the meantime, I would often see your Dadu stroll by our street every evening when I stood at the veranda. He would stand at the telebhaja dokan — the fried food stall, where our narrow by-lane dipped into a curve to meet the main road. At first, I found this very strange as this was clearly far out of the way from where he lived. Gradually, I understood why he came all the way and my heart blossomed in love. We hadn't spoken much and I wasn't sure if his love was strong enough. But I took that as a sign. Maybe he did love me! By then I was desperate. I needed to make a decision by the end of that month.

Should I suppress all my emotions and marry Rajat? Or did your Dadu love me enough to stand by me?

On Ashtami, the second and most important day of Durga Pujo, my mother was entrusted with the job of cooking Pujo'r bhog for our neighbourhood Pujo. She was making bhog'r pulao — an exquisite dish made with rice, roasted cashews and plump raisins. This sweet pulao was made with pure ghee and studded with dry fruits like cashews and raisins. My mother made this dish with utmost devotion and didn't eat a morsel until the bhog had been cooked and offered to the goddess. The aroma of that bhog was so divine that I was sure Durga would never leave my mother's kitchen.

To serve with the mishti pulao she made five kinds of bhaja eggplants chopped in rounds and deep fried, potato fries, sautéed spinach, florets of cauliflower fried golden and potol fried crisp. With that there was also a thick ruby red tomato chutney made with plump tomatoes and sweet dates and paramanna — paayesh made with milk, short-grained rice and jaggery.

On Nabami, she would make niramish mangsho — a succulent mutton curry for the Goddess cooked without onion and garlic.

While the neighbourhood ladies were busy helping my mother with the bhog preparation, I quickly draped a new saffron-coloured dhonekhali sari and slipped out to the pandal. I had a hunch that your Dadu would be there too. If he wasn't, I told myself I, would accept my fate and marry Rajat. And guess what? There he was. His palms together, his eyes closed, his lips silently murmuring, bowed before the Goddess. He looked so handsome and humble standing there that my heart fluttered in nervousness. Ma Durga's face was glistening and I thought I saw her smile, smirk rather.

I pushed forward to stand beside him. The rhythmic beat of dhaks mingled with the shrill sound of conch shells as the priest uttered the mantra for the anjali. I leaned towards him slightly and whispered, 'I have to ask you something.' He was so startled that he almost jumped. I didn't care. This was my only chance and I wanted to give it my all. My heart was beating faster than the dhakis could beat their drums.

'Do you think you love me enough to marry me?' I whispered under my breath. The sound of drums had reached a crescendo and I wasn't sure if he heard my words.

Your Dadu was so shocked that I could see the beads of perspiration on his forehead. You know those were different times, girls didn't go around proposing marriage like that. It was natural for him to be nervous. He looked at the Goddess and then at me, and stuttered a 'YE-E-SS'.

I did not wait for anything more and rushed home, my heart beating faster than my feet could carry me. I decided I would tell Ma to call off my wedding and if she didn't agree I would elope with your Dadu. My face was flushed with happiness. I didn't even notice the car outside or the chatter of excited voices as I went flying through our front door.

'Ma, slow down, and stop running around in the hot sun like this. See, Rajat's parents are here. Rajat is going away to London and they want you two to at least have a registry marriage before he leaves day after tomorrow!'

Ah, the hand of fate works in ways we can never foresee!

I will tell you the rest of my story later, now my fingers are aching, I think it is the arthritis. Lately, the pain has increased and none of the homoeopathic doctor's potions are working. I am sending you the recipe of mishti pulao and niramish mangsho — goat meat cooked without garlic and onion. Try cooking them during Pujo. For the mutton curry, set aside at least two to three hours of your time. It is best when cooked on slow heat until the morsels of meat soften like butter. For the best things in life you often need to wait to get your reward.

Bhalo theko,
Didan

I am so engrossed in thinking of the pulao and Didan's letter for the entire drive that I don't even realize I am just two houses away from my own. That lady must have had some nerve to take the first step and propose like that. I wonder if she got away from marrying that egotistical, rude Rajat eventually. But who are they? Will I ever be able to find the writer of these letters? I question myself in vain knowing well that the answers are no longer easy to find.

As I pull up, I can see the gold and orange maple trees in our front yard have caught the setting sun and are glowing like smouldering embers. The house, framed by the flaming trees, looks magical with its green-shuttered windows and old-fashioned chimney. It was those high windows and flaming maples that had sold the house to us. I can see a car in the driveway too, a navy blue Toyota sedan. The sun is in my eyes, I squint and look again.

Is it my house? Yes! Is it our car? No!

I am trying to figure it out when a man in a charcoal-black suit steps out of the car. He takes out a suitcase from the trunk and bends down to talk to someone in the driver's seat. His posture is a bit slouched, the seat of his pants creased and unkempt.

Oh my God! It is Sameer and that is his Uber ride. Wasn't he supposed to come later in the night? Like after midnight! He probably took an earlier flight then. Why is he home so early?

I gently pull my car to the curb instead of my usual spot in the driveway. The Uber driver is backing, his hand raised in a friendly parting gesture. I wait for him to pull out and then step out of my car. Sameer is already on the porch fumbling for the door keys in his pocket. His gait is slow and uncertain.

'Sameer, you are early,' my voice croaks. I am not prepared for this. Not yet. My plan for the evening was different. I had imagined a pulao in the backdrop of our conversation.

'Shubha,' Sameer turns around to face me. I don't know if he notices my hair. He isn't really looking at me, his eyes just glaze over to the sky beyond. And then for just an instant, a fraction of a second, our eyes lock and I see weariness and fear in his.

As I walk up the few steps, I notice how different Sameer looks today. Not his usual sharp confident self at all. There is defeat and tiredness writ over his face. Cast in the afterglow of the sun, his face looks so vulnerable. I want to hold him and stroke his hair and feed him before anything else. One part of me wants to mother Sameer, to cradle him in my arms, and shoo away anything that is bothering him. But the other part is nervous and angry, not sure how to react if he brings up the 'break'.

I can hit him on the head with my heels and knock him out cold if needed, and that vision does look deeply satisfying. But on the other hand, smiling icily and saying 'Whatever' might send him writhing in an invisible grip of guilt and remorse. Either way, what was going to happen, would happen.

'Shubha, I have something to tell you.' Uh-oh, there it goes, I think. The moment I have been dreading for. But the setting is all wrong. My resolve is weakening and I cannot be all cool and strong right now. I totter in my heels and grab him by the arm to steady myself. My heart is banging against my ribcage so loud that I am afraid he can probably hear it too.

'First, we will have mishti pulao and kosha mangsho,' I manage to utter with an air of confidence. I elbow him aside and lean a little to put the key in the front screen door. Sameer steps back behind me, waiting.

'What have you done to your hair? It looks like magic,' he says.

Facebook

I have uploaded a photo of my head, hair carefully spread across my back; my face not in view.

Glitter and shine. #newbeginnings

104 likes. 15 wows. 27 comments. Anju is not one of them.

Jai messages me on FB Messenger saying his son is coming at the end of the month. He reminds me of my doi maach promise and then mentions that my hair looks gorgeous. Yikes!

Neela has messaged me, 'See, the keratin did the trick. Next come with me for Hollywood wax!'

Niramish Mangsho

Niramish mangsho or vegetarian mutton curry would sound like an oxymoron to most. But not to meat-loving Bengalis, who found a way of offering to gods – a mutton curry cooked sans onion and garlic and thus labelled as 'vegetarian mutton curry'.

The roots of this dish go back to the Hindu ritual of animal sacrifice and offering it to the gods. In Bengal, this ritual was a part of the ninth day, Nabami on Durga Pujo and Kali Pujo. The sacrificed animal was considered as an offering to the gods and cooked without any onion and garlic (considered non-veg as per tradition), the mutton curry was deemed as 'maha proshad' – 'food blessed by the Supreme Being'. This recipe serves four to five adults.

Ingredients

Mutton – 2 lbs / 1 kg (buy cuts like front shoulder or back leg)

For Marinating the Mutton

Thick yogurt – ½ cup
Ginger paste – 2 tbsp
Turmeric powder – ¼th tsp
Red chilli powder – ½ tsp
Garam masala powder – 1 tsp, loosely packed
Salt to taste
Mustard oil – 2 tsp

For Tempering I

Bay leaves – 2
Cloves – 4
Green cardamom – 4

Cinnamon stick – 2' stick
Dried red chillies – 2

For Tempering II

Ginger – 2' knobs of ginger grated to almost 2 tbsp of it
Asafoetida – ¼th tsp
Kashmiri mirch – 1 tsp, loosely packed
Mix the above spices in a little water to make a paste.

Making the Masala Paste

Cumin seeds – 2 tsp
Coriander seeds – 2 tsp
Fennel seeds – 1 tsp
Dried red chillies – 2
Soak all the above in lukewarm water for 15 to 20 minutes and
then put in a blender to make a wet masala paste.

Others

Tomato – 1, ripe and juicy
Green chillies – 2 or 3
Garam masala powder – ½ tsp
Nutmeg powder – a pinch
Javetri or mace – 1 petal
Salt to taste
Sugar – 2 tsp
Mustard oil
Ghee – 1 tbsp

Marinating the Mutton

Buy and wash goat meat thoroughly.

Place the washed mutton pieces in a wide, open-mouthed bowl.

Add all the ingredients listed above for marinating the meat and toss the mutton pieces, making sure the pieces are coated with the spices.

Cover and refrigerate overnight.

Cooking the Mutton

In a wide-mouthed pan, heat about ¼ cup of mustard oil.

Add two tsp of sugar and swirl it around until it browns.

When the oil is hot, add the whole spices for tempering.

When the whole spices sizzle, add the grated ginger, hing and the Kashmiri mirch paste.

Sauté for 30–50 seconds. It will give off a lovely fragrance.

Now add the chopped tomatoes and sauté for a minute.

Add the mutton pieces, reserving the marinade liquid for now.

Fry the mutton pieces at medium high heat until the meat pieces lose their raw colouring.

Next, mix the wet masala paste with ¼ cup of yogurt and whip it well. Pour this into the pan, stir and mix the spices and mutton.

Cook at medium heat for around 15 to 20 minutes, stirring frequently.

For the next steps, you can continue cooking it in the pot or you can switch to a pressure cooker. It will take an hour or more in a pot and about twenty minutes in a pressure cooker. Transfer everything to a pressure cooker, if you choose to go ahead with the latter.

Add the marinade liquid and 1-1½ cups of water at room temperature to it.

Add the garam masala powder, nutmeg powder and mace. Mix well.

At medium heat let the gravy simmer and come to a boil. Taste for seasonings and add salt/sugar as needed. Soon you will see a fine layer of oil floating on top. Add the green chillies then.

Put the lid on the pressure cooker. Cook for five whistles in a whistling pressure cooker. In a Futura-like pressure cooker, once the steam builds up, the mutton will be cooked in about 15 to 20 minutes.

Serve with steamed rice or pulao.

7

Times are tough!

Sameer has been let go from his job. A job where he spent almost 90 per cent of his waking hours. A job which he breathed even while he slept. Apparently, his latest product idea, which their company had invested billions in, had to be recalled. The very core scientific theory on which the idea was based had been proven false and, so, all their clients had cancelled further work on the project. This resulted in a domino effect, and all of the top people involved in the project were let go – bam, bam, boom!

So, that was the 'break' he had meant all along – a break from his job. Well, more like a forced one really. In another life, I would have freaked out at this news. Mortgage! Car loans! I would have panicked. But now all I can think with immediate relief is that it is not that kind of a 'break', thankfully.

Not a break from me. Not a break from us. I keep telling myself.

He wasn't having an affair after all. Neither was he thinking of separation or divorce. There was no brunette in Miu Miu heels. Not that I wanted Sameer to have an affair (I promise I would never want that), but I had put in so much of thought in confronting Sameer with the choicest of words that this version of 'break' seems slightly boring.

In fact, when I brought up that piece of letter (I had tucked it away safely beside my spice jar of panch phoron) and bluntly asked him if he had been having an affair or maybe at least a fling, he looked at me with tired eyes and slowly said, 'Shubha, I was so fucking busy that anything to do with love, marriage or relationship was not even on my mind.' There was such exhaustion writ on his face that I felt remorse, and waves of pity rushed through my heart like the Ganga descending from the Himalayas. Here the poor guy was just super stressed and busy working, and there I was overanalysing his behaviour and doubting his fidelity. What was wrong with me?

Perhaps it was my hormones that were going all ding-dong at forty. I should check with my doctor about this unnecessary anxiety. Maybe he could suggest one of those anxiety pills. Why else couldn't I let go of 'Love, F' even after all that explanation? Something did not feel right.

So, I had gently nudged Sameer further. 'But why does the note say "Does she know about this?" Am I supposed to know something?' I had asked in a thick-honeyed voice, looking at him with innocent eyes.

He looked past me, rubbed his middle finger across the rough salt-and-pepper stubble that shadowed his chin and blabbered something about his boss and some secret that had to be kept from her due to high security surveillance and someone called Mrs Freeman who was helping him in this endeavour. I wanted to believe this, but honestly, it sounded kind of lame. There was a piece of the puzzle that was missing.

Was Sameer involved in some underhand dealings then? Was that why he had lost his job? Sameer's phone rang interrupting my thought process. His ringtone, I noticed, had changed from his usual hurried and jarring *Fast & Furious* ringtone to Beethoven's Moonlight Sonata. He glanced at the caller ID with his brows knit together, extended his arm to pick it up and then pulled back. For the first time in the last five years, he let it ring.

Today is the third middle-of-the-week day in months (or maybe years) when Sameer is home and not glued to his phone! He has got a decent severance and has decided to take a couple of weeks' break before he gets on the job hunt. I think Sameer had half hoped that once the news of his layoff was out, other tech companies would come grovelling at his feet, offering him dream jobs. Phones would be ringing off the hook. Offers would be pouring in. After all Sameer Gupta had been a big honcho in his tech world.

Nothing like that has happened. At least not so far. But I think he still hopes it will happen. He doesn't want to talk much about it anyway and clams shut if I ask anything. 'It will be okay, Shubha,' is all he says, watching *Star Trek* for the nth time on cable.

This is the part of Sameer that bothers me. He just goes into his shell and refuses to discuss or ask for any help. I think the three most difficult words in Sameer's dictionary are 'I don't know'; 'I need help' comes a close second. One time, in the days before GPS, when we followed the Road Atlas, Sameer had gone off-map during one of our road trips in India. It was somewhere in the remote Northeast and after about thirty minutes we had realized that we were just going round in circles. There was a small beat-up tea stall and I wanted to go there to ask for directions. But

Sameer had said, 'No, we will figure this out, honey.' He couldn't and almost two more hours later I had walked up to the local tea shop and found out that the road mentioned in the map had closed a few months back and we were supposed to take a new one only a mile away. Something that could be solved in minutes took hours because he didn't want to ask for help.

I am worried that he is off-map this time too and expecting too much. Now that he is settling into unemployment, I am also worried about our expenses and have been making spreadsheets and recalculating our budget like a maniac. If I am not careful, the severance package will run out sooner than we want it to.

It amazes me, the exorbitant amount of money we have been wasting. One hundred twenty dollars every month for Piyu's fusion kathak and jazz dance classes? What was I even thinking? Who needs to learn kathak and jazz? How does that rate as a life skill? Does it get a college scholarship? And why does Riya need swimming lessons any more? She is twelve. I have been driving her to swimming classes since she was four, and she still needs classes?

I then check our monthly grocery bill, something I started keeping track of since last month, and am alarmed. I have spent five hundred dollars at the organic store Great Foods alone. I scan through it again to verify that there is no mistake. How come I never noticed it earlier? And I am sure all I bought was a bunch of Kale, two kiwis and maybe some artisan cheese. Maybe also that big bag of organic cookies languishing in the pantry which tastes like sawdust. I must stop going there. Maybe I will change my route to work so that I don't even see Great Foods and get attracted to it following Newton's law.

I slash off rows and highlight them in red on my spreadsheet. Red alert. But even with all the red alerts the numbers don't add up. There is a chasm between our monthly expense and the earning if Sameer's cheque stops coming in, which will happen in about six months.

My eyes are puffy and groggy from all the red flashes on the screen. I have been holed up with my laptop since morning. Calculating operational budget. Recalculating expenses. There seems to be no way to adjust the deficit. Sameer is in the kitchen. I can hear the sizzle and phissh ... of the pressure cooker. He is humming a 1970s' Hindi song to himself and cooking lunch. He seems to be happy as he grates pearls of garlic and ginger for the mutton curry oblivious of all the red alerts. In fact, I have not seen him this relaxed in months!

But I don't know how he can be so cool about it. Yesterday, I spent two hours scanning through the job search sites and bookmarking the positions I thought would suit him. I even asked him for his résumé so that I could start applying for him. I did all the grunt work that he would have to pay a personal assistant to do, and all he did was give me a look as if I was the crazy one in the family.

I should start looking for a job for myself too. A job with a fixed salary, more than what my current 20 per cent stake in Right-to-Write could ever bring in. Money that could at least pay the mortgage.

But jobs are not that easy to come by. I mean, I have been out of the corporate world for a while now. I have not even been to a single interview in the last fifteen years. I don't know what to do. And then I went and promised Kajol that I will write the book. Yes, that thing is full and final now. No more backtracking. Kajol even made me sign a contract of sorts. Arrgh! I have my fingers in too many pies and none of the pies seem remotely edible.

I haven't told Sameer about the letters from Panchanantala, Kolkata, yet. Or about my project. I kind of feel guilty with all these secrets but I am waiting for the right time, for something more concrete to take shape. But if I'm being honest, I am not feeling that bad about keeping my secret any more. I have a feeling Sameer has not been fully honest either. Secrets can ruin your marriage they say … but what the heck!

Anyway, I don't have time to dissect this further, there is too much on my plate, but first I must get ready for tonight. For my first cooking lesson at Jai's home. Kajol is coming along too. 'Careful, Shubha! Don't do anything that you will regret later,' she had told me when I had first confided in her about the cooking lesson.

'I will only be teaching him to make doi maach, not sleeping with him!' I don't know what she was thinking, but my heart was beating just that much faster. 'It will help me practise my skills for the book,' I had added.

Kajol had pondered for a minute and then said, 'I will come along too. The book is our project, no?' She has been mighty pleased since I have committed myself to the book. I think she is just happy that she is not the one writing it.

I had sent Jai a long list of things beforehand that he needs to procure for tonight's menu. I hope he has got them right. It is 6.30 in the evening and I have spent the last one hour getting ready. I am not comfortable cooking when people are watching me and am tense already. My only solace is that neither Jai nor Kajol will understand if things go wrong. At the most they might decide that the end result is not like their mother or grandmother's but then whose is? Now if I had someone like Sameer as a student, my inexpertise would have not gone unnoticed. He would have laughed if I jumped back every time I slid a fish to fry in the hot oil.

After changing four times, I have decided to wear a simple kurta with black leggings for tonight and my hair is held up with a big clamshell clasp. Dangling lapis lazuli held in tiny silver claps with tiny beads adorn my ears. When I look into the mirror and remember Jai's message on Facebook, the clasp is undone and I let down my purple and gold keratin hair. I have no idea why I am doing this. It's not that I am trying to flirt with Jai or anything.

When I come down all dressed up, Piyu, Riya and Sameer are all huddled up on the couch watching *Despicable Me*. There are tall glasses of hot chocolate and a big bowl of popcorn on the coffee table. They are all having a good time. None of them have seen my budget projections into the future. They have no idea that next year by this time we might be homeless. I try to calm myself down and practise doing pranayama standing up right there.

'Are you okay?' Piyu asks as she takes a long sip of her hot chocolate. 'Why are you breathing like that?'

'Nothing, it is something my yoga teacher taught me. Helps clear the brain,' I say, exhaling through one nostril.

Piyu rolls her eyes. 'Mom, you cannot do yoga at the drop of a hat just like that. Pranayama means expansion, "ama", of the life force, "prana". When done correctly you can reach a higher stage of spiritual development. What you are doing looks more like you have asthma!'

'Just because you are fifteen and can use Google, you've become a yoga expert?' I say crossly. 'Seriously, do you girls think

I am some stupid oaf who's just been introduced to modern civilization?'

'There is nothing modern about yoga except your yoga mats bought off Amazon,' Piyu comments.

'Where are you going, Mom?' Riya asks me. She has wedged herself into a comfortable position under Sameer's right armpit. Even at twelve, she is like a little girl with her dad, finding comfort in cuddles and hugs.

'I have to catch up with some friends. You guys have dinner, don't wait for me,' I say, feeling guilty about my secret.

'But, Shubha, I thought I will make your favourite aloo posto tonight. I even soaked the poppy seeds,' groans Sameer, a note of disappointment in his voice.

'Maybe for lunch tomorrow?' I suggest, suddenly wanting to plonk myself on the couch and cancel my own plans tonight. It feels very different to have Sameer back home in the evenings.

'Okay,' he says, and the next minute they are all engrossed in the movie.

I go to the kitchen, grab the chhalni, the big round spoon with small holes to fry fish, and head out into the evening.

Jai's neighbourhood is a thirty-minute drive from my home. It is much closer to downtown, where the tree-lined main street houses all the big stores and independent boutiques. I quite like his apartment block. Charming two-storey buildings in a red and white brick facade nestle among looming evergreen trees and well-tended flower bushes. It's mid-October and there is a chill in the evening air. I shudder as I step out from the warmth of my car. The apartment is on the second floor and one has to climb a set of polished wooden stairs to reach his private landing. I don't see Kajol's car in the parking lot and wonder whether I should wait for her, but then I decide to go ahead.

When I ring the bell Jai opens the door immediately and I can see he has really spent the day making sure everything looks good. There is the same minty fresh look about him and the house looks spotless. The living room has comfortable leather couches and the coffee table is all dusted and gleaming. The small knick-knacks on the console, from the Dokra Ganesha to a Swiss cowbell, are all set up very tastefully. Faint strains of sarod fill the air from his iPod dock.

He looks around sheepishly as I exclaim, 'Wow!' I really had expected a sloppy bachelor's den with piles of laundry, but this was way tidier than my own house.

'Do you want to go to the kitchen or wait for your friend?' he asks. Jai is in a polo-necked T-shirt and shorts, a plaid kitchen apron tied around his waist, very different from his standard attire of shirt and jeans.

'Umm ... kitchen,' I say, trying to sound confident. 'I just want to check that you have got all the things on the list.'

The kitchen is fabulous too with gleaming stainless steel appliances and black counters. I see that he has laid out all the ingredients neatly. The fish pieces have been defrosted and cleaned. The cardamom, cinnamon and bay leaves are sorted out in small stainless steel bowls. Mise en place.

'What is with you? You are giving me a complex.'

'I try. Do you like it?' he asks, and I sense a note of hope trembling on the edge of his words.

'This is fabulous. Really impressed.' I smile at him, shaking my head. Jai grins, his smile is so disarming, like he is genuinely pleased with the comment. I have this strong urge to pat him on the head. He is too nice.

Soon Kajol joins us, a bottle of red wine in hand. She is in a flowing black skirt and a kurti top in red and black thread work. Her hair is cropped short and miniature silver flutes hang from her ears. After the introductions are over, she settles herself in a bar stool in the kitchen and gets busy sipping her wine which Jai has poured out in tall crystal flutes.

I dust the fish pieces with turmeric powder and salt, and ask Jai to chop the onions. Kajol does not seem interested to partake in the cooking process and declares that she would rather learn from a distance. 'Like distance learning, you know,' she says, waving her hand and taking gulps of wine.

I show Jai how to slide the fish pieces gently in hot oil and fry them until golden brown. Surprisingly, I feel confident. I seem to know exactly how to maintain the right amount of heat and to make sure the fish doesn't splatter oil that much. Soon the kitchen is redolent with the rich smell of fried onion and ginger.

'Are the onions organic? Did you measure the circumference of the onion? The readers would benefit from all this information, you know,' says Kajol sipping her wine.

'Are you writing a book?' Jai enquires, his voice incredulous.

'Well, kind of…' I trail off, almost embarrassed at the thought.

Jai doesn't give up, he keeps pestering. Eventually, between Kajol and me we tell him about the letters, the crisis our tiny publishing company is facing and everything else. He looks quite impressed.

'You girls are amazing. Small business heroes.'

'It all sounds very idyllic, but is far from so in reality.' I sigh as I add the cloves, cinnamon and cardamom to the hot oil. 'The book might not really save our business. No one might even buy it. A book needs so much more these days than just being written. Who will do the PR, media and hoopla for us? It is not a *Fifty Shades of Grey* that people will queue up in bed to read it. What then?'

'Oh Shubha, I thought of something. I am going to send out the book synopsis to a couple of my friends who are literary agents. It would help if we could tie up with a bigger name to publish it. Co-publishing is the way to go for us. More publicity, bigger reach, etc., and maybe some money upfront too,' says Kajol wistfully. The cloves and cardamoms dance in the hot oil.

Kajol always has these big dreams and for my own sanity I try not to get dragged into them. Instead I concentrate on the fish curry and ask Jai to make a paste of yogurt and cashews. Then I ask him to mix half of the onion-ginger paste with the yogurt and beat it until it is smooth.

Just before adding yogurt into the hot pan I instruct him to take the pan off the heat and wait for a minute, to let the oil cool a bit. 'Now when you add the yogurt, it will not curdle. It is the high heat which makes it do that,' I say, surprised at my own voice. Do I sound like Sanjeev Kapoor? I mean, the female version of him? Where the heck did I get that confidence from?

While the doi maach simmers on low heat, I make dal. Actually, Jai makes the dal; he is pretty good at it and needs little help. The rice is already waiting in the rice cooker. We are done cooking an entire meal in an hour and a half which, frankly, is excellent timing.

I am hungry and cannot wait to dig into the rice and doi maach. It looks gorgeous. By the time we sit around the dining table, tasting the fruit of our labour, it is already ten.

'Men are such jerks!' Kajol declares out of the blue, and then while carefully deboning the fish, adds, 'This is fabulous, Shubha. Couple of more such practicing occasions and it should be ready for the book.'

I know Kajol well enough to understand that this is a cue for her rant. She has had too much wine and too many boyfriends to arrive at this decision at the end of the day. I am about to ask her to elaborate so that she can continue her rant when Jai says quietly, 'My wife thought I was one too. Maybe she still does.'

Okay, so he doesn't know about Kajol's cathartic process. I open my mouth and then clam it shut in fear that I would utter something wrong.

'I am sorry, I didn't mean all men.' Kajol is taken aback at this unnecessary obstruction to her own rant.

'No, it is okay. Everyone has their own reasons. I am sure my wife had too.' Jai's words are slow and measured.

And then he can't stop himself. He sniffs and sputters out his life story without a single pause, like a fire hydrant gushing water. 'She wanted a faster paced life, more power, more money and more parties. I was the opposite. I stuck to a job where I could leave by five every evening. I liked spending my evenings in our garden, planting flowers, removing weeds, and I hated cocktail parties. My wife thought I was lazy. She was doing very good as the marketing head in her company and would travel almost three days a week. On other days, she had parties to attend after work. She wanted me to go along but I absolutely hated those cocktail parties. We hardly saw each other. And then one evening, when I came home I saw her waiting for me. This was unusual and I was happy that we would have an evening to ourselves. That evening she told me she wanted a divorce. She had the papers ready. All I had to do was sign. When I asked her why she wanted one, all she said was "You are such a jerk."'

There is an awkward silence at the table. No one knows what to say. The evening has taken a totally new turn and all because of Kajol. Not that Kajol is showing any intention to admit that and make things better. Suddenly, I feel an urgency to go home, to be with my family – for better, for worse, in sickness and in health!

'But why did you sign the papers?' I break the silence, wishing the evening to wrap up faster.

Jai rubs his eyes with the tips of his long fingers. He looks deflated like a balloon hanging around long after the birthday party. 'I didn't at first. But in the end, I just wanted peace.'

I can hear the resignation in his voice and feel sorry for Jai and his little boy. I hope that Jai remembers the recipe of doi maach for the sake of Ananda.

Facebook

For better, for worse, for richer, for poorer, in sickness and in health, to love and to cherish. #quotablequotes #lifemantra

42 likes. 42 hearts.

Neela has commented 'Love you, both.'

Karthik
(October – November)

It is late in the evening and I am still in office. Claire and Samantha left an hour back. Kajol is switching off the lights, shutting down her computer and wrapping up. I don't budge and keep typing furiously on my computer.

'We won't have money to pay the electricity bill next month,' declares Kajol. This is her way of telling me that I am wasting company resources and should go home instead. She makes a lot of rattling noises and pulls out the printer plug, which if you ask me is totally unnecessary.

But I don't say anything. The thing is I can't go home. Not now. Evenings have become the most chaotic time at our home now that Sameer no longer has a job. Every evening, he either plans a movie night or a cook-a-thon with the girls, replete with popcorn and fresh ice cream shakes that he himself makes in the Vitamix. He seems to be hungrily making up for the time he lost with the girls.

Sometimes, even Piyu's friends drop in. Sameer feeds them fish koftas smeared with hummus. 'Never knew your dad is so cool,' they keep saying. On some evenings, he just welcomes random neighbours for a drink and mixes exotic cocktails like Negroni spiced with paanch phoron. The look on their faces afterwards is of pure torture and I feel sorry for them.

Pots of curry simmer merrily on the hob splattering yellow polka dots on the white and blue backsplash. Gossamer-thin garlic skins flutter around like butterflies in my terracotta tiled kitchen. By the end of the evening, the house looks like a frat house with popcorns wedged between sofa cushions and half-empty cocktail glasses on windowsills. I have extreme OCD about such things and it takes me hours to wipe down all the surfaces and make sure that there are no rings left on the coffee table.

Just as I think the last unwanted guest has left and try to vacuum out bits and pieces of samosa crumbs from my kilim rug, Sameer hollers above the din of the vacuum, 'Shubha, don't bother with the vacuum, I just invited Mr Bhosle for Bijoya dinner. I am making a Maharashtrian fish curry. He said he will be thrilled to join with his nephews.'

There is a constant buzz of shuffling feet and high-pitched laughter as boys and girls, men and women stream in and out throughout the evening. It gives me a headache. Both the constant chaos and the mess. Oh, and the expenses of it all! Just when money is tight Sameer decides to feed hormonal teenagers keema shingara, stuffed with spicy chicken mince. Does he have any idea how many each of them can devour? But Sameer is so oblivious to everything that I cannot even explain it to him. He has been behaving like an attention-grabbing puppy, happy to please these people who drop in. I understand that he misses his hectic work days, easy camaraderie over client dinners and the rush of breakfast meetings. My hunch is that to compensate for all that he simulates this environment at home.

Due to all that din, I was not able to write a single page all of last week, and I know I am seriously behind on the draft. Without a draft we cannot pitch it to the big publishers we are targeting next month. Since the company is currently running on a shoestring budget, Kajol has decided to go for a co-publishing agreement. We will pitch the book to a bigger publication house, Right-to-Write will share publication costs, but in return we will get the advantage of their expertise, a bigger platform and more profit. So now I have decided to stay back at work until the hullabaloo at home subsides. That way I can at least get ahead with my draft and Sameer can party his heart out.

Kajol finally leaves after exasperated sighing to show her displeasure. With the click of the door closing behind her, a delicious silence descends around me. It is precious. I stretch my limbs, stand up and try to touch my toes to shake off the lethargy and get to work. Of course, I can't touch my toes but if I try hard enough, the tip of my fingers kind of brushes my ankle. That is good enough, right? I make myself a cup of tea and get the pack of Parle-G out from the drawer. I am surprised that I am enjoying the silence so much! Wasn't it just last month that I was complaining about Sameer being away and pining for a full house? The human nature is strange indeed. Now that I know Sameer doesn't want a break from our marriage, I am all for me-time and solitude.

Kajol switched off all the main lights when she left and so I have to work by the light of the table lamp on my desk. The letters over the last seven months are neatly piled on one side of my desk. On the other side, I have a tottering pile of books I borrowed from the library. They are all cookbooks with history of Indian food. I need them for my research to cross-check the ingredients and recipes mentioned in the letter.

For instance, I learned yesterday how the Portuguese brought cheese to Bengal when they settled in a colony in Bandel, along the banks of River Hooghly, almost 50km north of Kolkata. Bandel Cheese, made from chhena and well salted, sounds a lot like ricotta. In fact it was the Portuguese who introduced chhena to Bengal by that whole process of splitting milk with lime juice.

And then today, I read about Goalondo steamer curry, the reddish-coloured spicy chicken curry that was cooked by the boatmen on the steamers plying the mighty River Padma from Goalondo ghat to Narayanganj. Sitting many miles away, I can imagine the deckhands (also known as Khalasis) preparing their midday meal while singing bhatiyali songs as the steamer ploughed down the river.

I can't believe how much I am enjoying myself with this project. It was all about 'No, I cannot do it, I don't write', at the beginning. And now I cannot wait for the evenings when I fire up my computer and start typing. I read and reread the chapters I have written and at times marvel at how the story is unfolding. On other days, I am highly critical and cringe at the words on the screen. 'Tch, tch, such cliché,' I tell myself and mercilessly delete paragraphs, editing away sentences.

The strange thing is though I am writing this book, I have no control over it. I am not the author who with the stroke of her pen can create heroes and villains. I am bound by the letters and the fate of the story does not lie in my hands. I am as much in the dark as anyone else as to what decision the old lady will take next.

I have accepted the arrival of the letters every month but I am curious as to how this will end. Will I ever know who the real 'Didan' is? With the deadline looming, I have so little time in my hands that I cannot afford to play detective right now. Instead I focus on the present.

As I open this month's letter, I can't wait to see if she agreed to the registry marriage. Or did she elope with Dadu? I definitely prefer the elopement but that was a different time and maybe she was tied by the norms of society.

Dear Moni,

How are you? When will you come to India? Next time come in the month of Karthik, I think the weather will be nice and cool for you then. Karthik is the first month of the season hemanta. Those days we had six distinct seasons. Sheet (winter), bosonto (spring), grishmo (summer), borsha (monsoon), early autumn sharat and late autumn hemanta — such lyrical names. Now all year it is either summer or rain.

Both the months of Ashwin and Karthik were of great joy to us as they were packed with back-to-back festivals and long holidays. Lokkhi Pujo would roll in right after Durga Pujo. Then came Kali Pujo and Diwali, the festival of lights. Soon after there was Bhai Phota, for the brothers.

The weather would cool down and there would be a distinct chill in the air. Early in the morning you could see glittery dewdrops gathered on the leaves and hanging on the edges of green blades of grass. At night, you needed something warm and we always had the softest silk quilts from Rajasthan, faintly smelling of naphthalene, to cover ourselves with.

That year the season was perfect but my life was tumultuous. The chill in the air was also enveloping my heart. My marriage with Rajat was registered before he left for London. Actually, we were at the registrar's office on the evening of Dashami and his flight left the very next morning. I tried to tell my mother that I did not want this marriage and that Rajat was in fact a cruel snob, but she was too caught up in the glamour and name of Rajat's family to listen to me. 'Pore shunbo,' my mother had said, egging me to wear the kanjivaram she had bought as part of my trousseau.

Since the registry marriage was a quiet affair with only the parents as witness, my in-laws did not force me to stay with them or wear many signs of a newly-wed. Neither was my marriage consummated in all that rush. This was my only relief as I continued my life as before, going to college and continuing my studies. I did not try getting in touch with your Dadu either though I often thought of him. It was too late ... what was the use, I would tell myself.

And then something that I would have never imagined happened. A couple of days after Diwali, I was in the kitchen helping my mother as she made sweets and savouries for Bhai Phota. Every year, my mother made all that was best in her culinary repertoire for her two brothers on that special day. The softest roshogollas from home-made chhana, triangular nimkis flecked with tiny black kalo jeera, dim'r devil where egg halves were cocooned in keema was followed by a lunch of fried rice, doi maach, chingri bhaape and chicken chaap.

We were making the nimkis that day. Rolling out the dough in layered triangles so that when fried they would puff up and you could see the layers. They were delicate beings, flaky and brittle.

It was one of those quiet afternoons when the sun would be directly above our lane casting short, stout shadows of the houses. The birds would have taken refuge in the cool shade of the huge banyan. There was a lazy silence only broken by raspy calls of 'Basanwala' or 'Chhuri-Kaanchiwala', the bangle and utensil sellers, as they walked the lanes and golis of Kolkata. I was busy following Ma's instruction of adding just enough ghee to the flour to make nimkis that would be crispy 'mooch mooche'.

There was a knock at the door. When I opened it, I was so surprised that I am sure I must have looked like an idiot. I can still recall your Dadu standing there, beads of sweat rolling down his forehead, his shirt sleeves rolled up to bare his strong forearms. My heart twisted in pain on seeing him and my voice choked with tears.

'Baba is in office,' I whispered, bravely blinking away the tears which were ready to roll down any minute.

'I heard what happened and I am ready to wait,' he said.

'For what?'

'I don't know. Maybe for you.'

I wasn't sure what he meant but it gave me hope and I was trying to say something more meaningful, when my mother walked in with a plate of nimki and roshogolla and started chatting with him. She kept looking at him and then me, but didn't say anything. Just as he was leaving, my mother called after him. 'Baba, don't come here again. She is married now and people might talk,' she had hesitantly added.

I cried so much after it that none of the nimkis turned out puffed and crisp. But don't worry, the recipe I will give you has the exact measures; yours will turn out perfect. Make the dim'r devil too, it's the Indian version of Scotch eggs and I am sure your kids will like them.

Bhalo theko,
Didan

Dim'r Devil

Devilled Eggs the Bengali way

Dim'r devil is not devilled eggs, though it owes its name to a similar root. They are more like the British Scotch eggs and the Mughlai nargisi kofta. It is a very popular snack for most Bengalis, where egg halves are covered in a cocoon of ground chicken, breaded and then fried.

Ingredients

Eggs – 2
Chicken keema – 2 cups
Potatoes – 2 medium-sized
Garlic – 6 cloves
Ginger – 2' knob

Spices/Seasoning to add to the keema:

Cumin powder – ½ tsp
Coriander powder – ½ tsp
Red chilli powder – ½ tsp
Garam masala – ½ tsp
Chat masala – a pinch
Salt to taste
Coriander leaves – 2 tbsp, chopped
Green chilli – 2 finely chopped

For breading:

All-purpose flour – ½ cup
Egg wash – made by beating 1 egg + 1 tbsp water
Breadcrumbs – ½ cup

Vegetable oil – for deep frying

Boiling the eggs

Put two eggs to boil in a saucepan. Once the eggs are boiled and cooled, peel them. Then cut them in half. So, now we have four egg halves. Sprinkle on the eggs some ground pepper.

Making the keema + potato for the coverage

Boil potatoes.
Make a paste of garlic and ginger.
Put the chicken keema/ground chicken in a bowl.
Add the following seasoning:
- Ginger-garlic paste prepared earlier
- Everything listed under spices/seasoning

Mix well and keep aside for half an hour.

When the potatoes are done, let it cool. Then peel and mash them smooth.

Heat oil in a frying pan and add the spiced ground chicken to it.

Stir it for a few minutes. When it starts to lose its raw pink colouring, add the mashed potatoes.

Stir and pat and mix again, letting the ground meat cook fully. The keema and potato mixture will take on a brownish tinge eventually.

At this point, taste and adjust for any seasoning.

Once it has cooled, mix the ground meat and potatoes once more with your fingers. The mix should be on the drier side and not too soft to hold shape. If you think it is too soft to mould, you can add some cornstarch.

Breading and frying

Set up a breading station with a plate of all-purpose flour, egg wash and a plate of seasoned breadcrumbs.

Take a ball of the keema and potato mixture on your palm and then flatten it out. The surface should be big enough to hold the egg half. Put the egg half in the centre of this. Now, mould the keema mixture so that it covers the side of the egg. Take some more keema mix and cove the top surface. Working with your palm, make sure that the entire egg half is cocooned by the ground meat mix and now looks like a covered egg.

Roll the chop/croquette in flour, dip in egg wash, roll in breadcrumbs.

Let it rest in the refrigerator for half an hour.

Now heat enough oil for deep frying. To see if the oil is ready drop a small speck of the keema dough in the oil. If it bubbles and rises, the oil is ready.

Gently suspend the croquettes in the hot oil and fry until both sides are golden brown.

Sprinkle the croquettes/chop with some chat masala or pink salt and serve with chopped onion, kashundi and ketchup.

Bite in and enjoy the magic of two cuisines meeting.

8

We have a meeting with Big Whales today. They're a big publishing company. Well, a medium one, but way, way bigger than ours. So, from where we are with Right-to-Write, which is way down in the totem pole, it seems huge.

I am so tense about this meeting that I wasn't even able to sleep well last night and have been up since five in the morning. It is usually Kajol who handles all our clients while I take care of the design and technical aspects of our business, so dressing up and mouthing niceties eludes me. This meeting is giving me the jitters. I didn't even want to go, but Kajol says they had specifically mentioned in the email that my presence is necessary.

A couple of weeks back, one of Kajol's many friends had pulled some strings and got an editor at Big Whales to read the synopsis and the sample chapters of the book that we had sent. They had liked it enough to want to discuss further with its author.

I am trying not to panic. There is nothing to panic about. 'Everything will be fine' – I am trying to chant this mantra over and over. Not that it is convincing me but chants have a quality in themselves. It is not what you say or mean but the continuous, monotonic, uttering hypnotizes you to believe in the impossible.

The days have turned colder and shorter. It is 5.30 in the morning and still dark outside. Sameer seems to be up ahead of me. I take a quick shower and try my best to tame my hair. Clearly all that keratin treatment had no long-term effect on my obstinate mane. After one whole week of fretting about what to wear, I have picked up a navy blue pant suit for today's meeting. It's been years since I wore one and I like the power the blazer gives me when I slide in my arms through its sleeves. I pull myself up in front of the full-length mirror hanging on my closet door and am hoping to preen at what I see.

I imagine a power lady, hair in place, determination on face.

A successful entrepreneur.

A bestselling author.

But nope, my mirror image has hair which has gone back to being frizzy and it is standing out with all the static in the air. My skin feels dry and flaky. The look on my face screams nothing but – nervous! I feel a bit deflated and my shoulders slump a little. On other days, I wouldn't bother with these details but when you are wearing a navy blue suit, everything else has to chime in. But nothing seems to be chiming in.

The one reason I got ready so early was that I wanted to creep out of the house before the girls were up and bombarding me with questions and criticizing my suit. I didn't want any teen style reviews. The day was just dawning when I silently came down the stairs hoping to wiggle out unnoticed, but there was Sameer in the kitchen. I wasn't expecting to see him first thing in the morning. Not after last night's argument.

I have been increasingly worried about his unemployment and last night I had said something to the effect that he is not trying enough to go out and get a job. I wasn't totally wrong as Sameer seems to be too comfortable pottering around the house in his pyjamas. He doesn't even shave regularly any more, which is the complete opposite of the clean-shaven, sharply dressed, nose-buried-in-his-laptop Sameer I have known for the last seventeen years. Surprisingly, he seems very happy in this new avatar and it bothers me. Okay, not because he is happy, but the fact that he is becoming too complacent. I think that is what triggered me to make that scathing remark.

He had looked at me angrily, wielding the silver-bladed Henkel knife which he was using to julienne or dice or do something to the potatoes, and had said, 'So, you think I am not trying enough? Do you know to how many companies I have sent off my résumé? Do you understand that each of them came back with a polite reply of how impressed they were but apologizing because I was not the right fit?'

I don't understand this about Sameer. He is so confident that he thinks confiding in even your own wife is a problem. Why was it that he had to bottle up everything? Why couldn't he have told me earlier the frustration he was coping with?

'I could have helped,' I told him, hurt and embarrassed at the same time.

'And what would you have done? I don't want anyone's help. I will figure this out,' he had said arrogantly. Sometimes Sameer can be so pig-headed that I really want to thwack him on the head with the back of a frying pan.

Now, with the first rays of the sun just behind him, he looks at me, his eyebrows arched, and says, 'This early?'

I fumble and wave my hands trying to say something vague about a client who wanted to meet us early at dawn. Best ideas come with the rising sun, after all. It sounds absolutely ridiculous, but Sameer doesn't question me.

'Have some tea and a toast, don't leave on an empty stomach.' He gets busy taking out the bread and putting the kettle to boil.

I want him to be more inquisitive, to ask more questions. That will give me the perfect chance to spill the whole story, so I say with an air of importance, 'Well, I am actually in a rush. This is a big client.' Sameer only nods his head, checks on the toast but doesn't ask anything.

I continue to persist, 'We are discussing a huge project and if we get the contract then…' I pause dramatically.

He narrows his eyes, pours out tea in my mug and briskly asks, 'Then? Do you want butter or cream cheese on your toast?'

'Cream cheese,' I mumble, feeling kind of deflated. I don't understand Sameer. Unlike me, he is just not curious. I grab the toast, pick up my car keys from the foyer table and click open the garage door.

———

Big Whales' office is in the DC metro area, so I am taking the train. It has been ages since I have worn a suit and taken a train this early in the morning. Despite all my nervousness, it feels very intoxicating.

The office is in an impressive Victorian building. The latent architect in me is mesmerized by the beautiful building and its intricate details. If I remember correctly this building is an example of the neoclassicism form of Victorian architecture.

While I am standing there, looking up and admiring the carved balustrades and parapets, Kajol arrives in her trademark leggings and kurti. She looks very cool and completely in charge.

I love this thing about Kajol. Her confidence. Her blatant disregard for conformation to Western society or for that matter any society. She can just be herself in any setting and still look cool. I wish I knew where she gets it from.

'Hi Shubha,' chirps Kajol and then lowers her voice to a whisper and says, 'I have gained some weight and none of my suits were fitting me, so I had to wear this.' With that she fishes out a tie-dye scarf and wraps it around her neck. 'Does this look better?' She frowns peering at her reflection in the glass door.

Big Whales is etched in raised letters on the frosted glass door with the sketch of a whale splashing in water. Looks more like a dolphin to me but must be a whale. We push open those heavy doors and the security directs us to a lounge where we must wait until someone comes to take us upstairs.

After we have waited for almost twenty-five minutes, and glanced through all kinds of magazines I would never buy, a young girl in pointed stilettos comes around looking for us. She looks as if she has just walked off a ramp and arrived straight into the office. Her stunning blonde hair falls down her back in a perfect cascade. As she walks up to us, placing one long toned leg in front of the other in perfect precision, I panic.

I curse myself for cancelling my salon appointment. I should have got my hair straightened as Neela had suggested, and lost some weight too. At least five pounds of it.

Miss Perfect Legs shows us into a room which looks kind of like a library with its walls lined with mahogany and glass bookshelves all around. They are crammed with books from Neruda and Márquez to Sophie Kinsella. There is a distressed oak coffee table at the centre and comfortable leather sofas with bright-coloured cushions around it. The setting is very informal and immediately I feel much more at ease. I can handle this. This is just a posher version of my family room.

A minute later, a tanned gentleman in his fifties walks in. 'Luke Murphy,' he introduces himself with a smile that reaches his eyes. Luke has close-cropped salt-and-pepper hair and he is wearing jeans and a pinstripe lavender shirt. He seems warm and friendly. Soon he is joined by a lady in her early sixties who looks very much regal, almost like Maharani Gayatri Devi, except this lady has auburn hair which she has tied up in a knot with a pencil.

'We loved your proposal, Ms Sen-Gupta.' Luke smiles at me. 'We are trying to diversify our work and plan to include more interracial fiction. You know fiction that will be our window to another culture. With the world being a global platform that is what we need. We loved the letters from the old lady, the grandmother, in your book. Very charming.'

'And we would like to offer you a contract. An advance of one hundred and fifty-five thousand dollars, half of which we will give you right now and the other half when you deliver the full manuscript,' says the lady – her name is Vera. 'Plus, you will get your royalty, of course' she adds hastily.

I am stunned. They liked the proposal! Big Whales is offering me a contract! To me, Shubhalaxmi Sen-Gupta who is a first-time author. This could be epic. I could be famous! I could use that money to pay mortgage. I am beaming but Kajol is looking at Vera with her eyes narrowed. She is smiling too but her smile is plastic, like something pasted on a toothpaste model. I don't understand why. She is the one who had pushed me into writing this book, the one who had pitched it and got this interview, so why doesn't she look happy?

'About the rights,' Kajol interrupts.

Luke and Vera exchange a quick glance and then Vera shifts her legs and says, 'Well, the rights will be solely ours, of course. The contract will be between us and Ms Sen-Gupta alone. I know you wanted joint publication but I am afraid we cannot agree to that at this point. The senior management does not think it is a good idea.'

Kajol looks stunned. Her face is as ash as a brown person can get. It is now a burnt sienna. She puts on a brave smile and says, 'In that case, I am very happy for Shubha.' And then she turns to me and says, 'Congratulations!'

I can feel what she is feeling. Towering over the joy I felt a minute ago, I feel her sadness; our sadness. This is her project as much as it is mine. This project was supposed to catapult our company to fame, okay, rather help it stay afloat. I don't know what to say. The advance amount is generous and in my current situation it would be of immense help but it feels wrong to go ahead with the project in this manner.

I bite my lip, unable to think clearly, and then look straight into Luke's eyes.

'Ahem ... this is all going too fast. Thanks for your very generous offer but I would need some time to think about it.'

Kajol shoots me a surprised look. I see Luke and Vera are a bit taken aback too but they quickly compose their looks to calm and smiling, and politely say, 'No problem, Ms Sen-Gupta, why don't you sleep over this and we talk in a week's time?'

When we are out in the sunshine, we don't talk. We were supposed to go for lunch after the meeting to celebrate but I don't know if it is still on. Kajol is a very independent spirit and I know this is hard for her.

'You don't have to do this, Shubha. We will manage something. Go, just sign the contract. I am really happy for you,' she blurts out.

'I am not getting the right vibes. I honestly need to think this through, Kajol. The money would be good, yes, but I want it for Right-to-Write, for all of us and not for me alone.' I squeeze Kajol's hand, and then add, 'Plus, according to my spreadsheet our family budget is good for the next four months. We should figure out something by then.'

Facebook

I upload a photo of a cute kitty playing with a ball of yarn. It paws off the ball every time it is thrown in its direction.

Missed opportunities. But there will be more. #ihavegotfaith

2 likes. 3 sad faces. 5 direct messages asking if everything is okay. Jai is one of them.

Agrahayan
(November – December)

Dear Moni,

I cannot believe it is almost Agrahayn, the seventh month of the Bengali calendar. You know, this is the harvest month in rural Bengal when farmers reap the first crop of rice. The first harvest is offered to Goddess Lakshmi along with milk, gur (jaggery), pieces of sugarcane and is called Nabanna – Notun anna – new harvest. It is a harvest festival celebrating rice, the main crop in the plains of Bengal.

Nowadays, in cities you don't even realize these things. Even Promila, my house help did not know anything about Nabanna. I asked her yesterday to make paayesh with the new rice and she told me not to get greedy. Do you see how impudent she has become? But Kolkata was not always like this. When I was young, most of the families had a close connection to the villages and so the festivals of the farmers of rural Bengal were also celebrated at our home. The first harvest of golden paddy with beautiful names like madhushala, sitashaal, gobindobhog would arrive at our home from our desher bari. What beautiful fragrance they had! I can still breathe in the fragrance of the first paayesh of the season, made with the new rice to offer to the gods.

That Agrahayan it had been two months since Rajat had left. In those two months, he had sent only one telegram, that too immediately after reaching London. After that neither any letter nor any trunk calls came from him. There was a change in his parent's demeanour too and my father was getting a bit antsy with their cold attitude. I was busy with my final exams and glad that I did not have to go to their house or talk to them.

Meanwhile, your Dadu stopped coming to the telebhaja shop near our house. Instead he got bolder and often stood outside the second-hand bookshops opposite my college. We walked together to the tram depot where I took the tram to Shyambazar and he went to Sealdah station from where he took the local train to Howrah. We talked about different things but he never brought up Rajat's name in the conversation and I didn't say anything either. One day there was some strike and so our classes had been cancelled. It was a beautiful day, with the first flush of winter making the city more vibrant in bright-coloured sweaters and scarves. He was going to meet his mother who lived in their ancestral home and asked if I wanted to accompany him.

I readily agreed and we took the local train to his home about two hours from Kolkata. As the train picked up speed, the city started peeling apart and ripe golden paddy fields lined with narrow rivulets of water dotted the scene. Moss green ponds with their surface covered in hyacinth leaves flashed by. I was excited and at the same time nervous about meeting his mother. Did she know that I was a legally married woman? What if she instructed her son to not see me any more?

I don't know what his mother thought of me that day but I was smitten by her earthy, gentle nature. She had prepared a very simple and rustic meal for us which she served in raised bell metal plates that shone like dull gold. We sat on the kitchen floor, our legs criss-crossed on mats which she herself had embroidered. Her kitchen was cosy, the dying embers in the coal stove radiating a soft warm glow. Outside, the slender leaves of bamboo trees trembled in the late autumn breeze and a lone ghughoo plaintively called upon her mates.

First, she served us rice from their own field. A reddish variety of aman rice named balam – harvested in the month of November. A small bowl of golden fragrant ghee was poured on the rice followed by a thick yellow moong dal and crispy fried bori, which she had made at home.

The ritual of preparing bori called 'bori deoa' is an age-old custom among Bengali women during the autumn and winter months when the sun is warm and strong but not scorching. Women of the household would bathe at dawn and then immerse themselves in the task of bori-making. It was a ritual made almost sacred with its demands on sanctity.

Large quantities of lentils were ground on the sil nora, then seasoned and whipped early in the morning. A large expanse of a washed and dried cloth, usually a sari, would be set out on the terrace, its edges secured by bricks. On this cloth, the women would put scoops of the lentil paste, ensuring a peak at the centre of the dumpling. My mother would always tell us to make boris with sharper centre peaks, the incentive being that the one whose bori had the sharpest peak would have a sharp-nosed husband. The little lentil dumplings were dried crisp in the sun and were stored away for later use.

That day I clearly remember a very unique dish that followed the dal. His mother had made kochupata chingri bhapa – made with the young green leaves of taro and tiny shrimps that burst into multiple flavours of mustard and coconut in my mouth. I learned the recipe from her later and you always loved to eat it. I think she also made some fish curry. Maybe it was an aloo-phulkopi diye koi – koi fish cooked with potatoes and cauliflower – but I am not sure. If I can remember I will give you that recipe too.

Everything was so simple and peaceful there that I didn't want to go back to the city. I wanted to start a new life right there in that village with your Dadu. But I did not have the courage to say that, Moni. And so, I took the evening train and came back home where an uncertain future awaited me.

Bhalo theko,
Didan

I fold this month's letter and add it to the growing pile of all the previous ones. My future is uncertain like Didan's too. I did reject Big Whales' offer last week, but now how would we find the money to get the book out there? We have pored over the math in the last five days and the future looks bleak! Even if we manage to print a few copies solo, we don't have the budget for advertising or marketing for that matter! Who would even buy the book?

I feel restless and want to run away to the idyllic village described in the letter. I try to envisage the lady's life in those times, the tumult she must have been going through, torn between a marriage she clearly abhorred and a man whom she trusted and loved. Definitely, her problems were far worse than mine!

As much as her strong character inspires me, I am not sure whether I should get the taro leaves and try out the kochupata chingri. All that effort somehow seems meaningless. I need to lose the pounds I have put on with all this cooking and tasting, and if the book is not happening then a detox juice diet seems more appropriate.

But before that I need a drink and someone to listen to my sob story. I decide to call up Neela and ask her whether she is free in the evening. After a stiff martini, I will tell her about the letters. Neela's eyes will grow wide like saucers and she will be itching for the moment to spill my secret to someone, but I know she will also have the right words of sympathy.

'Shubha, don't worry, we will figure something out.' I hadn't noticed when Kajol had come in and stood behind me. Since the meeting at Big Whales, Kajol has mellowed down a bit. She even offered to make me a 50 per cent partner.

'Yes, Shubha, we will all help. I will get the word out to all my family and friends, and believe me they make up at least 20 per cent of the US population,' chimes in Claire and walks up to my desk. 'I will make every member of my freaking Italian family buy that book.'

Sam squeezes my hands and rubs my back. 'Thank you, Shubha, for saving my job, we will fight this together.'

The whole scene is so freaking emotional that I start crying. Yes, it is also my PMS time. But I never ever cry in public. That is just not my thing. But today, fat tears roll down my cheeks. I am in such a mess that I have to wipe my nose on Sam's scarf but she doesn't mind. Or at least doesn't complain. Soon all four of us huddle together and sob. I don't know what we are crying for and how crying will solve our problems, but it does feel good.

I think everyone should try this crying therapy. I don't understand what people, men in particular, have against it; I mean against crying. Honestly, they should try it more often and companies should make 'volunteer crying' part of their team-building activities. Lacrimal glands hold a lot of healing power.

Facebook

I join three groups on Facebook – Detox and Lose Weight, Forgotten Food from Bengal, Self-Publishing Group.

Kochupata Chingri

Shrimp cooked with tender kochupata aka taro leaves in a sharp mustard and coconut paste is a dish from 'opar bangla' or what was once East Bengal. The sharp mustard oil, the even more pungent mustard paste and then the colocassia leaves which gives some an itchy throat — clearly indicate that this is not a dish for the faint-hearted. This recipe serves six.

Ingredients

Kochupata/taro leaves/colocassia leaves — 6-7 medium-sized
Shrimp — 15-20
Mustard seeds — 3 tbsp
Poppy seeds — 1 tsp
Green chillies — 8
Grated coconut — ¾ cup or more
Lime juice — 2 tbsp
Mustard oil — ¼cup
Salt to taste
Turmeric powder — ½ tsp

Procure tender taro leaves or kochupata. In the US, you can look for paatra leaves in Indian grocery stores.

Peel and clean shrimps. Dust with salt and turmeric powder.

Making the Shorshe-Narkol Baata (Mustard-Coconut Paste)

Soak mustard and poppy seeds in water for 30 minutes.

In a mixer jar add:

- Drained mustard and poppy seeds

- 4 chopped green chillies
- ¼th cup of grated coconut
- 2 tbsps of lime juice (or white vinegar)

With a splash of water, make a smooth paste. This is shorshe-narkol baata.

Making the Narkol Baata (Coconut Paste)

In the same mixer jar, add half cup of grated coconut.

With a splash of water, make a thick paste of coconut – narkol baata.

Chopping and Boiling Kochupata

To chop it, first remove the thick vein that runs through the centre. If you find any more thick veins, remove them too! Next, roll the leaves and chop them in chiffonade.

Now, with kochupata there is always a lurking fear that it might cause your throat to itch. So, as a precautionary measure we will do the next step. Put a big pot of water to boil. Once the water has come to a rolling boil, add the chopped leaves. Boil the leaves for 6 to 7 minutes. Drain the water and keep the boiled leaves aside.

Cooking Kochupata Chingri

Heat mustard oil in a kadhai or frying pan.

Lightly fry the shrimp until they lose their raw colouring. Remove and keep aside.

Sauté the boiled leaves in the same oil, until they have softened.

Make a coarse paste of half of these sautéed leaves. Keep the other half aside.

In the same frying pan, add some more mustard oil.

Once the oil is hot, add slit green chillies and the shorshe-narkol baata (mustard+coconut paste). Sprinkle turmeric powder. Sauté for 2 minutes.

Add the narkol baata (coconut paste) and sauté for 2 more minutes.

Now add the coarsely ground kochupata as well as the rest of the sautéed kochupata. Sauté for 8-10 minutes with splashes of water as needed.

Add salt to taste. Now add the shrimp and mix well. Add some more grated coconut.

At this point drizzle a little mustard oil, add some slit green chillies, cover the pan with a tight lid and keep cooking at medium heat for 30–40 minutes.

Serve with steamed white rice.

9

I love December. The joy in the air gets into my bones and makes me all pink and fluffy. That there is a white-bearded guy who is responsible for bringing happiness to all takes a lot of responsibility off my shoulders. I feel pure nirvana at the thought that I am nothing but a minor data point in this vast universe. My purpose is not to make anyone happy or sad. If you are disappointed that is because you have been naughty and so Santa didn't get you anything. If you are happy that is because of your good karma and Santa, of course. Simple!

I feel light-headed with the load lifted off my shoulders. I don't worry too much about Sameer's joblessness either. I mean he doesn't himself, so why should I? I don't even stress about the book. Or the dangerously sliding house budget. Or that scrap of paper signed 'Love, F'.

I am becoming this whole new person and the first step towards that is to learning to let go. It is all in the Gita anyway, no wonder our forefathers had such wisdom. I mean I haven't exactly read the entire Gita but I have checked out SparkNotes and the main idea is about 'letting go'. That will do for now.

But what if Sameer is worried 'within', you know like on the inside, and only doesn't show it. Instead of worrying about getting a job, he whistles and chops mutton liver to cook a spicy mete chorchori. But do we know what exactly lies beneath that veneer of happy tunes? That there isn't a black hole of worry gnawing at his heart? What if he is on Ambien and is hiding that from me?

Okay, wait, now I am worrying about his worry. This doesn't even make sense. I have to let go, I remind myself. Then I smile, which could be termed beatific, and try to conjure an image of Baba Ramdev doing pranayama. I draw in a huge puff of air. It smells garlicky. What does Baba Ramdev's air smell of? Definitely, no garlic there. Maybe hing – asafoetida – I think. And then I blow the air out of my nostrils in a big whoosh. In and out. In and out.

'Shubha, do you remember when you were pregnant with Piyu and became anaemic, the doctor suggested that you eat iron-rich foods like beets, spinach and mutton liver? You completely ignored the beet and spinach and focused only on the "mete". I had to cook a mete chorchori for you every week and that too a spicy one,' Sameer looks up from the chopping board, his voice rising over the roar of the chimney fan.

I am practically raising a tsunami sitting at the breakfast table, doing the whole in-and-out breathing but Sameer doesn't seem to notice my pranayama. All he can think of is mete chorchori.

He seems very happy though, with a kitchen towel thrown across his shoulders and serious concentration on his face as he slices the purple onion in perfect half-moon slices, each slice of the same thickness. I have to admit that this layoff has not been all bad. There is one good thing that has come from it. It has changed Sameer. As in, changed him back to the old-seventeen-years-rewind-Sameer. He looks more relaxed these days and has developed this habit of fishing out anecdotes from the past, nuggets from our years together, like this whole 'mete' thing, and keeps saying 'Shubha, remember this ... remember that'. It almost seems like he is sorting through his album of memories, pulling out the old ones from the bottom of the pile, dusting them and putting them on the top – like a memory curator.

Most importantly, Sameer is laughing again now. Laughing with his head thrown back, eyes crinkled – his heart in that laughter. The lines around his mouth deepen with his laughter and the ones on his forehead disappear. His face looks softer when he does that and boyish, even with that salt-and-pepper hair. I can clearly see streaks of the old Sameer then, the one that I loved with all my heart even on days when he was not perfect.

'Yes, and then I became so constipated eating only mutton liver that the doctor banned it from my diet and put me back on five servings of spinach and beet instead. The things I had to go through while pregnant with Piyu,' I sigh, breathing out on cue.

'All for good. All for good. That colicky baby is now turning a beautiful sixteen. Can you believe it?' he says wistfully. 'I had thought I had lost her when Piyu was saddled with her angsty teen attitude, and then did you see how magically it all mellowed down in the last few months. It was just as if a cocoon morphed into a pretty butterfly. She even hugged me yesterday and said, "Baba, don't worry things will sort themselves out."' Sameer was now tipping the onions into hot mustard oil.

The sharp aroma stung my eyes and I blinked away the tears. Piyu is turning sixteen in a week. Sameer is right, she has really matured into a lovely person over the past year. Not that I thought Sameer had the time to notice any of the morphing in between his late nights and travels, but looks like he did.

Piyu is the easier one of my two girls. Even her roll-your-eyes teenage syndrome wasn't too bad to begin with. Yes, we did have our fair share of yelling and shouting and she complaining about what a nag I am, but she never did put on Goth make-up or smoke marijuana in the bathroom. She followed the rules and rarely did anything to raise my hackles. But lately, she has become more like an amiable, nice and positive person. The kind you would want to hang out with when you are feeling low. She hasn't even asked for a sweet sixteen party like her friends. Money is tight right now and she understands.

But we have decided to throw her a surprise party anyway. Nothing fancy, just us, a few of her friends and Neela. Piyu loves Neela aunty and her cool fashion sense. I have also invited Jai and Kajol. We will have the party at home and Sameer wants to cook. He has been watching cookery shows and reading up blogs, searching for the perfect dishes for a sixteen-year-old. Sometimes I think he just overdoes it. I have already told him I will make khejur gur'r paayesh. The Bangladeshi fish store has got fresh stock of khejur gur, date palm jaggery, and Jai got me some. Now I only hope that this month's letter has the perfect recipe for paayesh.

The first snow of the season falls softly on the morning of Piyu's birthday. Just like the day she was born, sixteen years ago. A pristine white blanket lay over the ground and rested on the bare branches of the tree, making the world look that much more magical. Only a few moments to savour the magic before life tramples in and turns it into a murky slush that needs to be shovelled.

I can hear Sameer in the kitchen already. The soft bang of pots and refrigerator doors as he goes about getting his ingredients ready. The girls are still sleeping. I go down the stairs softly, still in my nightdress. The kitchen looks like a place of worship – scrubbed, cleaned, bathed in a soft ethereal light that only comes with the first snow. There is a blue flame dancing on one of the stove burners and a pot of hot water gurgling softly on it. There is something holy about the whole scene, reverent even.

Sameer hands me my tea in my favourite mug. His face is close to mine and I can smell his familiar cologne. Still citrus. Delicious spiced lemon. I cannot resist myself and throw my free arm around him. He is taken a little by surprise and then he holds the small of my back and pulls me towards himself. Even after all these years, my tummy clenches and there is … ahem … a tingling in my nether regions.

We are just about to have the best kiss on a snowy morning just like it was sixteen years back … when Riya walks in.

'Mommy, Baba, guys you should seriously get a room or something,' Riya snaps. 'Today is Didi's birthday and all you are interested in is this?' She points an accusatory finger at us, as if we are hormonal teenagers trying to sabotage her sister's birthday.

'Umm, well, so to jog your memory, we are the parents, the reason behind your sister's birth and we are doing our best to make her birthday as memorable as possible. What are you doing?' I move two steps away from Sameer and take a long sip of my tea.

Sameer looks at me and then back at Riya and gives her a wink. Really? Now he is conspiring with my daughter behind my back? The two have a plan and I don't even know about it!

'I am baking Didi's birthday cake. Baba knows already,' Riya proclaims proudly. 'I tried to ask you, but you said "Don't bother me". Remember?' she adds testily. This younger fruit of my womb is going to give me far more tough times, I can tell already. I dread the day she comes out of her room with black eye make-up and seven piercings.

I try to conjure up Ramdev again. It is not easy given that he is no Brad Pitt. But my motto for December is to be calm. To be like the swan who doesn't let water rest on her back. I toss aside any anger or disappointment that I feel with this daddy-daughter clique and try to be the bigger person here. The person who will make paayesh, the star of the birthday party, okay, maybe a tiny star.

I busy myself, measuring out the milk, smearing the grains of rice with ghee just as Didan had said in her letter. I soak a fistful of golden raisins in water, waiting for them to swell up. I have to keep a close watch on the milk, practically babysit it. So, I stand guard with a ladle, stirring the milk, making sure it doesn't boil over or scald the bottom of the pot. There is a thin line separating these events and a moment of carelessness can lead to the whole paayesh getting ruined. I stir the milk and from the corner of my eye watch Riya and Sameer.

My God, Riya and her dad are really good. They are gliding around the kitchen efficiently measuring flour and separating egg whites like Nigella Lawson. I gape in wonder. While Riya bakes a chocolate cake, her sister's favourite, Sameer is getting ready to make sixteen dishes that Piyu has adored in the sixteen years of her life. Yes, sixteen different dishes. This man is a freaking genius.

Menu

1. For year one, he is making a blueberry puree and apple sauce dip to be served with adult-friendly crackers.

2. Year two was when Piyu loved eating khichuri and finger food like aloo bhaja. So, Sameer is making an adult version of khichuri weds risotto, studded with nuts, raisins and topped with wafer-thin parmesan crisps.

3. Year three – mashed potatoes. Yep, you got it right, our very own Bengali alu sheddho. That with butter and rice plumped up Piyu in year three as it does to most Bengali toddlers.

4. Year four, Piyu started preschool and got introduced to mac and cheese. She was so much in love with that gooey mess that mac and cheese was all she wanted for all her meals. I have never been a fan of the dish but Sameer is making his gourmet mac and cheese with bits of ham which is to die for.

5. Year five saw Piyu become a big fan of a simple chicken stew and rice. It was one of those rare recipes of my mother's that I actually cooked. She loved to have that stew with rice and called it 'chicken-jholu bhaatu'. Sameer made a stew in

honour of that. His stew is, of course, more full-bodied and flavourful and will be served with sourdough bread.

6.   Year six – dal chawal. No, seriously, there was this one whole year of unconditional love for lentils. Sameer took this a step ahead and is making a Moroccan lentil soup tempered with panch phoron.

7.   Year seven – Maggi. I don't know a single child with Indian parents who does not have this fondness for Maggi. It has been a part of my childhood as well as my girls, I remember the first dish that Piyu learned to make was Maggi. She would make a bowl for Riya and herself on Friday afternoons after school. This one today is getting an adult avatar with bits of bacon and green onion.

8.   Year eight – paneer butter masala. It was Delhi Garden, a very small, typical Indian restaurant's orange glow paneer butter masala that my daughters were hooked on to. Lots of cream, neon orange in colour, mild in flavour, sweet in taste to please the Caucasians with low tolerance of heat. Every other night, they would ask for this dish. I tried making it at home and yet they always preferred Delhi Garden's.

9.   Year nine – mutton curry and rice. Piyu loved the simple Bengali mutton curry that Sameer made on Sundays. He would make a pressure cooker full of mutton curry, a reddish thin curry with potatoes bobbing in the gravy. This one, he did not want to modernize and, so, Sameer's trademark mutton curry is on the menu tonight

10. Year ten – tacos. Homemade ground chicken chilli and black beans in store-bought crunchy taco shells. This was a hot favourite with the girls for at least a few years in a row. It was

also my staple dish, easy, quick and I always got a compliment on taco nights.

11. Year eleven – pork chops. Thick, fatty pieces of pork chops – marinated with loads of garlic, black pepper, ginger and salt – cooked on the skillet with lots of onion. My mouth waters at the thought of it.

12. Year twelve – salmon in herbed garlic butter sauce. By twelve, Piyu had developed a deep interest in two TV channels. Food Network and HGTV. You could see it in her choice of food and decor, both getting refined. She was always asking me to try out recipes beyond Rachel Ray. This was one of them and she couldn't stop eating salmon that whole year.

13. Year thirteen – shrimp scampi. How can we forget the year of shrimp scampi?

14. Year fourteen – roasted asparagus with pesto kashundi. This was the year Piyu went vegetarian. Yes, it was hard for us. She refused to eat meat, fish, eggs and was on the edge of going vegan. We kind of pulled her back from the vegan camp but she still stuck to vegetarianism. But thanks to her, I discovered new ways to eat the same old vegetables. Sameer just notched asparagus up several levels with his kashundi in that pesto.

15. Year fifteen – the transformative year. The year of morphing and nothing more or less than sweet paayesh flavoured with khejur gur is fitting.

16. Year sixteen – the finale with a luscious ganache covered chocolate cake.

By evening we are ready with all the food and party decorations. The house looks festive with white Christmas fairy lights strung across windows and shiny helium balloons. I have made a photo booth where the guests can pose with Piyu's baby photos as props. I have cute bibs with yellow duckies and glittery sippy cups. And large 9'x11' prints of a six-month-old chubby Piyu in diapers.

It seemed like the cutest idea of all until yesterday but now I am no longer sure. I have a feeling that Piyu might cringe and get embarrassed by her photos in diapers and binky in mouth. The more I think of it, the more I can see her giving me dagger looks afterwards. So, at the last minute, I am googling and printing out photos of hot, young male celebs. I am sure sixteen-year-old girls still like hot male models.

'Shubha, what are you doing?' Sameer comes in with a bunch of printouts in his hand. In each of them one or the other bare-bodied hunk with tight six-pack abs is looking out at the world with narrowed eyes. His brows are knitted in consternation and his voice is lowered to a hush.

Oh no, no! 'Hey come on, not what you are thinking! This is for Piyu's photo booth.' I roll my eyes.

'Photos of these half-naked men are for Piyu's photo booth? You must be kidding me.'

Okay, so what does he think? They are for my entertainment? 'Sameer, these are not any men, they are famous … err like stars.' I stress on the word S-T-A-R-S. 'Do you realize Piyu is SIXTEEN? At that age, you are supposed to have crushes on celebrities especially hot ones. When we were that age, we used to swoon over Aamir Khan and Tom Cruise.'

Sameer isn't convinced but to my utter relief he decides to let go. 'If you say so,' he shrugs and looks around suspiciously. 'I still think those baby pictures were a better idea. I miss that binky.' He is clearly moping now.

'Aww Sameer, she will always be your little girl, you know. You will always be the centre of her universe,' I assure him and then I pick up the stack of photos, hold them like a flag above my head, and proclaim '...and these will be mere sidekicks.' It doesn't sound very convincing but Sameer is not paying attention anyway. He grabs my laptop and settles down on the bed.

I sort through the printouts quickly, dumb – recycle bin, dumb but cute – maybe, dumb but solid six-pack – keep for photo-booth, not dumb and yet a solid six-pack – save for myself!

'Why did they have to grow up so fast, Shubha? I miss those tiny toes and fingers, that angelic look on her face when she slept,' Sameer is scrolling through all the baby photos on our hard drive now. Tiny Piyu grinning a gummy smile, drool dribbling down her chin. Naughty Riya in the dishwasher, smiling at the camera. Angelic Piyu all dressed for annaprashana. Piyu and Riya together sucking thumbs.

'I was so busy with work that I missed out on so much. I missed all the little moments because I thought I was doing some big thing. But in the end, all that matters is right here.' He jabs at the screen, his voice all muffled.

'Are you okay?' I ask cautiously. Honestly, I am not that sad about the growing up. I am actually glad that those diaper changing and potty training years are over. And God, the every-two-hour feedings at night. I am not going back and doing that again! Nope. I am very, very sure about that.

But Sameer is not okay. He sniffs and rubs his nose, all emotional and teary-eyed. Is he going through a perimenopausal stage? Do men even have that stage? I must google this.

'Hold on, let me get you a glass of Chianti. That will pep you up,' I tell him in a very soothing voice. I must get Sameer out of this funk before the guests start coming in and alcohol seems like the best idea at the moment. If Chianti doesn't work, I am going to pour him a Scotch!

Facebook

Happy sixteen to the best sixteen-year-old. Sweetie, your time has come ... spread your wings, fly. #birthday #motherofsixteenyearold

108 likes. 99 'Happy Birthday Piyu' wishes.

Poush
(December – January)

Piyu's party was a huge success. She was thrilled to bits. Everyone who came to the party raved about the food. Piyu's friends went 'ooh' and 'aaah' over everything Sameer had made. He even got an offer to cook for one of Piyu's friend's sweet sixteen which is next month. Sameer was mighty pleased with all the praise and was gloating all evening.

Later at night, when everyone had left, and we were alone in the kitchen, our elbows covered in soap suds and hair smelling of herbs de Provence and garam masala, he asked, 'Shubha, are you okay if I take up the catering offer? You know, to keep myself busy until I get something more … more permanent.' Tucking in the last dish in the dishwasher, I could feel the hesitation in his voice.

I know how hard it is for him to say this. For Sameer, the one who doesn't like asking for suggestions or discussing problems, this is a huge leap. I am gradually realizing that the market is bad and it is getting increasingly difficult for him to get a job in the tech industry. It might be a while till he gets an offer that is right for him, if at all.

'I think it will be fantastic. Do you really want to do it? This is different from cooking for family and friends, you know.' I tried to test the waters. Sameer loves cooking but I don't think he knows what catering to other people's food choices is.

'Of course, I know. I think I am ready to spread my wings. I have lots of ideas and this will give me an opportunity to try those out. I can even hire some help.' His voice got more and more excited and I could see the dream in his eyes.

'I was tired of what I was doing, Shubha. I loved the challenge of what my brain was pushed to do, but at the end of the day I was being wringed like a wet cloth. I missed my time at home with you all. Now that I have a second chance, I want something different. Maybe, just maybe, this could even become my second career, what say?' Sameer grinned at me.

I knew then that that was what he wanted and I felt this deep desire to push away all obstacles that came in his way and help him succeed. I wanted to tell him about our project too, the letters and the book I am writing. But then I was no longer sure what was going to happen with it! It might all go nowhere so I kept quiet.

And guess what? The very next day there was finally some good news for our book too. See, that whole 'letting go' idea of mine seems to have inspired the universe. And things are falling into place. Well, not exactly in place but is getting there. Slowly.

So here's what happened. Jai came to our office last week. He had an interesting proposition, as he had told Kajol over the phone. We weren't sure what it meant. I just hoped that it had nothing to do with him 'proposing' to Kajol. I mean yes, they did meet a few times since that cooking lesson and seem to have hit it off, but still a proposal would be too much. Kajol would outright reject him and the poor guy would be devastated. Jai is a sweet guy and I know Kajol pretty well. I love her, but she can be harsh. I imagined all of this in my head but, of course, I did not say any of this aloud.

Jai came around lunch with a big grin on his face. Uh-oh, I thought.

'I have good news,' he started off, looking shyly at Kajol and then me. I was sitting across from him, beside Kajol, and tried my best to shake my head and mouth 'Not now'. As a friend, I felt a responsibility towards him, to protect him or rather his feelings.

Jai looked quizzically at me and said like an idiot, 'What are you saying, Shubha?'

Naturally I gave up all hope and slinked down in my chair.

'So, this is the thing. I have a friend from my schooldays I am very close to. He lives in Kolkata and is one of the founders/partners of a publishing company. Well, it was a kind of middle-tier publishing company, but recently one of their imprints was sold to a Bollywood movie producer and so they are getting a lot of attention.' Jai paused, looking at us expectantly, probably waiting for us to react.

I had no idea where this was going so I gave a polite smile. At least this was not the kind of 'proposal' I was thinking. Kajol was staring intently at Jai, elbows on the table, slightly leaning forward. Really, it is hard to know what goes on in this woman's mind.

'So, don't you want to know why am I telling you all this?' Jai asked a bit impatiently.

'Yes, yes, of course.' Kajol flashed a smile and leaned further forward. Her face was barely two inches away from Jai's. He leaned back a bit, clearly uncomfortable. Did I read this whole thing wrong? I don't know, I am bad at predicting human relations.

'So, I was talking to Abhishek, my friend – the founder of the company – the other day and I was telling him about your current project. One thing led to another and now he is very interested to collaborate with you, I mean with Right-to-Write. He will take care of all the printing, marketing and media coverage. Everything! And he wants to have a meeting with you both over

Skype ASAP.' Jai finished the last sentence in a single breath and beamed at us.

My jaw had started inching open in slow motion and was now wide open. Kajol was speechless. This was a bolt from the blue. A good bolt, an amazing one, but still a bolt.

After a moment of pin-drop silence, Kajol gave a shrill shriek, jumped up from her chair, hugged me tight and started kissing my cheek. The girl really goes to the extreme. It was so embarrassing. Then she flung her arms around Jai and squeezed him tight, saying ridiculous stuff like 'You are my angel from heaven', 'You are the cream on my whoopee pie', 'You are the kashundi on my fish chop'. Jai stood like a wooden soldier, stiff and clearly in discomfort but Kajol was undeterred as always. It was the funniest thing to watch.

So, we had a teleconference last night, with this Abhishek, Jai's friend. Their publishing company is called Bong Reads. Not very imaginative, but to the point. The Skype video didn't work because of poor Internet connection on their end and so we couldn't really see each other's faces.

'Please call me Ovshake,' said Jai's friend, rounding out the first letter of his name. 'Madam, the main thing in the publishing industry these days is marketing – and we do that really well. You can write utter crap and we will still have your book at number one on Amazon.'

'I did not write utter crap, I worked really hard on this book. It is pretty good,' I said defensively.

'Aha, don't get angry. Just saying *ar ki*,' Ovshake or Abhishek cackled on the other end. Kajol rolled her eyes and signalled me to peace out.

The important thing is we had a good discussion and they want to be in. It means, they are going to do the printing and marketing and all such things related to publishing the book. They are okay with doing joint publishing and though I am not getting as much money as Big Whales was offering, this thing can be big if the book is a success.

Kajol is breathing somewhat easy. There seems to be some hope on the horizon at least, and maybe some money. First time in months, Kajol suggested that we go to a restaurant for our monthly team lunch. Even though we only went to the Indian Lunch Buffet where it costs $10.99 per person, I would take this as a positive improvement over the single topping pizzas.

Now there is only one more thing to be done. The last step to finish my book. I have to find out who's been writing those letters. By 'who' I mean the old lady whose life story unravelled each month and whose story helped me write mine. Even though the letters were never meant for me, I must admit they changed my life like no other. I want to thank her for that. I cannot finish the book without her blessings and without knowing how her story ends.

———

Dear Moni,

How are you? It has been very cold here in the past few days. This year winter just rushed in like an express train with the onset of the month of Poush. Didn't even give me time to sun my quilts and blankets. Sometimes, I am not sure if it is the cold that is more brutal this year or it is my old bones which cannot stand the icy wind any more. At night, I cover myself with two thick quilts and the soft blanket that you sent me and yet I shiver as if there is ice in my blood.

How I miss the winter of my youth. It used to be the best time of the year, you know. We would wear our heavy south silks, wrap colourful batik scarves around our neck, cardigans knitted in the latest fashion and make most of the Kolkata winter. It was the time to enjoy the crisp outdoors. Picnic at the zoo, Christmas at Park Street, cake from Flury's, stroll through Hogg Market which would have the most colourful wares on display – ah, those were the days.

Even the local haat would be dressed up, strutting their prettiest and fairest vegetables as if it was a veggie fashion show. All kinds of leafy greens, shiny green cabbages, ruby red beetroot, slender orange carrots, fat snap peas with their emerald-like peas snuggled inside, purple eggplants with skin so silky that sunlight would slide off them.

You know what was the best part of Poush? Khejur gur, date palm jaggery! The cold weather would trigger the palm tree to make its sap, which would be harvested fresh early in the morning by village folks. That sap was then stirred and thickened to make khejur gur, the nectar of the gods. Aha! What a taste it had! What fragrance! The whole house would be redolent with the sweet fragrance of gur on the days I made paayesh. The khejur gur they sell in Kolkata these days is all fake, no flavour, no taste, no nothing! I think they make it in a factory with chemicals.

So anyway, what was I telling you in my last letter? Did I tell you that Rajat was in London and I had not heard at all from him since then? I could not have been happier with this arrangement, actually. It looked like God had heard my prayers finally.

Then that Poush Sankranti, his parents came to our house. It was a sudden and unexpected visit. My mother had just finished frying the last batch of her famous gokul pithe and was in the kitchen sorting them to *be distributed to our friends and neighbours. I can still see her, sitting on a low wooden stool, her fair skin glowing pink from the fire, her fingers quick and deft, rolling small discs of dough, stuffing them with kheer, patting them to flat discs and then frying them in hot oil. She then quickly dunked them in a sugar syrup she had ready in a humongous brass dekchi. Those gokul pithes were so delicious, one bite of the thin exterior cover and you would be treated with the creamy kheer interior. She had fried the last of the pithe when the doorbell rang.*

It was Rajat's parents standing at the door. My mother-in-law's eyes were puffed up and her face was a blotchy shade of pomegranate. My father-in-law was grave and sombre. They had come bearing the news that Rajat had been in a fatal accident. He was hit by a car in Trafalgar Square and had died on the spot. One of his British friends had sent a telegram with the news. He had specifically insisted that since the body was badly hit there was no point in them going to London and the friends would take care of the last rites.

His parents left and just like that I became a widow. Now, it wasn't a news I should have been happy about. But to tell the truth, I felt an odd relief, a happiness, the kind that comes on becoming free. I felt my shackles were finally broken. So many years later, I feel no remorse in saying that I was very happy hearing this news then. It gave me a new lease of life.

A year later, I heard from one of our neighbours that his son was visiting London and he had actually seen Rajat at Hyde Park. He was there with a blonde lady and the two seemed very close, holding hands and hugging each other. So Rajat was still very much alive but he had just made up that story to get out of the marriage! I still don't know if his parents were part of the plan. But I didn't care, did I? I didn't even share this news with anyone and asked the neighbour to say nothing to my parents.

Being a widow had given me a new lease at life. My second chance. And I did not want to lose it.

Today I will share two recipes of pithe with you. One is a savoury pithe, where the dough is made of rice flour and then filled with snap peas. Working with rice flour dough is a bit tricky, you need to mix the dough with very hot water and shape it immediately. The other is my mother's famous gokul pithe — you might find making them a little difficult at first but trust me you can do this. And even if you mess up at first, remember, like I said, you get a second chance.

Bhalo theko,
Didan

Gokul Pithe

Pitha or pithe are a special variety of rice cakes associated with the harvest festival of Makar Sankranti or Poush Parbon, celebrated in Bengal. Though the primary ingredients are rice, coconut and jaggery, pithe is also often made of wheat flour like the gokul pithe. It is a fried pithe, made of wheat flour and a sweet coconut-kheer stuffing and then fried and soaked in hot sugar syrup. This recipe makes 25-30 gokul pithe.

Ingredients

For Stuffing

Grated coconut – 2 cups
Khoya – 12oz almost 2 cups (ideally homemade khoya/kheer is best but store-bought khoya works fine)
Sugar – 1 cup

For Batter

All-purpose flour – 2 cups
Ghee – 1 tsp
Baking soda – ¼tsp
Whole milk – 1 cup
Saffron – a pinch

For Syrup

Sugar – 4 cups
Water – 4 cups

For Frying

Vegetable oil

Making the Stuffing

Heat a kadhai or frying pan.

Add coconut and sugar and lower the heat.

Mix the grated coconut with the sugar lightly pressing with your fingers till the sugar melts and mixes with the coconut.

Add the khoya. Keep stirring till the mixture becomes light brown and sticky. It should easily come off from the sides. At this point, take a little bit of the mix and see if you can fashion a flat disc out of it. If it is too sticky you may have to cook it a bit more, else you are good.

Take a little of the mix, roll a small ball between your palms and then flatten between your palms to make a disc about 2" in diameter and thickness of a ½". Make about 25-30 discs of this size.

Making the Batter

In a wide-mouthed bowl add:
- All-purpose flour
- Ghee
- Baking soda

Mix it lightly.

Now add a cup of whole milk and a cup of water. Mix scraping the sides to form a batter. You will need about one more cup of water but add this gradually till you get a batter thick enough like a pakoda batter.

To this batter add a generous pinch of saffron.

Making the Syrup

Boil 4 cups of water and 4 cups of sugar till you get a syrup of one-string consistency.

Add a few drops of kewra or rose water to the syrup to get a sweet smell.

Frying

Heat enough oil for deep frying in a skillet.

Dip the coconut-khoya discs in the batter so that they are well coated. Now fry them in the hot oil like a fritter. Remove with a slotted spoon when both sides are golden brown. Dunk in the syrup and remove when they become a little soft.

In one version of gokul pithe you can make the sugar syrup thicker and then coat the fried pithe with the syrup instead of soaking them in it.

Enjoy!

10

I am going to India. Kolkata, to be precise. I finally decided that I had to go back to those very roots that I have wanted to avoid and at least try one last time to search for Didan, the grand old lady whose magical letters have changed my life. It is not that I have too much hope of tracing through the lanes and by-lanes of a Kolkata neighbourhood and finding her. I have done everything possible virtually and nothing has come of it. But though my mind understands the futility of all my efforts, my heart still lives in hope.

What if I walk the roads, the narrow lanes weaving through lost neighbourhoods, the sleepy back streets that probably slunk out of Google Maps and find her? What if I actually find myself at 253/5 Panchanantala Lane and see her, sitting on a four-poster bed with a gleaming brass box of deep green betel leaves, her round-rimmed glasses resting on the edge of her slightly upturned nose, as she bends over a blue inland letter where she writes in tiny pearl-shaped rounded Bengali letters. What if ... I recognize that face of hers? Is it like my own grandmother's, lips stained scarlet with betel juice and spider web wrinkles around brown twinkling eyes? I try to focus on the face, but it is a blur and I can barely make out the outlines of a large red dot on her creased forehead.

Shucks! The face somehow always eludes me in my visions. Concentrate, Shubha ... concentrate. I scrunch my nose, close my eyes and try my best. I can see thin strands of her silver hair pulled back and tied in a bun. Her sari is of white cotton, with a broad border in green and red, just like the ones my own grandmother would wear. She is so real that I can now almost touch her ... graze my hand across the folds of skin on her arms ... but the face ... it is still a blur.

The more I do this thinking exercise, the more real it seems. I am not dumb, I know it is all in my fantasy and that I am just adding to my heartbreak by painting all these lifelike scenarios, but I can't seem to stop myself. Miracles do happen, so why not this one time? My fingers twitch and I have this strong desire to know when I hug her will her skin feel fragile like a scroll of ancient parchment or will it still be soft and satin like a ball of luchi dough that I can now expertly make. One thing I am certain about — I need to meet her if I have to finish this book.

Okay, so, there is another very selfish reason why I am desperately holding on to fragile strands of hope, why I keep believing in happy endings. I am scared. Scared to land in Kolkata after eight long years. The last time I was there, it was for Baba. There was an early morning call one sunny, winter day, and I had thrown clothes into a suitcase and rushed to the airport to get a seat on whichever flight was East-bound. The girls were little, four and eight, and I didn't even think twice before rushing off to the airport all alone. As I slogged through layovers and securities in three different airports before reaching Kolkata, I had earnestly hoped that Baba would survive this stroke. Most people did. Heart attack was a common thing these days.

'You have to stop eating all these sweets, you know. Only oatmeal for breakfast from now on,' I would say in my stern but caring voice, adjusting his pillow.

'Shubha, get your facts straight. Do I have diabetes? My sugar level is perfectly okay. Why should I then not have jilipi and milk for my breakfast?' My broad-shouldered, tall and handsome Baba would dismiss my concern, adjust his black thick-framed glasses and dive into the pages of the *Statesman*. Then everything would go back to as it was before.

But it didn't. Baba didn't live to have his jilipi breakfast the next day. He breathed his last while I was at Kolkata airport, jet-lagged and tired, scribbling on my customs form and declaring that I had nothing but love in my heart to export.

I have never gone back to Kolkata since. We do come to visit Sameer's parents in India every other year, but they live in Bhilai – a small township in Chhattisgarh. We fly to Delhi and then straight to Bhilai. Thankfully, it is far enough from Kolkata and opposite in its culture, to remind me of the city. I have erased Kolkata from my itinerary in the past eight years and I never thought I would have the courage to step back into the city again, until now.

It was hard enough for me to take the plunge this time. 'It is now or never,' Sameer had said, when I finally confided in him about the project, blurting out about the letters, the forgotten recipes, the whole saga from A to Z. I was feeling a bit contrite and thought he would be upset that I had not said anything to him earlier. On the contrary, he was very excited about the whole thing.

No sulking. Not a single emotional 'We have been married for seventeen and a half years and yet you keep secrets from me'. Not even a sentimental one-liner like 'You should have told me'.

All he said was, 'Ah, now all that cooking falls into place!' I was quite offended by this lack of distress on his part. I mean which guy is excited that his wife has kept such humongous secrets from him? Shouldn't he have been worried that maybe I have more secrets? Like, maybe I have secret admirers even?

I guess I will never really understand men, even my own husband. And then he kind of pushed me to book the flight tickets and make this trip! 'You should make this trip, Shubha. If you think you need to find her, you must go find her. I know you can do it!' Seriously, dude, how do you know it?

Despite Sameer's pep talk, I am not yet sure how I will feel walking through the airport this time. Will the city be as cruel to me as the last time? Nope, I don't want to think about it.

'Anything to drink ma'am? Coffee or tea?' I am jolted from my reverie by the no-nonsense voice of the air hostess, on the second leg of my flight.

'A single malt, please.' Yeah, good decision, Shubha, I pat myself on the back.

The stewardess sets a glass with perfect cubes of ice and a tiny bottle of whiskey on the tray table. The balding desi gentleman on the other side of the aisle gives me an appreciative look. He must be in his fifties and looks overly interested in other people's affairs. I twist open the cap and drink the single malt straight. From the corner of my eye I can see the guy's jaw inching open. I gulp down the drink thirstily and look straight into his eyes and say, 'Cheers!' He gives a wide grin that almost touches his ears and asks, 'Kolkata?'

The overhead light slides off his pate, plunging his features into a shadow and I am not sure if he is being plain nosy or trying to be flirty! Look at my luck, even when there are people flirting with me, it is balding, bellied men. Bleh! Had it been Kajol, there would be hot Spanish guys with dreamy eyes and black gelled hair ready to do the samba with her.

Anyway, I decide I am not fond of balding middle-aged men even when they are attempting to flirt with me. I don't want to indulge him any further and so I nod my head, draw the scratchy airlines blanket up to my chin and go to sleep. A deep dreamless sleep.

I must have slept for the entire last leg of the flight, from Dubai to Kolkata. I am awakened by a sharp nudge. I stutter and look up to see it is that same gentleman across the aisle. Seriously, what is his problem? 'Get up, get up,' he says, 'here is Kolkata. See the glittering lights, all three-pronged like London, set up by Didi.' He proudly points to the window where I can indeed see a string of lights in the pitch darkness around. The three-pronged lights rise faster and faster and I can see more of them now, lining what seems to be neatly laid-out streets from this altitude. All around me people are waking up – stretching their arms, brushing off crumbs from shirts and getting ready to face what Kolkata has to offer them. I am glued to the seat by some unexplained law of attraction and show no such signs of enthusiasm.

Soon the airplane lands with a thud and barely as the wheels touch the tarmac I can hear the flick of mobiles and the tap-tap of the keypads. Everyone seems to be calling home announcing their arrival.

'Hyaan dinner was good. They served biryani, and gulab jamun for dessert. You go to sleep, I will take an Ola.'

'No, no, I already had dinner. Yes, yes, they gave biryani this time. Chicken. Yes re baba, chicken biryani.'

'What did you say? You made rui mach'r kalia for dinner? Okay pack it for lunch tomorrow.'

Unwittingly my lips curl up in a smile and I know things will probably be all right this time. If not, I will take what is given to me and make the most of it. A city that has food in its soul cannot be cruel to anyone.

———

By the time I am done with customs and baggage, it is almost dawn in Kolkata. I step out into the streets of the city with my pishi and her house help. At the ripe old age of eighty, my aunt is sprightly and has come all the way to the airport to receive me in spite of my repeatedly telling her not to. She looks wiry and tiny in her leggings and oversized kurta. But I know not to get fooled by that façade. She does tai chi, runs half marathons and is probably more fit than me.

'Shubhaaa, I am so glad you decided to come. Wish you had brought Piyu and Riya too. But girl, you need to take better care of yourself. Don't you follow the yoga videos I send you on

WhatsApp?' These are the first words Pishi utters, as she envelops me in a tight hug.

I mumble and feel a bit guilty. I have not watched even one of the 'good morning' videos she sends me every morning without fail.

'Ah, let's go home and I will make a routine for you.' She gives me a sweeping glance and then turns to her house help, 'Ratna, don't forget to soak some chirota for Didi. She needs to drink that on an empty stomach every morning.' I absolutely hate bitter chirota but am secretly relieved that Pishi is there and I feel reassured holding her thin, bony wrist curled up in my palm. I have been a bad niece and not visited her in eight years, but I know she understands.

It is the end of January and the air outside is cool and heavy. It smells sweet like a mix of overripe fruits and smoky like someone is hosting a barbecue party. I roll down the window of the tiny Maruti, and peer outside as the car rolls out of the airport area and on to a broad two-lane road. The road is relatively empty this early and is lined with ample street lights, three-pronged, just like the gentleman on the plane had pointed out. Glossy colourful billboards, with slim, pretty models selling clothes or cars, loom every few feet. I take a big gulp of the familiar city air and watch mesmerized as the car speeds exactly on the centre of the street markings, dodging sleeping cows and dogs, and ignoring any traffic lights that come in its way!

'Close the window, close it!' Pishi shouts. I am surprised by the panic in her voice. 'Oh ho, there is so much pollution. You will fall sick. You are not used to it any more.' Pishi leans over and rolls up my window.

I feel like a child again and realize how much I miss being one. On an impulse, I squeeze her tight and feel the coolness of her palm on the back of my head. She strokes my head gently and I feel a drop of warm tear on my forehead. And then I am crying too. All those tears that I had held back so long, tears of anger against my parents for going too early, tears of sorrow for leaving me alone, tears of regret for not having to spend more time with them, all come out gushing in streams of salty warm water. I wring my heart out, squeezing out the last tear from my eyes. My body racks as I sob. And then just like that it is all over. My tears take a bow and leave the stage. Just like that they are gone.

I sit up straight, wipe my grimy face and fish out a Kleenex from my bag to blow my nose. I feel much better, as if a load has been lifted off my heart and I can breathe free again. I was so busy bawling that I had forgotten about all the other people in the car. I look around to see Pishi staring at me with an incredulous look in her eyes. I cannot see the driver's face but from the look of his stiff shoulders, he seems to be very tense. The house help, Ratna di, on the front passenger seat seems to have acquired a frozen posture. OMG! Was I that bad? Did I think I was in the back seat of someone's limousine, where I could bawl in complete privacy?

And then, Pishi throws back her head and starts laughing. She slaps my back and chortles, 'You can still cry like your six-year-old self. No wonder your mother called you a crybaby.' At this, Ratna Di lets out a giggle. The driver's shoulders sag a bit and settle down in a slope. I sulk a little at being called such awful names and then I join in the laughter.

For the next two days, I do practically nothing. I sleep through most of the day only to wake up at odd hours, and irrespective of which hour I wake up, I am forced to eat a big meal. I tried to feebly protest the first time, but with Pishi it is just plain easier if I fall in step with her plan. Also, Ratna Di is a fabulous cook, and I don't have the mental strength to shy away from a jhaal-jhaal, spicy, tyangra fish chorchori with slender purple eggplants, huge jumbo prawns – golda chingri in their bright orange shells cooked in a delicious mustard paste, or a plain aloo posto tempered with nothing but nigella seeds and green chillies.

After two straight days of pure leisure, my biological clock finally adjusts to the Eastern world, and I am awake at my normal time of 6.30 in the morning. I can hear Pishi practising tai chi in the living room, following lessons on YouTube. I step out on to the balcony with a steaming cup of tea that Ratna hands me without even asking. She is like a magical genie, I cannot remember the last time someone brought me a cup of tea in the morning! I wish I could export her to the US. I don't mean the illegal way, I mean via all the official process like visa, etc.

A crow is cawing incessantly on the balcony, pausing for only a few seconds between each raspy call. That sure sounds like a sign. An ominous one. In the early hours of the morning, the city is draped in a fine gossamer veil of fog and the sun is kind of meek like a watery egg poach. I can see patches of green across the highway and more tall buildings around where I stand. Pishi lives in a gated community of four multi-storeyed buildings. Her flat is on the seventh floor of the second tower. This part of the town is more modern and newer than any of the Kolkata I know. Pishi was not able to manage her huge sprawling house in an old

North Kolkata neighbourhood, and so a few years back she sold her home to move to this apartment. It seems like a nice place with well-tended lawns, plentiful trees and clean sidewalks.

I open my laptop and connect to the sketchy Wi-Fi only to be bombarded with fifty unread emails from Kajol. That woman is truly hyper. She has arranged a meeting for me with Abhishek at 2 p.m. today, without even asking me. God! Kajol can be such a control freak, I grumble to myself.

By noon, I have showered, dressed and am ready for my meeting. 'Dress Indian to be safe.' Kajol had insisted in her micro-managing voice. I wanted to ignore her but then ended up in simple black leggings and a turquoise Fabindia kurti. She has a way to put these things into your head – one moment you are protesting and the next you are on autopilot following orders, forgetting to even think for yourself. I pull my hair back with a barrette and put on my long silver fish earrings. We had looked up the address earlier on Google Maps and Pishi figured out that the Bong Reads' office was located in College Street, right across Presidency University and on the street behind the first row of bookshops. Pishi is extremely adept at technology and seems to adore Google.

'Ask Gogol,' she keeps telling me.

I can feel the excitement mounting during my cab journey in the afternoon.

#1 Of course because this partnership has the potential to solve our publishing house woes and propel me to stardom. Amen to that!

#2 Also because College Street holds a special place in my heart. Every summer vacation when I would visit my maternal grandmother, Dida, in Kolkata, she would take me to College

Street and let me loose, buying me all and any book that I wanted. I would stroll between Dasgupta, Rupa and the myriad other stores picking up my annual stock of books.

#3 My first so-called date with Sameer was at Coffee House and I am sure good things will happen here today too.

As the Ola driver cruises through the newly built flyovers and weaves through the narrower lanes of old Kolkata, with rickety trams chugging along the centre of the road, I feel a whole wave of nostalgia sweeping over me. Old majestic houses, with green shuttered windows and roots of banyan sprouting from their wall, stand shoulder to shoulder just like always. Mishti'r dokan, sweet shops, with their glass front shelves loaded with trays of nolen gur sondesh, emerge at every corner. Throngs of people on the sidewalk and screeching buses careening dangerously. And then comes College Street, with its pavements teeming with tiny stores each boasting tottering piles of books on all subjects. Nothing has changed. And yet so much has.

I arrive at my destination, in front of those huge gates of Presidency, almost fifteen minutes early. My cab ride was super entertaining with my cabby discussing his son's love life, state of political affairs in India as well as the US, and then finally Sourav Ganguly. By the end of it, neither of us were happy with the ride getting over. I sighed and got down to browse through my favourite bookshops before going to Abhishek's office.

Though Pishi had clearly pointed out the Bong Reads' office on Google Maps, now I find it hard to locate. After asking a few people, I am pointed to a door so narrowly wedged between two busy bookshops that it could be the platform 9 ¾ of Harry Potter. The door leads to a rickety staircase flanked by walls stained with betel juice and graffiti. My heart sinks at the sight. Ahem ... so this is the upcoming publishing house which has signed up an award-winning, movie-making author.

I am now having serious doubts on how well Jai knows this friend of his. Maybe this Abhishek is a fraud after all. Maybe his situation is worse off than Right-to-Write and he is trying to lure in our dollar money. Wait, what if he has goondas at the top of the stairs waiting to loot me? Not that I have anything much on me anyway. But what if he kidnaps me and asks Sameer for a ransom! Oh no, the poor dude doesn't have the money for ransom any more, my red highlighted Excel spreadsheet looms before my eyes.

I am in two minds now but then my hitherto unseen woman power raises its head (I didn't even know it existed) and I climb those stairs with steely determination.

Oh boy! I am so glad I did. The stairs open up to a very posh lounge which looks more like a lavish family room with antique upholstered sofas, Victorian wingback chairs resting on heavy clawed foot, huge paintings hanging from the walls and piles of books resting on mosaic-inlaid side tables. One entire wall of the room is lined with a ceiling-high mahogany bookcase whose shelves are neatly stacked with books and magazines. There is a corridor leading to the back and beyond that wall. From where I am standing, I cannot see what lies there. I cast my gaze around and realize that two intellectual-looking men with beards and jhola-type cloth bags are sitting on one of the couches intently peering at a MacBook screen. They are so still and quiet that I am not sure if they are part of the décor. I deeply inhale this stale, sweet smell of old books and papers and whisper, 'Errm ... I have a meeting with Mr Abhishek Bhattacharjee. Where can I find him?' I dare not raise my voice and break the library-like silence in the room.

'Obhishekdaaa ... visitor,' one of them shouts without moving his eyes from the Mac.

'Coming...' I hear a voice and then the owner of the voice comes rushing out of a dark corridor on the other side of the bookcase wall.

He is bald, wearing a maroon T-shirt tucked in his trousers, and looks somewhat familiar. Where have I seen him before? I try to think. Or does he resemble someone I know. I rack my brain, flipping faces I know in my mind.

'Shubhalaxmi Sen-Gupta? Shubha?' He extends his hand, the smile on his face wide and almost touching his ears.

And then I freeze right there, my hand stiff midway in the air. This is the baldy from my flight. The same guy I had ignored and had cursed my luck for lack of in-flight Spanish hunks! I don't remember what else I must have told him. I was drunk. Oh God! Why did he have to be Abhishek! What must he think of me? What if he cancels the contract? I feel so embarrassed that I can feel drops of sweat trickling down the hollow of my back.

'Your face looks familiar. Were we on the same flight last Sunday?' He knits his brows in concentration.

'Maybe ... maybe not ... that was in air, this is on land, separate worlds ... we can never be sure about these things, can we?' I mumble.

He shrugs and says, 'Ah well … let's get to work, shall we, Ms On-Land-Sen-Gupta?' I don't like the way he stresses on the 'on land'. Who does he think he is?

Abhishek leads me into a room, which looks like his office. A huge whiteboard with hundreds of Post-its cover one wall. On the other end, near a huge window is a vintage writing table in honey-coloured wood piled with headphones, a projector, a huge iMac monitor and a MacBook.

He does not waste time and flicks open his laptop. 'I have everything planned. You will see,' he says in a very superior kind of way and then pulls down a screen on the other wall to project a slide show.

He is quite thorough with his plans to market the book. I must give that to him. Media coverage, social media, book launch, book promos, he has everything on there. I watch mesmerized as he points here and there and waves his little laser dot across graphs that shows curves in various colours rising up, up and up. I imagine my meteoric rise up those steep curves and feel a shiver of excitement. Well, the guy is balding and middle-aged and kind of cocky, but he seems to know what he is doing.

'I have the manuscript. Do you want it now?' I say when the presentation is over and Abhishek leans back on what looks like a very expensive swivel chair.

He looks at me quizzically, 'Why?'

'To edit and, you know, suggest changes if you want …' I trail off.

'Ah, the editing is your responsibility and Right-to-Write's. Once it is ready, you hand it over. We do the layout, we both review it and then it goes to print. Bas!' He ticks off on his finger.

'Abhishek Bhattacharjee does not read books,' he announces, rather pompously proclaims, and swivels his chair so that his back faces me now.

'Well, there is one small issue,' I gulp and lay down my cards.

'Now what?' He swivels back at me.

'We have to find Didan, the grandmother whose letters are the core of the book.'

'Isn't that your grandmother who sent you those recipes and letters?'

I shake my head slowly. 'I have no clue who she is.' The guy clearly had not paid attention to half of our story.

'Hmm. Then there is the whole copyright and plagiarism issue. What if we publish the book and the actual grandmother and family barge in and sue us for infringing copyright? We can't do this.' He leans further back, bringing his surprisingly short fingers together in a rhombus and tapping their ends. 'Nope, not happening.'

I panic. What does he mean not happening? What about the contract and the money and my stardom and Right-to-Write's future? I feel angry now. I am still a bit jet-lagged and that nagging irritation fuels my anger.

I lash out at him. 'What do you mean not happening? Is this some kind of a joke? We have a signed contract. I have left my family and flown all the way across oceans to get this done and now you say not happening?' My nose is all flared up and my head pulsates with disappointment. 'I am going to find who sent me the letters. And you will help me. In three weeks' time, the book goes to print.' I spell out the sentences through clenched teeth.

I could be a good villain in a Bengali movie. I never thought I had the potential.

Abhishek is a bit taken aback. I am sure he didn't expect me to get so angry. He struggles to say something. But I don't wait for him and storm out of his office. I have an old lady to find!

Facebook

I upload the photo of a mishti'r dokan, sweet shop, I had taken earlier in the day.

82 likes, 32 hearts, 15 sad emojis.
Twenty people have commented about how they miss Kolkata!
Neela and Jai have asked to bring back some Nakur'r sondesh.

Maagh
(January – February)

Dear Moni,

Did you see how the year passed quickly? It is already Maagh, the tenth month of the year. This is also the last of the winter months. I am so glad that winter will finally be over and soon it will be spring. Everyone says it is already warm, but I can still feel the chill. I sit on the terrace all day with my back to the sun and they say that I am turning brown and crisp like a toast!

But what else would I do? I don't go into the kitchen any more; my eyes are not strong enough to do knitting; and if I read a book I forget the beginning by the time it ends. I can feel my mind going soft at the edges like a half-boiled egg. They tell me to go for those religious talks at Mandirtala, run by some sadhu, but you think I am interested in their mindless chatter? How I wish your Dadu were here and I could cook for him again.

So, you know, after Rajat's fake death, I was the object of everyone's pity and sympathy. All my family members tiptoed around me, being extra nice. They assumed I was very sad and fragile. No one asked me how I really felt. Well, except for one person who knew me inside out – your Dadu!

He knew the relief I felt, and he also knew the sad charade I had to put up in front of my people. Women had a difficult life in those days, Moni, and a widow had so many rules to follow. Though my mother tried protecting me from the ire of my relatives, I was not served meat or fish at meals. I was not even allowed to be part of any religious ceremony, wedding or any auspicious occasion. It was getting more and more difficult to stay amongst my relatives under such scrutiny. The final straw broke when a distant aunt suggested that I should shave my head as my luxurious dark hair was not suitable for a young widow.

On your Dadu's suggestion, I took a job as a schoolteacher at a small girls' school in a village 120 miles away from home. My parents were worried but agreed to let me go. I arrived there on the fifth lunar day of Maagh, the day of Saraswati Pujo, when we celebrate the Goddess of learning. What a perfect start to my second life!

Staying far from home helped both me and my family to come to terms with the situation. That was the best time of my life. I was independent, earning my living and doing things I loved. I loved teaching young girls and I taught them much beyond their textbooks. I taught them to be strong, independent and brave.

The girls in turn taught me so many little things like fishing for tiny prawns in the muddy water with a piece of woven cloth called 'gamcha', climbing trees to pluck topa kul — berries which ripen just around this time and how to make kulfi by keeping a bowl of thick milk out on the terrace all night in the cold month of Maagh.

I taught mathematics and music to those girls for one whole year. Your Dadu would come and visit me every first Sunday of the month. He was a good friend, always there in my times of need and never ever did he try to take any advantage. I would cook for him with all the little fish and vegetables available locally. Fresh green pohi leaves with pumpkin; crispy fried mourala; freshly caught baby rui that glittered like a silver anklet, cooked with potatoes and cauliflower. Your Dadu made sure that I ate fish and lived my life like any other twenty-one-year-old.

I was so much in love with him, Moni. But even then, I was not sure if we could ever live the life of a married couple. How would the world take it? What about his mother, his family? Would they accept if their intelligent, handsome son married a widow?

But I never lost faith, Moni. Faith in our love, in your Dadu. Don't ever lose faith, Moni, it gives you strength when you feel you have none.

Today I will give you the recipe for gota sheddho — with whole baby vegetables and lentils. This is my mother's recipe and very popular among the neighbourhood ladies who waited for their share every year. She would cook it on the day of Saraswati Pujo and the cold gota sheddho would be served the next day on Sheetol Shoshthi. That was the day she gave her kitchen a rest, wrapped her shil nora in a piece of new yellow cloth and worshipped Ma Shoshthi. This one-pot dish was supposed to be an immunity booster, for the onset of spring brought a lot of new diseases in those days.

The way she made gota sheddho was by boiling kali urad (with skin) known as maashkolai in Bengali with five different vegetables in season which were to be added whole, little salt, sugar to taste, some pieces of ginger and a drizzle of raw mustard oil to finish off. The vegetables most commonly used were small red potatoes, small eggplants, hyacinth beans, whole green peas in their pod — and baby spinach. It was a simple dish and looks a bit unappetizing but brimming with good health. Way better than the salad you say that you eat in the US.

Look after yourself and eat healthy. Take my blessings.

Bhalo theko,
Didan

———

Late into the night, while Kolkata sleeps, I lie wide awake. I can hear Ratna Di's musical snores from the study just across mine. Unlike me, she sleeps peacefully after an honest day of cooking and feeding us. Pishi is a light sleeper and I hear her fidgeting every few hours – opening the fridge, turning on the bathroom tap. It's three in the morning and I toss and turn, replying to texts from Piyu and Riya or scrolling through the photos Neela has sent of Saraswati Pujo in her basement.

Everyone's life seems to chime in with perfect rhythm, except mine. My mind is in a quandary. In a moment of arrogance, I promised Abhishek I will find the old lady within the next two weeks. But for the life of me I don't know how that is going to happen. If it will happen at all.

I reread the last letter that had arrived just before I left for India. I am so proud of the feisty 'Didan'. She gives me hope. I try to look for hidden clues in the postmark. And then as the first rays of sun touch Kolkata, I fall asleep. I dream of my mother on a four-poster bed at 253/5 Panchanantala Lane, writing thousands of blue inland letters.

Gota Sheddho

Gota sheddho is a very simple and earthy dish cooked by boiling together a particular variety of lentils and five different vegetables unique to the season. The vegetables are cooked whole and the dish has barely any spices, not even turmeric. Traditionally, this dish was had on the day after Saraswati Pujo.

The day after Saraswati Pujo is Sheetol Shoshti. Shoshthi is the goddess of fertility and worshipped by mothers as a guardian angel of their offspring. 'Sheetol' in Bengali means cool. And on the day of Sheetol Shoshthi, the kitchen is given a rest and cold gota sheddho that had been cooked the previous day is to be had by all mothers worshipping Ma Shoshthi. Saraswati Pujo heralds the advent of spring, and with spring came many diseases in those days. This gota sheddho was definitely an immunity booster for new mothers and kids, brimming with nutrients from the steamed, fresh, vegetables and lentils.

I have adapted the recipe to our taste, it serves four people.

Ingredients

Green moong or black urad lentil – ½ cup
Whole vegetables

- Small red potatoes – 4
- Small round eggplant – 2
- Whole peas in their pods – 10
- Sheem/hyacinth beans (remove strings) – 5-6
- Baby spinach with stems – 1 cup

Whole green chillies – 5-6
Fennel seeds – 1 tsp

Ginger – 2" piece

Salt to taste

Mustard oil – 2-3 tbsp

The day before cooking, soak half a cup of green moong in water. The authentic recipe asks for black urad.

The next day, soak the dal a big pot. In my case, this was the pressure cooker.

Along with the dal, add all the whole vegetables. No chopping or cutting.

Ideally each vegetable should be added in sixes. But I do not follow this rule.

Pour enough water in the pot to cover the veggies and dal.

Add salt to taste and five or six whole green chillies.

Add 1 tsp of fennel seeds (mouri) and 2' inch piece of ginger, pounded in a mortar and pestle. This gives an amazing flavour.

Cook till dal and veggies are done. Since I do it in a whistling pressure cooker, I cook it for about five whistles on low-medium flame.

When done, dry off excess water if you wish. Add sugar to taste. Drizzle enough mustard oil. Serve hot or cold.

Instead of raw oil, I heat a tbsp of mustard oil in a separate kadhai. I temper the hot oil with four dried red chillies and then add it to the cooked dal.

11

It has been two weeks since I landed in Kolkata. Two hectic weeks. Now I have only one more week until the deadline that I very haughtily gave Abhishek at his office.

But some other things have happened in these two weeks. I have become some sort of a social media celebrity. Yes, in only two weeks! Abhishek and his team pulled all kinds of strings in getting me the media attention as planned. And boy, I must admit, even if grudgingly, they did good. Actually, very good!

I was instructed to spread my social media wings beyond Facebook and WhatsApp and join Instagram, Snapchat and Twitter, where I am supposed to engage potential readers and lure them into reading my book.

It is all super exciting, but keeping track of all these social media accounts is a bit overwhelming. I totally get now why Riya is glued to her phone all the time. I am smitten by Instagram filters and am checking out SRK's stories on it half the time. My thumb is aching with all the typing and I might have just developed carpal tunnel. But that is not important. What is important is that I still managed to get some ten thousand followers out of thin air. Even with my sore thumb!

As a result of all this social media outreach, my photo has now been on the centrespread of two major dailies published here. Yes, two! One Bengali, one English.

'NRI in Search of Grandmother's Recipes', says the English article in huge garamond font. Okay, so the photo is not exactly how I intended it to be. I don't know what the photographer was trying to do but he caught me with my mouth open, shoulders slouched and a blank look in my eyes. I didn't even get time to suck in my tummy! That look is not exactly one that will excite the readers, but thankfully some mustard oil brand put in a huge ad right on the centrespread, which kind of obscures my photo. You can't tell if I am awestruck by the oil or am generally demented.

The Bengali newspaper has taken too much liberty and introduced me as 'An accomplished chef with deep knowledge of historic Bengali recipes'. Wrong! Wrong! Wrong! I sound like a total fraud when put that way. Heck, I had no clue how to even cook a decent shukto before April. I was in two minds about sending a correction to the newspaper but Abhishek insisted that I let it go. 'It will do the book good, madam. These are small, small things. You look at the big picture.'

So, concentrating on the big picture, last week I was interviewed as an 'expert Bengali Chef' on the very popular FM channel Radio Beguni. It was all very casual and the RJ was super sweet and cheeky; and just as I was thinking I have conquered the heart of every Bengali in Kolkata with my in-depth knowledge about the origin of chhana and chhanar roshogolla, some extremely know-all, paka, listener called in to ask, 'Shubha Di, have you cooked mocha? Can you tell me the difference between mocha and thor?'

Honestly, I had no clue. My mother did make mochar ghonto and I know that it is banana blossom, but I have no idea who thor is. The only Thor I know is the hammer-wielding Norse God of thunder and lightning but I was sure that wasn't what he meant. The RJ was looking expectantly at me, with great respect at that. Time was ticking. I could feel a knot in my stomach and then I had my eureka moment – this was radio, the listener can't see me. So, I did what any intelligent human being would do. I fished out my phone, googled and gave a very erudite answer about thor the banana stem, that seemed to satisfy the listener.

But that was only the beginning. The next one with an anxious matronly voice asked, 'My niece lives in Atlanta. She was asking if she can use panch phoron instead of radhuni in her shukto.'

Seriously this was getting too much. Who did they think I was, the Rabbi of Bengali food?

'I don't think she can get a radhuni in Atlanta. Bengali radhunis are not easy to come by in the US. Now if she wants a Mexican cook, that would be very easy…' I tried to explain earnestly.

'No ma'am, we can send her radhuni from Kolkata if it is absolutely a must for shukto.'

I was bewildered by this person's dedication towards shukto. He wanted to send his niece a radhuni – a cook – just to make shukto? Who does that?

'But how will you get a visa for a radhuni?' I was really curious now. If it was that easy maybe I could take Ratna Di too.

The young RJ in her blue jeans and Fabindia kurta was giving me an incredulous look and quickly cut me off with an ad jingle.

'I think the gentleman was asking about radhuni the Bengali spice,' she hissed.

Bengali is such a weird language. Radhuni means both cook and a unique spice mix. How was I supposed to know what the caller meant? I was getting a bit fidgety at this point and fervently hoping the show would wrap up, when the RJ cheerfully announced, 'And now our last caller is on air asking a question that we are all eager to know.'

I could sense the trickle of sweat down my back. What were they so eager to know? Have they found out about my fraud? That I am no expert in Bengali cuisine? Oh God! How would I explain?

The caller cleared his throat, yep, on air, and slowly asked, 'Have you found out who wrote you those letters yet?'

I swallowed a couple of times and sipped water that the cheerful RJ very helpfully offered. 'Umm ... we are looking. Soon, very soon we will find her,' I croaked.

But apart from these few hitches, I am actually liking all this attention. I can now totally understand how a film star feels. But I am also panicking. Six more days to find Didan or the contract is off. Only SIX! I cannot imagine the look on Kajol's face if that happens. The contract is off means no book, no money, and Right-to-Write closing its shutters. Oh God! I cannot let this happen. What will I tell Sam and Claire? They will be devastated. I cannot go back home if the contract falls through. I have to make this happen somehow.

Time is ticking away faster than I think. I have been trying my best. In fact more than best. I have combed the oli-golis, lanes and by-lanes, of Kolkata on Google Street View. I have eaten phuchka at dubious street corners from Manicktala to Belghoria, tactically asking the Bihari phuchkawalas about Panchanantala. I have gone to the local Baranagar post office where the young postmaster put on a very stern look and shooed me away – 'Na, na, there is no Panchanantala Lane here.' I have posed the question on all my social media accounts. The newspapers have mentioned it. And yet no luck.

I have given up almost all hope as I sit on the sofa chewing on Ratna Di's beguni, fried crisp on the outside and buttery on the inside, racking my brain to think of one more strategy, when Pishi says, 'Why don't you try the GPO? You know the central post office. They have a record of all streets in Kolkata. My friend used to know the postmaster general there, let me see if he can help you.'

This seems like such a logical solution that I cannot believe my ears. All the time that I have been out in the sun walking the streets, worrying myself to death, Pishi has had a perfect solution tucked up her sleeves. 'Pishi, you are such a saviour! But why didn't you tell me earlier…' I am almost on the verge of crying in frustration and joy. This is my last straw and I fervently hope it helps me stay afloat.

'*Aami ki jani?* How would I know? I thought you had a plan in place already.' Pishi shakes her head in disbelief and rummages around on her phone to find the friend with the GPO connection.

Finally, after a series of phone calls to friends, friends-of-friends, nephew-of-friends-of-friends, a connection to the high official in GPO has been established. Just as I am thinking that I have to go meet one more government official who may or may not have an answer, I snatch a part of the conversation where Pishi seems super excited.

'Panchanantala Lane had been renamed? The new one is Rani Rasmoni Road? Aha, the one behind the Shib Mondir, the narrow lane that goes on to a dead end…'

We finally found it. We found it! It has been there all the time, right under our nose but with a new name. I grabbed Pishi and twirled around the living room in excitement. Tomorrow, tomorrow I will know.

Facebook

I travelled miles, for many a year,
I spent a lot in lands afar,
I've gone to see the mountains,
The oceans I've been to view.
But I haven't seen with these eyes
Just two steps from my home lies
On a corn of paddy grain,
A glistening drop of dew.

— *Rabindranath Tagore*

104 likes. 50 hearts.

Falgun
(February – March)

I couldn't sleep well last night; the excitement was too much. I kept thinking how I should react when I meet the old lady. Should I be, like, all calm and cool – 'Hello, so your letters were delivered to me by mistake. Thank you for helping me to cook and giving me a new direction in life. Goodbye.' Or should I be all emotional and teary-eyed – 'I love you so much! I cannot thank you enough for what you have done. You have given me a closure to my past and the courage to learn new things. You have changed my life. Please adopt me.' I twitch and turn, not sure of what exactly I should say.

I am up early morning today, way before the crow could start its morning raga on the balcony. I make myself a cup of black tea and try doing some of my faux yoga. It seems to work. My mind is clearing up. It will be fine, I tell myself. Just go with the flow, tell her what you feel, what wells up from within you when you meet her. I also decide to do the trek by myself. I don't want a witness to my personal moment.

By the time I reach Panchanantala Lane aka Rani Rashmoni Road, the sun is higher up in the sky, wrapping the earth in its warm, toasty glow. I feel hot, given that I am now used to twelve inches of snow in February. The streets are relatively empty, taking a breather after the morning office and school rush. Older men, woollen scarves wrapped around their thick short necks, sit on stools in front of roadside chai stalls, basking in the sun and drinking copious amounts of sweet milk tea. A few young men, either unemployed or dropped out of college, are hanging around taking down a pandal made with logs of bamboo and sheaths of yellow and white cloth. Saraswati Pujo was last week and this must be the neighbourhood pandal. Time seems to flow at a slower pace here.

Panchanantala Lane is a very narrow street for cars to manoeuvre and so my cabbie drops me off at the junction from where the lane branches off in the east. I walk down the narrow street, and feel how close the houses are to each other. If I stand bang at the centre and stretch my hands, I can practically touch the buildings on both sides. I can hear a girl practising the harmonium, her untrained voice slipping off the keys often. From another window wafts in notes of methi and hing phoron sizzling in hot oil. I can faintly hear a woman's voice, taut with anger, shouting at someone, probably the house help who in response bangs and clatters utensils to create a din and the woman's voice softens.

The fifth house on the left is 253/5. It is very unassuming with its faded salmon pink exterior and green shuttered windows. It looks like any of the other houses on this street – sentinels of grander days, now old and craving for some serious TLC. The paint is peeling off in places, exposing bricks, which must be at least a hundred years old I think. There is a sliver of an open veranda in the front which has seen better days and is now dusty and full of pigeon droppings. I don't think I can do this any more. I feel a knot in my stomach and my heart is beating so fast that I am afraid everyone else can hear it. Just when I am thinking, whether this is the moment I should just turn and go back to my regular, safe life, someone opens the forest-green wooden door.

'Are you Shubha? Come in, I have been waiting,' says that person. I am so shocked by this that I am almost about to faint. Is this some kind of magic? Maybe black magic? How does she know my name? Oh wait, the letters were addressed to me by name Shubhalaxmi Sen-Gupta. But ... but how does this person know that I was supposed to come, that I will be here today?

I walk inside, pulled by some strange laws of attraction. It is cool and dark inside. My pupils take a few seconds to adjust from the harsh sunlight outside and as I focus on the woman smiling at me, I realize she is no grandmother. I mean she is not old enough to be a grandma. Clad in a handloom sari, hair in a neat bun with a few grey strands around her forehead, she has an intelligent and sweet face. But she is definitely not as old as I gathered from the letters. Maybe a few years older than me, but that's it. Unless of course Didan has exercised, eaten right and kept herself looking thirty years younger. In that case I need to know her secret. Or maybe she is just another person and Didan is bedridden or dead or something.

I have no clue what to say and so I wait for the lady to speak. She knew I was coming anyway.

'Do you want something? Water or some sherbet? You look very pale,' she says with a concerned look on her face.

'No, no, I am good.' I compose myself and look around. This is the living room as I understand from the furniture. Heavy brocaded sofas and antique chairs with curved backs are neatly arranged on one side of the huge room. The furniture looks old but expensive. I look up at the high ceiling and see dangling crystals from a chandelier, now dusty and grimy. It seems the house belonged to a rich family but has now fallen to hard times.

The lady sees me eyeing the chandelier and says, 'I live here by myself. No longer do I have the energy to clean all this heavy stuff. Honestly, I am just waiting for a buyer to sell it to and move to a smaller flat.'

I don't know why she is even telling me all this, but I politely nod my head. Since she doesn't even mention Didan, I gingerly broach the topic again. 'So, I have been getting a few letters since April of last year, Boishakh in Bangla, and...'

'Wait,' the lady cuts me off and leaves the room. Maybe now she will bring back the old lady, in a wheelchair or something, I hope. But she returns almost immediately, two blue letters in her hand. I try to peer behind her but don't see anyone else. 'Here,' she says, 'Falgun and Chaitra, the last two months you must be waiting for.'

I open and close my mouth like a fish gasping for air and no words come out.

'So, you really don't know who sent you these letters? Sameer didn't tell you anything?' She seems a bit surprised.

Sameer? Where does Sameer come in the picture? My mind is all woolly and I cannot think straight any more. Too much for my forty-plus brain to process at this point. I shake my head in silence, indicating negation.

'I sent you the letters,' the lady continues, 'but I didn't write them.'

Another piece of puzzle. This whole thing now looks like a 1000-piece jigsaw puzzle and I have no energy to solve it. Seeing my blank look, the lady probably takes pity on me.

'Okay, so let me tell you the story. I am Falguni, Sameer's cousin, second cousin actually. My grandmother and his grandmother were sisters. Very close sisters too. When Sameer was little, he spent a lot of time at my grandmother's home, whom he called Mashi-dida and sometimes Didan. They were thick as Marie biscuits and cha. Sameer would be the sous-chef, toddling around with ladles and kadhais, always tagging my grandmother around her kitchen. My grandmother actually adored Sameer more than any of her own grandchildren. Mashi-dida would cook her best recipes for Sameer. She would wait all year for summer vacation when Sameer would come and stay with her.' Falguni paused.

I am slowly trying to fit in the puzzle. So, Mashi-Dida, Sameer's great-aunt, has a connection to these letters?

Falguni softly continues, 'Towards the end of her life, she feared that she was losing her memory. She was still a very fiercely independent old lady, but after my Dadu's death, she started forgetting things. Small things – like she would forget the name of her oldest son, or the name of her favourite serial on TV. Scared that it was an onset of Alzheimer's, she started writing letters to save what was most precious to her. Her recipes and the story of her life.'

Falguni's grainy and soft voice is that of a storyteller, full of emotions and inflections in the right places. I am mesmerized and as she narrates, the story leaps to life in front of my eyes. I try to remember Mashi-Dida from my wedding, but most of the faces are a blur and I am not sure which one of the many elderly relatives she was. I have heard Sameer speak fondly of her in those early days and now I remember how he grieved on her passing.

'She wrote these letters for Sameer but never remembered to post them or give them to him. At that point, her memory was failing fast. Sameer had just left for the US and so communication was rare too. She never even mentioned anything about those letters to him. Probably, she forgot about them herself. Mashi-Dida passed away almost fourteen years ago. This was her home during her last days, she lived in a room upstairs. After her, that room became kind of a storage room for us. But last year, while sorting through all her old stuff, to sell off to the kabariwala or at the curio shop, I came upon a bunch of these letters wrapped up in a muslin cloth at the bottom of her trunk. They were all for Sameer and I immediately called him and told him about them. I knew how precious these memories were for him.'

Falguni pauses to take a breath and smiles at me. I am so bewildered with where the story is going that I wait with bated breath, afraid that a breath of air might change its course.

'Sameer came and looked at them last year. He was stunned by what he read. And then he said, "I want to gift these to Shubha. She is the one person, I know, who will cherish them. And who knows maybe it will inspire her to cook those recipes that her mother once did. Shubha turns forty in April and I want it to be a surprise for her. But if I just give her these letters, she will not pay much attention to them. So Falguni Di, I need your help. You have to do this for me. Please."' Falguni stops for a second and sips water.

I hang on to her every word, my mouth so wide open that a fly could have easily gone down my oesophagus.

'Sameer is our youngest cousin brother, very dear to me. We had not seen each other for many years as I was away with my husband on his assignments across Africa. His plea was so full of love that I could not refuse what he asked of me. The letters were old and the papers were yellowed, so he asked me to rewrite these letters every month, beginning in April, in a blue aerogramme and send them to you.'

I cannot understand what Falguni is telling me. I really can't.

Sameer was the mastermind? He was the one who arranged that the letters be sent to me? All this time that I was thinking we were growing apart and there was a burgeoning chasm between us, he was instead thinking of what would make me happy. I feel a wave of love sweeping over me and pulling me into deeper waters. I don't even know what to say any more. My eyes are hot with tears and I am crying. I don't know why exactly I am crying but big, fat, salty tears are flowing in rivulets and staining my face.

'And so, every month since April I sent you the letters. I was always worried if I was doing my job correctly. When you sent back the letters, I panicked and wrote to Sameer asking if somehow you had unearthed the secret. But you know, in my heart I knew you would come here one day seeking the truth … only I didn't know when.'

I can't hear her clearly. Her words are getting all muffled up in my ears. All I can hear is Sameer telling me weeks ago, 'You should make this trip, Shubha. If you think you need to find her, you must go find her. I know you can do it!' He knew. He knew all this time!

Between my sobs, I manage to ask, 'When you wrote to Sameer, did you sign them as, "Love, F"?'

Falguni Di smiles. 'You are good at puzzles, I am surprised it took you so long.'

Dear Moni,

At last Basanta is here. I cannot tell you how happy I feel that the brutal winter is finally over. Spring is short-lived these days and soon we will be in the throes of sticky hot summer, but until then we can enjoy nature's rebirth in all its glory. 'Phagun legeche bon e bon e,' Robithakur had said – the forest is aflame with colours of spring.What a beautiful verse!

The neem tree outside my window has sprouted tiny copper red leaves. I wish you could see them.These leaves are of great medicinal value and I still remember your love for bitter neem-begun. I told Pratibha to cut some eggplant in small cubes and sauté them in mustard oil with these tender neem leaves. It is a delicious dish, but Pratibha pretended not to hear me.

You know, the month of Falgun brings new life not only to plants and trees; it had also given me new life. This was the month when he, your Dadu, finally proposed to me. Now, don't think 'propose' like as they show in serials these days. Nothing of that. It is just that one day he came to the village where I was still teaching and said, 'This is not working. I cannot stay far from you anymore. I want to be with you forever.'

I was too embarrassed to say anything. I mean I did try to tell him that society would not accept and such stuff but he just brushed those excuses aside. 'I don't care,' he said. He was always like that. Fearlessly, did what was right and true.

But there was an issue. I was in a conundrum. I did not know what my legal marital status was.Technically, I was a widow as Rajat had 'died' in a fatal accident. But then, he had actually 'fake died' as a few of us knew and in that case, he was still my legally wedded husband.What if Rajat came back in the near future?What would I do then?

It did not seem safe for us to marry and stay together in Bengal.All my relatives, Rajat's family, their friends were here. So, after much discussion, we decided to move to southern India crossing the Vindhyas. In those days, not many Bengalis settled in the southern part of India.

On the day of Dol Purnima, the full moon night of Holi, we got married at the Kalighat temple and then went straight to Howrah station, all our belongings packed in two tin trunks. No one knew about our marriage, not even my parents or his mother. It was too much of a risk telling anyone. How different my wedding day was from the usual affair. No shehnai, no flowers except for the hibiscus as the Goddess's offering, no new saris or jewellery. And yet I was the happiest.

We finally arrived in Madurai where the famous Meenakhshi Temple is and your Dadu took up a job with the postal service in the town. Soon I too got a job as a mathematics teacher at a local school. We set up our new home, far away from our own. Every day was a struggle to learn a new language, new culture and traditions. Food was the most difficult to adjust to. But human beings are the most adaptable species and we did adapt.

I learned to make sambhar which I sweetened instead of adding tamarind. We ate idli for breakfast and fell in love with it. Since banana was easily available there, I often made mochar ghonto with banana blossoms and kaanchkolar kofta with the green plantain. We hardly ate fish as it wasn't easily found, and cooking fish was not allowed by our landlord anyway. But we found places famous for Madurai's kari dosai with minced meat and mutton kurma that helped us satiate our taste buds.

Your Baro Mama was born a year later and then your aunts, Baro and Chhoto. Such wonderful days those were. Gradually, we also connected with my parents who forgot all past squabbles once they met their grandchildren. His mother came and stayed with us in her later years. If I had one wish, it is to go back to Madurai and see the house where my children grew up.

Today I am sending you the recipe for mochar ghonto, made of banana blossoms tucked inside the deep purple banana flower. The difficult part of this recipe is cleaning the flower. Put mustard oil on your fingers and then peel the purple outer layers. Next, remove the florets. In each floret, you will see the longest string with a round head called the 'stamen' and the translucent thin cover – remove those. Now chop the florets in small pieces and soak in water for a few hours. Once you are done with this, the cooking part is easy and you can make anything from a mochar paaturi with mustard paste or a ghonto with coconut and black peas.

Don't get dejected by the difficulty of it, keep at it and you will succeed. Life has a surprising way of working out its problems. The only thing you have to do is have faith and keep at it.

Bhalo theko,
Didan

Kashundi Narkol Mocha – Banana Blossoms

Mocha, the blossoms of a banana plant, is a much-loved vegetable in Bengal. The only difficult part in cooking this dish is prepping it, which needs some patience.

Mochar ghonto, where the banana blossoms are cooked with potatoes, horse gram and coconut, is a very popular dish. In this recipe, I have cooked the blossoms with narkol aka coconut and kashundi, a sharp mustard condiment. If you don't have kashundi you can use a full tablespoon of mustard paste to get the same result. This recipes can serve up to six people.

Ingredients

Mocha (banana blossom) – 1
Potato – 1 large
Grated coconut – ⅓ cup
Kashundi – 1-2 tbsp
Green chillies – 4
Grated ginger – 1 tsp
Turmeric powder – ½ tsp
Salt to taste
Sugar to taste

Spices for tempering

Bay leaf – 1
Small green cardamom – 2
Cumin seeds – ¼ tsp
Dried red chillies – 2
Mustard oil – 3 tbsp for cooking

Prep the vegetables. Buy mocha banana blossom, a purple-hued conical object, from your vegetable seller or Indian grocery store.

At home, make yourself a cup of tea, roll out a newspaper, place a chopping the board on that paper and turn on a movie. Prepping these blossoms will take some time!

If you have manicured hands, then wear rubber gloves before chopping the mocha. If you don't have gloves, smear mustard oil on your fingers and then peel the purple outer layers.

Next remove the florets. In each floret, you will see a matchstick-like long string with a round head which is the stamen. Remove that. Each floret also has a translucent thin cover, remove those too.

Chop the blossoms into small pieces and soak them in water with a little turmeric powder and salt.

After two hours, drain the water and steam the blossoms. In a pressure cooker, it takes two whistles.

While the mocha is cooking, chop the potato into small cubes.

If you have frozen grated coconut, defrost it and pulse it further in your food processor until it is finely grated. If you have fresh coconut, grate it whichever way you wish.

Cooking the mocha

Now heat mustard oil to smoking.

Temper the oil with bay leaf, small green cardamoms, cumin seeds, dry red chillies.

Add the potato to it. Sprinkle some turmeric powder and fry the potato until golden.

Next, add the steamed banana blossoms and sauté for 3 to 4 minutes.

Add the grated coconut, kashundi and green chillies. Mix well and sauté for 4-5 minutes.

Add a little salt. Kashundi will have some salt, so be careful.

Now add grated ginger and a splash of water. Cover and let the potatoes cook.

Check intermittently that all vegetables are cooked.

Add salt and sugar at the end, according to taste.

12

The book has gone to print.

I feel like a piece of my heart has walked out there and I am both happy and anxious for it. Everyone is super excited. Kajol, Samantha and Claire have already sent out excerpts from the book to hundreds of libraries across the US and the response has been very encouraging. I have given numerous interviews and done other book promotions across all media.

Ratna Di thinks I am some celebrity and keeps asking me what I want to eat. I have taken full advantage of the situation and asked her to make everything from muithya to mocha!

Anju has texted me asking if Right-to-Write will publish her memoir. 'I have a very interesting and sizzling story to tell,' she'd added.

The pre-order link for the book is up on Amazon. Jai and Neela have already pre-ordered forty copies each! For what, I don't know.

I have butterflies in my stomach. 'Mom, don't worry, do your pranayama,' Piyu had advised over FaceTime. 'Your author photo on the back cover looks weird! You should have styled your hair at a salon,' Riya had added. I can't wait to catch my flight and go back home tomorrow!

'Come back home, Shubha. We miss you,' Sameer had said. I can't wait for him to see the book in print – he will roll his eyes and cringe. The dedication page of the book says, 'For Sameer, the wind beneath my wings.' Yeah, totally sappy!

I still cannot believe the whole surprise plan Sameer had hatched. The lengths he had gone to get the letters delivered to me. I know our marriage is not like one of those rosy romcoms I love, and yet at present it looks better than anything a romcom director can even think of.

My heart is so full that I can completely grasp what 'brimming with love' feels. It is like a terracotta pot filled to the brim with creamy, sweet mishti doi. It is like that perfect plate of mutton biryani from Shiraz with a hunk of subtly spiced potato hidden amidst the fragrant rice. I can feel the happy energy radiate through my pores. My steps are light and I drink chirota with a smile on my face. I don't even bargain with the hawkers selling their wares at Ballygunge market and leave the phuchkawala a hefty tip.

As I pack my suitcase – trying to fit in hand-embroidered lehengas with kalamkari borders for the girls from boutiques at Park Street; woven tassar sari in parrot green with a red pallu for Neela; sequined dupattas for the Right-to-Write girls; jharna ghee, meetha ittar and bhaja masala for Sameer; tupperware boxes filled with Nakur's sondesh – Pishi comes in with a brown leather diary in her hand. She doesn't say anything, but I see her eyes are moist, her dark pupils shine like tiny flames flickering in a shallow pool. I give her thin, toned arm a tight squeeze. I had asked her to come with me, for at least a holiday, but she has a perfectly balanced ecosystem here, which she didn't want to disturb. I have promised her I will visit again next year.

Pishi hands me the diary, it looks ancient. The mahogany leather feels soft and aged under my fingers. I carefully open it at the middle, and yellowed cuttings from old magazines and newspapers with frayed edges tumble out. The paper is fragile and looks like even a small shift in pressure can crush it to smithereens. Caramel pudding in pressure cooker. Bread pakora. Plum cake. Recipes cut out neatly from magazines of yesteryear. As I flip through the much-thumbed pages carefully, I come upon notes scrawled along the margins, snatches of recipes and home budget calculations in neat rounded numbers. I look at Pishi with hope in my eyes and she nods at me.

I know then. It is my mother's diary – the one where she kept her accounts for the washerman and monthly grocery. The one which was a silent witness of her daily life until that dreadful day when it was cut short by an irresponsible auto driver. I turn page after page of how she planned her budget, notes on her saffron-scented biryani masala learned from a Muslim neighbour, the recipe for that face pack to cure acne which she made for me in high school. I hold it close to my nose and take a deep breath. It smells like old paper mingled with the smell of my mother's turmeric-stained cotton saris. I don't remember that smell exactly but I have a feeling it was something like this.

'Your mother always made the best caramel pudding,' Pishi reminds me.

'The one with the burnt brown top and scented with orange rinds?' I try to recall the sweet dense taste of the pudding and its citrus fragrance.

'And her cakes were always moist and soft. She had a knack for baking. Remember her Christmas fruit cakes with dry fruits soaked in rum? Even your father grudgingly admitted they were as good as Nahoum's,' Pishi reminisces.

I smile and flip through the diary, remembering that UFO-style contraption my mother had as an oven. In our very middle-class Bengali neighbourhood, she was the adventurous one trying out cakes and cookies that we had never heard of, following recipes from foreign magazines. Neighbourhood ladies would often flock to our home for afternoon tea, their powdered faces mesmerized by what my mother churned out from her electric oven. Once, when I was enamoured by the mention of pizza in one of the many American books I read, she made something akin to a pizza in her oven. It was a spectacle with ketchup, Amul cheese and lots of onion – all piled on a roti.

I tell Pishi about my first pizza and we laugh over our ignorant selves in those simpler times. Dusk sweeps down gently over Kolkata and from the seventh-floor window I can see the horizon turn a dusty pink. Far below, buses and autos blare horns as mothers and fathers hurry back home to cook dinner and sort out homework. Young children linger in the park for a last chance to shoot a ball before darkness falls. Ratna Di brings us a plate of warm chicken patties and steaming cups of ginger tea. I hug the diary close and a feeling of contentment descends over me, wrapping me in its soft cocoon. It has been many years since I have been in such complete peace!

Kolkata has been too kind to me this time. The city has done all she could to erase my past sorrows and bring me joy. The City of Joy has taught me her secret. I have learned to not go searching for joy outside – it is there right within our reach, in the people around us, in the heart within us. All we have to do is know where to look.

Facebook

Thank you, City of Joy, for everything. #Calcutta #CityofJoy

500 likes. 200 hearts. 150 'Congratulations'.

Chaitra
(March – April)

Dear Moni,

It's been more than a year since I have seen you. Already it is the month of Chaitra, the year is crawling to an end. Soon Boishakh will be here and with it the new year. Why don't you come and celebrate the New Year with us? I won't be able to cook your favourite dishes but I can teach Pramila to make them. Not that she will listen to me, she is very stubborn!

You know the last day of Chaitra, Chaitra Sankranti, was celebrated with as much importance in our home as was the New Year, Poila Boishakh. Food cooked for Chaitra Sankranti was usually mild and vegetarian – five different kind of fries, dal, vegetables and sweets. My mother made a dish called pachon – with myriad of different vegetables that were particularly found in the month of Chaitra and dried beans. It was almost like a panchmishali, but unique in taste.

For sweets, she made sondesh with homemade chhana, curdling whole milk with lime juice, and then cooking the chhana with jaggery at low heat to make norom paak'r sondesh. And then she shaped them like flower petals, conch shells and even fish, with the variety of stone moulds that she had.

Your Dadu loved sondesh. Rajat too. He never liked Bengali food but when it came to sondesh there was nothing stopping him.

You know, the other day it was very hot, so I was standing in our second-floor balcony looking out on to our narrow street. At least you can feel the breeze there. And guess who did I see? Standing by the telebhaja shop at the corner was Rajat and your Dadu. Yes, both of them! Rajat in his suit and tie like always and your Dadu in his usual kurta with sleeves rolled up and dhuti. They were sipping tea from small earthen terracotta cups and chatting merrily.

Moni, I can't tell you how shocked I was! What if Rajat wanted to come home and meet me? What would I say? I had never told any of my children about him. I was scared to death. Should I act nonchalant and offer him sondesh and snacks if he knocks at my door? I wasn't even sure if we had any sondesh at home!

I was so nervous that I called your uncle – Baro Mama – out in the balcony. 'Do you see your father there at the telebhaja store? And that man in a suit with him?' I asked, pointing towards the store, where our narrow lane dips and turns towards the main road.

Your uncle looked at me strangely, held me by the shoulders and said, 'Ma, he is dead. My father, your husband, passed away five years ago.' For a minute, I just kept staring at him. Then I remembered, of course your Dadu was no more. What does he think? Am I foolish?

But Moni, strange as it was, I did clearly see them – Rajat and your Dadu, walking away towards the main road, further and further from our house. They became smaller and smaller, little specks of black and then I couldn't see them any more. It seemed like they just vanished around the bend.

I wanted to join them too and walk away from all this. I have had a good life. A full and happy life. Yes, things were hard at times but everything turned out to be all right in the end. And that is what matters, Moni. Everything will be all right in the end. If it isn't, then it is not the end.

You come, Moni. I will make sondesh for you – shaped like a fish with my mother's sondesh mould. You will love them. And then I will make some for your Dadu and Rajat and carry them with me.

Bhalo theko,
Didan

At a height of 32,000 feet above the Hindu Kush mountain range, I read the last of the letters again. The metal bird is hurtling towards its destination at an impossible speed. A fluffy blanket of clouds floats beneath the bird's wing as if it is a magic carpet transporting us to a future where we can savour wonders only if we know the magic words. The air hostess has just served lunch. A nondescript plastic tray carrying factory-made chicken biryani, raita and a single sondesh waits for me.

But there is a catch in my throat and I can't swallow any of the food. My eyes are fogged up in a veil of tears. I am happy that it has all ended well. My tears are not tears of sorrow. Nor are they tears of joy. They are tears for loving dearly.

I can't wait to get home!

Facebook

Everything is all right in the end. If it's not all right, then it is not the end. #takeyoursecondchance

195 hearts. 100 likes.

Sondesh

Sondesh is a popular Bengali sweet made from fresh chhana aka homemade paneer also known as curdled milk solids. The chhana is kneaded with sugar and different flavourings to make different varieties of sondesh. Different kinds of kneading from smooth to grained gives different types of sondesh.

Traditionally, only delicate flavourings were used for sondesh like rose or saffron and notun gur in winter. While the raw flavoured and sweetened chhanna is made into kaancha golla, the kneaded chhanna is put back on heat and cooked further for different durations to make different kinds of sondesh. The first sondesh was introduced by Bhim Nag in 1826, but Nakur Chandra, Sen Mahashoy and Balram are some of the oldest and famous sondesh-makers of the city.

Though khoya/kheer is not a necessary ingredient in sondesh, it is added in a particular variety called kheer'r sondesh. This recipe makes about 25 sondesh.

Ingredients

Whole milk – 2 litres
Lime juice – 2 tbsps
Vinegar – 1 tbsp
Khoya – 6 oz or 150 gm of store-bought khoya (in the US, we buy a 12 oz block of nanak khoya, half of which is used for the purpose).
Sugar – ½ cup
Khejur gur (Bengal date palm jaggery) – ½ cup

Note: Add the sugar and jaggery to your taste. You can use no sugar and all jaggery instead as well.

Step 1: Curdling milk

Bring two litres of whole milk to boil.

When the milk is boiling add lime juice and vinegar. Lower the heat. Almost in seconds, you will see the milk curdle and clumps of white milk solids forming. When you see the greenish water separating, take the milk off the stove. Let it sit for thirty seconds or so.

Step 2: Draining chhana

Now line a colander with cheesecloth and drain the chhana. The greenish hued whey is great for making roti dough, my mother says.

Next, lightly rinse the chhana with water to remove the lemony taste and let it drain.

After a few minutes gather the ends of the cheesecloth to form a purse-like shape and squeeze out the remaining water from the chhana. Then put it on a flat plate and weigh it with a slightly heavier object and let it remain like that for the next hour. I used my mortar for weighing down, I remember my mother would use her nora.

Step 3: Kneading chhana with sugar

Knead the chhana with the heel of your palm for about 5-10 minutes. Your palm should be oily at the end of the kneading and the chhana should have come together.

Add about ½ cup of fine sugar and knead for 4-5 minutes more until the sugar is totally mixed with the chhana. At the end of this, the chhana will look like a smooth ball of dough.

Step 4: Getting khoya ready

Soften the khoya in the microwave. Crumble the khoya and put it in the mixer with a tbsp of milk and blitz it to get smooth khoya.

Step 5: Paak or cooking chhana

Now we will do the 'paak' or cook it. Since I am doing a norom paak'r sondesh we will not be cooking the chhana to hardness. We will also add the khejur gur at this point.

The khejur gur is usually solid, so in a microwave-safe bowl, add ½ cup of loosely packed khejur gur and a tbsp of water. Microwave for a minute or until the jaggery melts.

For the paak, put a non-stick pan on low heat and pour the khoya and the liquid jaggery in it. Stir for a couple of minutes. Then add the kneaded, sweetened chhana. Mix with your fingers. Keep the heat at low so that you can mix with your hand.

After you see that the khoya and chhana are mixed together, raise the heat to medium and stir continuously for the next 15 minutes. The chhana mix will slowly come together and will no longer stick to the pan. When you can take a little of it and make a ball, you know it is done.

Step 6: Shape cooked chhana to make sondesh

Now take out the warm chhana and immediately shape with moulds or just toss into balls. If you wait longer, it will harden and you cannot shape it. If you have the sondesh moulds, grease them with ghee. Put a ball of sondesh on the mould and press to flatten it out so that it takes shape. Gently pry it out and put on a plate. Keep a bowl of water handy to dip your fingers and proceed with the next ball.

For more decoration, you can warm a few strands of saffron in drops of milk and dot each sondesh with the saffron or add pistachios. Enjoy the sweet results warm or cold.

Acknowledgements

In no particular order, this book happened because of the following people.

My lovely daughters, Sharanya and Ananya, who made sure that I finished writing this book instead of watching Netflix or looking over their homework. Love you both.

My husband, the H-Man, who read the first draft, then the second and finally the third draft, in flight, at airports and sometimes at meetings — reassuring me that this was a book for any time and all places. Thank you for cooking dinner and doing dishes, while I played the 'I have to finish the book' card.

Ma and Baba, for inculcating in me a love for reading and for always being my cheerleaders.

My friend and forever editor Neelini Sarkar, who believed there was an interesting book in the first rough draft I had sent her and gave me the confidence to go ahead with it. Words cannot express my gratitude to her for always being my adviser, mentor and friend in the world of book publishing.

Kanishka Gupta, my agent, to whom I was introduced by Neelini, and who then did everything to get the book noticed. Thank you!

Big thanks to Swati Daftuar, my editor at HarperCollins, who gently guided and suggested, and made the book better. Thank you for making the remote work process smooth and effortless with your calls and WhatsApp messages. Tanima, thank you for taking care of all the minute details, recipe layouts and noticing all the little mistakes. Amit, thanks for the fabulous cover design. Thanks to the entire team at HarperCollins India who worked as hard as I did, to bring the book to fruition.

And finally, the most important of all, readers of my blog 'Bong Mom's Cookbook', who have always enjoyed my writing and pushed me to do more, this book is for you. Thank you!

About the Author

Sandeepa Mukherjee Datta is the Bong Mom, the nom de plume behind the blog 'Bong Mom's Cookbook'. She has been entertaining her readers with food and stories for over ten years, and is the go-to source for Bengali cooking on the Internet. Her previous book, *Bong Mom's Cookbook*, was published by HarperCollins India in 2013.

An engineer by profession, she lives with her family in New Jersey, USA.